CREDARA

RISE OF THE KRAYLEN

The Water Edition

JE HENDERSON

**Arc-Pen
Publishing**

ISBN - 13: 978-0-9882494-4-8

Arc-Pen Paperback Water Edition, 2018

Main Title Typeface: Evanescent by Aeryn
The text type was set in Adobe Garamond Pro

Image source: Dreamstime.com

<u>Image Artists</u>
Akv2006
Kmariok7
Mimimilch
Davthy
Hypermania37
Dimedrol68
Nomadsoul1
Ikarth
Graphixparanoid
Olimayer

SITCIAN [si-chee-<u>uh</u>n] adjective, noun — Of or from the angel warrior forces of God, Masters of the Hamen Fighting Art.

<u>Example:</u> The Sitcian Angels put down the rebellion of Lucifer, cast him out of Heaven, and forever into Hell.

...forever is a long time.

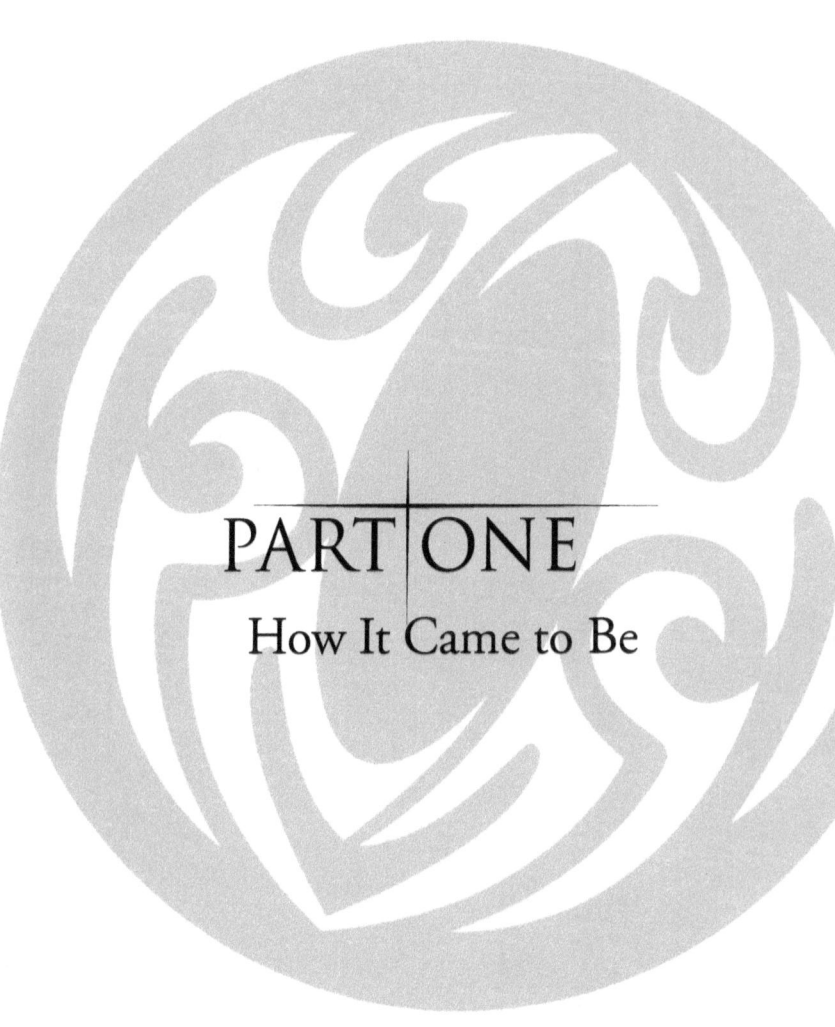

PART ONE
How It Came to Be

chapter one

In the Beginning There Was War

As the arrow's tip entered its body, every cell instantly and violently ripped itself from the next.

For a warrior in battle, there are things which strike the senses like a blade to flesh; the clash of sword against shield, the drawing of an archer's bow, the thunder of a steed's hooves against the earth. But nothing more so than the inimitable sound of pain and anguish. And why should this battle have been any different?

The sound of it rose into the air mixed with the dust of struggle and death; penetrated only by the relentless rays of a blazing sun, and a lone majestic hawk which soared across the sky. Beautiful and sounding off with a familiar screech, this hawk was special. The sacred gold pendant that hung from his neck bore the Arc-Pen Symbol. God's symbol.

Since the very beginning the Arc-Pen Symbol has represented all that was of God, whether in Heaven or on earth, and why such a sacred symbol adorned such a special creature. The heavenly hawk, Flittorin.

As long as all things have existed, Flittorin has traveled the realm of the angels. God's Heaven. On this day, he soared above Heaven, screeching and making all aware of his presence. And on this day, above that which was the end of the Great War, the air reeked of the stench of dead angels.

With a cloud floor at their feet, Sitcian Angel warriors of white, with golden swords, bows, arrows and shields, all bearing the Arc-Pen Symbol, and with the Hamen Mark of Sitcian upon their necks, surrounded thousands of defeated angel warriors of grey. Grey because their hearts had become impure, with those impurities now visible upon their very being. The grey angels scurried backwards, forming a tight huddle as they were cut off from escape, flanked on all sides of their ranks. Sitcian archers continued to unleash a deluge of arrows into the pack of helpless angels. Every angel struck fell in a cloud of ash, smoke and grey feathers at the feet of the others; who themselves stumbled, exhausted from battle. Their dirty and heavily damaged wings stood out in stark contrast to the brilliant white wings of their Sitcian subjugators. In their eyes, defeat - and an expectation of the worst.

Leading the Sitcians was a young, handsome warrior — God's strong, dark-haired General, Archangel Michael. His eyes burned of victory and, were he to have it his way, he would have quickly ended the existence of every one of these enemies of God. How could they believe they would succeed in this reckless betrayal of the One who created them?

Michael clearly understood His orders. Extermination was not one of them.

Just steps ahead of his Sitcian legion, Michael approached as if wielding the might and authority of God himself. Then, he raised his sword. All at once the Sitcian legion came to a dead halt.

Michael scanned the horde of rogue angels. His disdain for them and their rebellious actions showed clearly upon his face as he sought out their leader.

"Lucifer! Lucifer, you will show yourself…" demanded Michael. "…or I will cut a path to you with the blade of my sword!"

Out of loyalty, the horde of rogue angel warriors began to squeeze closer together, closing their ranks in an effort to protect their leader. Suddenly Lucifer's voice rang out from the pack. "Step aside!" The angel warriors of grey stepped aside, making an opening and revealing God's defeated nemesis.

Lucifer. A bit older than Michael, he was a strong, dark, evil being in both appearance and demeanor. Tall with dark hair, broad shoulders, and a muscular build, he embodied the very definition of warrior. As their eyes met, Michael's heartbeat quickened and his anger built. He could not understand why God would not allow him to vanquish this one — one whom He loved and trusted, only to see him become a traitor to His kingdom. Michael's thoughts turned to the past when he and Lucifer were the pride of the Sitcian force. He had looked upon Lucifer as a brother as they joined together on many of the most important assignments given by God himself. He recalled how he and Lucifer had captured and imprisoned the most destructive force of evil ever to find its way to God's kingdom. Where Lucifer had once stood tall in God's favor as one of His top Generals, he had now allowed that very same evil to seduce him. It had corrupted him, rotted away his goodness, and brought to Heaven the Great War.

Lucifer approached with arrogance and stood forward as the leader of the defeated angels.

"So what now, Michael? Death? Or, as I suspect, something far more interesting?" Lucifer asked.

"Were it my choice, you would no longer exist. But He decides all things. Something you would have been wise to have remembered. Nevertheless, know this: whatever happens here today, Lucifer… it is of your own doing," Michael said, returning the arrogance. Lucifer turned his head and spat.

Just as the tension peaked, the sound of a heavenly horn broke the silence. Michael maintained eye contact with Lucifer as the Sitcian Angels stepped aside to form an opening. With another blow of his horn, the Archangel Gabriel, a young, handsome, blond-haired messenger of God, glided in and landed beside Michael. Along with his beautiful golden horn, he carried an item wrapped and tied in gold and white cloth. Gabriel did not display the same anger as Michael as he faced Lucifer. His demeanor was much more administrative. At least this is how it started out.

"Lucifer," said Gabriel.

"A rare honor indeed to stand before messenger and executioner for judgment," Lucifer said.

"You were His most loved Sitcian, Lucifer," said Gabriel.

"Do not part your lips to speak to a warrior," Lucifer responded. "It is I who swore to defend His kingdom. I who should share in the power and glory. Yet you, Messenger, are allowed to know His secrets. Do not speak to me of His love. You have it, and you deserve none of it." Lucifer angered Gabriel with his words. "Let there be no doubt, Messenger. It is I who should choose to love Him!" Lucifer proclaimed angrily.

Angered, Michael instantly spun, drew his sword, and

parked it's point within the open space between Lucifer's lips. "Hold your tongue, Lucifer! Or I will remove it!"

Lucifer held his arrogance, eyeing Michael with contempt. As Michael lowered his sword, he closed in on Lucifer until they were face to face. He then untied a pouch on Lucifer's waist and removed a small thin book with the Arc-Pen Symbol burned into its leather cover. His eyes met Lucifer's again. For a moment Michael thought about the punishment for defying God's orders and considered slaying this heretic right where he stood. His breathing accelerated. Lucifer smiled at Michael. He knew what he considered.

"Did you feel it, Sitcian? Does it surge through your blood?" Lucifer asked. "A fleeting moment of standing apart from Him. It's like ice and fire all at once, is it not? Defy Him, Michael. Do it!" The very thought of defying God rattled Michael to the core. It horrified him. Then, he gained control over his thoughts as his breathing calmed.

"You no longer deserve such an honor," Michael said, holding up the book. Having decided against the act of defiance, Michael backed up to Gabriel, never turning his back on Lucifer, never breaking eye contact. He handed the book to Gabriel, who placed it in a pouch on his waist.

Gabriel looked Lucifer directly in the eye and proclaimed, "You want to rule, Lucifer, and so you shall. But it shall be over a kingdom not of good men, but of your own kind. And you shall never again know His kindness, nor His mercy - only the putrid fire of your own greed and jealousy."

Gabriel handed Michael the wrapped item. Michael untied and uncovered the item, revealing what few, even in His Kingdom, had ever had the honor of beholding. The Credara. A beautiful, ornate urn, slightly larger than Michael's hand, made of glistening silver metal and glass. Upon it, the Arc-Pen Symbol. Within it, precious water giving the Credara powers which can be wielded only by a Sitcian. The beauty of this vessel was overwhelming even to Archangels who had seen its beauty before, and knew of its power.

Michael held up the Credara as a gesture of honor, then tossed it onto the cloud floor near Lucifer's feet. Lucifer appeared frozen as the Credara created gold sparks and burned through the cloud floor. It then began plummeting to earth.

The Credara fell like a meteor cutting through space. It began to glow and trail fire. Then, in an uninhabited area, it struck the earth, creating a great opening with shock waves rippling from it. Suddenly a tremendous blast of bright light shot upward from the opening and into the clouds. The light struck the clouds just beneath

Lucifer's feet and quickly burned through. Lucifer felt the cloud floor beneath his feet begin to give way, but before he could react, the light created an opening through which he began falling to earth.

Directly down through the beam of bright light Lucifer plummeted, flailing about and yelling as he began a painful transformation. His wings flared out and began to be pulled harder and harder until they were ripped torturously from his back. His skin began to smoke and burn as his muscles deformed and grew. His face pulsed and cracked as bones throughout his entire body broke and reformed. Additional vertebrae formed from his spine and burst forth from his lower back to form a long scaly serpent-like tail. As he screamed out in excruciating pain, his eyes turned blood red and horns exploded from his skull. His skin sweat and settled into a deep dark red tone as he transformed from angel warrior into the horned dragon-like figure known... as Satan.

As he drew closer to earth, he continued growing larger; larger and more horrid until finally, fully transformed, he fell through the opening in the earth. All that was heard were monstrous screams of horror as Lucifer was cast into the eternal fires of his new kingdom. A place over which he would now have eternal dominion. Lucifer's Lair. Hell.

His red eyes descended into the darkness and fire as

the opening began to close. Lucifer's screams became more distant as two five foot thick stone plates, forming half circles, began sliding together, closing the lair entrance. A metal pillar positioned in the center of the stone plates, with the Credara on top, began rotating and descending, until finally the two halves slammed shut. The Lair Entrance was locked. The Credara, now the key to Lucifer's Lair, sat atop the entrance. Dead silence.

All at once the ground trembled as the earth around the entrance began to build up. From barren earth, dirt and rock formed until it became a small mountain covering the lair entrance entirely. The crest of this new mountain formation bore a uniqueness all its own. The Arc-Pen Symbol.

All eyes were fixed on the hole formed in the cloud floor as it slowly closed. Lucifer's young General, Licronus, stepped forward. Strong and dark like Lucifer, Licronus had a dusty complexion and wasn't as muscular. What he lacked in size, he made up for in fearlessness. And Licronus had an air about him which was much more sinister.

Despite what he had just seen, Licronus stared defiantly at Gabriel and Michael for a moment. Then, arrogantly, he began to laugh, mocking their actions against Lucifer. He then stopped, replacing his laughter with another defiant stare.

"So. What is to become of us, oh great Sitcian," Licronus asked, "now that you have your victory — for now?"

Gabriel confronted Licronus. "You could have been one of us, Licronus. An honor you chose to waste on Lucifer's lies and deception." Licronus smirked, almost laughing again.

"Do you doubt my words, Licronus?" Gabriel asked.

"I doubt everything, Gabriel," Licronus replied.

Gabriel became more serious. "You shall pay for your crimes, Licronus. You and your brethren."

Licronus interrupted, "And your blood, Gabriel, yours… shall travel the length of my blade."

"You and your horde shall be known from this day forth as Kraylen, after the filth and refuse discarded after the creation of the heavens and earth," Gabriel continued.

"Every Sitcian will fall!" Licronus declared.

"Look around, Licronus!" Gabriel continued. "See the beauty of Heaven for the last time. For He has said: 'You shall never set eyes upon it again.'"

Licronus sneered at Gabriel, "We shall see about that."

Gabriel then lifted his hands and conjured a tremendous force of light and energy. The wind whipped through as the energy built to its peak. Then, with one step forward, pushing, Gabriel directed this force to Licronus and his angel warriors. Explosively, all angels of grey were propelled up and outward in all directions.

Licronus and his rogue angels tumbled and fell uncontrollably from Heaven towards earth. As they fell, they, like Lucifer, began to painfully transform. Their wings remained intact but burned and turned from grey to jet black. Their skin turned leathery and darkened to the color of something dead. Their faces changed to those of ugly, demonic versions of their former selves — an unmistakably evil appearance to anyone setting eyes upon them. In every corner of the earth, they landed with great force and in crumpled heaps.

A fisherman and his young son were trolling for net floats not far from shore in the chilled waters of the China Sea. Just as the man reached for a float, a strange light and sound drew his attention. He and his son looked to the sky just in time to see a Kraylen land with tremendous force in the water nearby, sending a plume hundreds of feet into the air. The initial look of shock on their faces suddenly turned to one of horror as the force sent a forty-foot wave of water rolling their way. They both scrambled to grab the oars and escape, but it was too late. The huge wave engulfed and capsized their boat.

Seconds later, the young boy popped up out of the water and immediately began calling out as he frantically searched for his father.

Suddenly, with the force of an active volcano, the

winged Kraylen erupted from the water, swooped down and began flying directly towards the boy. The young boy's look of horror returned when he saw the ugly creature coming towards him. Just as it was about to decapitate him, the boy ducked under the water. The Kraylen missed its target and continued flying towards the shore, deciding not to return for another try. The boy popped up out of the water and watched with fright as the creature soared off into the distance.

In the sunlight of a clear sky, the leaves of a tropical forest glistened from an afternoon rain. A troop of chimps enjoyed a meal of fruit, leaves and buds from the abundance of trees. They happily swung from limb to limb, interacting during the course of a typical day.

Several of the chimps spotted something strange above the tree canopy. An opening in the thick canopy allowed them to see several trails of bright light in the sky. This resulted in a flurry of near panic among the troop as they all clamored to see. Only one of the light trails streaking across the sky was of interest to the troop: the one headed in their direction.

As it approached, the chimps somehow knew they were directly in the fireball's path. An alert went out and frantically hundreds of chimps made a mass exodus through the trees and brush to get out of its way. And not a moment too soon as, all at once, the fireball blasted through the tree canopy and landed, cutting a fiery swath through the forest floor. Trees burst into flames and exploded into the air as the fireball plowed a deep chasm through the earth's soil. Finally, it came to rest.

For a brief moment there was silence. Then, as quickly as they ran for cover, several of the chimps came back into the area to satisfy their natural curiosity. When the Kraylen emerged from the crater, smoking from the heat, the chimps again ran for safety. The Kraylen flexed its wings and then tucked them away. He then walked out of the crater and along the deep chasm formed by his landing.

As did the others, Licronus transformed as he streaked across the sky. He landed in a rocky deserted area, smashing into a huge boulder. A huge dust cloud emerged as the boulder quickly turned to rubble.

Licronus crawled from the rubble and dusted himself off, almost as if annoyed by Gabriel's actions. Could Gabriel possibly believe such a pitiful act would destroy them? As he continued dusting himself off, Licronus caught a glance at his hands which had taken on their new look. He then touched his face, feeling, searching for some iota of his former self. He found little. The fury within him rose as Licronus realized he had been changed, horribly disfigured. With great anger Licronus released a loud, frightening scream that resonated throughout the mountains. Fuming with anger, he spread his now jet-black wings and prepared to take to the air as the echoes diminished. Then he paused to think. Now was not the time to allow his anger to take over. Perhaps it would be best to preserve his energy. This world was not his. He had been cast out from his rightful home in Heaven. He knew the humans would not look kindly upon an ugly winged creature such as himself. So he tucked his wings away, drawing them into his body, and began walking.

Days and nights passed as he trekked through the dry rocky landscape, stopping for neither food nor water, his anger barely at bay, until one day at dusk he stumbled over something in his path and fell face forward to the ground. Licronus spat out dirt and brushed off his face. He turned to see what it was that had tripped him. A human. A man, wearing a warrior's garb, face down in the dirt. These pitiful humans know nothing of true war, he thought. They are given everything to exist peacefully and they make a mockery of it, destroying the greatest gift He has given them. Life. They should be made to pay.

Licronus stood and slowly moved closer to the man. He then reached down and turned him over, confirming his suspicions. The man was dead, the blade that had pierced his heart still within him. Licronus noticed the man's hand. The thick scar on the back of it was contrast-ed by a large unique ring on one of the fingers.

"Ahh. Something from this wretched world I actually want," Licronus said.

Licronus reached for the ring. As his hand neared the man's, suddenly a strange feeling rushed through him. A familiar feeling he couldn't believe was happening. Trans-formation. He closed his eyes until this brief moment passed. Then, he reopened them. When he did, he con-firmed something he had never expected. His hand had been transformed into an exact copy of that of the dead man; ring, scar and all. Licronus then touched his face. Exactly like that of the dead man's. He now realized that somehow, despite the burning and deforming exile from Heaven, he had kept his power to transform.

An enviable power, Licronus always viewed the abil-ity to transform, to shape shift to any human form, as a curse. Put to use whenever an angel was given a mission on the surface with the humans, it allowed an angel to blend in. Licronus would reject these missions whenever he could, as he despised the human creatures. He could never understand God's love for them. As an angel, he felt the humans were beneath him, literally and figuratively. So why? Why was this power not taken away? And what of the others? Then, Licronus realized. Again, his anger escalated.

"A cruel joke. The power to fit in unseen among these filthy humans," Licronus said. He stood and looked to the heavens.

"You bury us among them! Lower us into the dirt that is their worthless existence! I will not let you forget us! We will have our revenge!" he yelled.

Licronus then closed his eyes and, focusing his energy, transformed back into his Kraylen form. Breathing heavily for a moment, he inspected his hands once again. Then, he looked at the ring on the dead man's finger. He knelt, removed the ring and placed it on a finger of his left hand. He clenched his fist as he stared ahead in anger. Licronus then removed the man's sword, stood, turned and continued walking.

Day turned into night as he traversed the rocky dry landscape, continuing until day returned. Then, appearing almost like a mirage, he saw a large caravan of Amorites in the distance.

Licronus moved in closer and then paused out of sight for a moment to study them; their color, hair, mannerisms and their garb. Then, he began walking directly towards them. After a few steps, Licronus transformed himself into his own human form, wearing their nomadic garb. For now, he would be one of them.

PART TWO
The War Within

chapter two
A Troubled Soul

THOUSANDS OF YEARS LATER
15TH CENTURY EASTERN EUROPE
GOD'S HOLY ORDER

The God's Holy Order monastery had existed for as long as anyone could remember. As no records of its construction could be found outside of its walls, it was said by some to have been built by God himself, at the time of the beginning. This place was, and felt, very old.

The monastery was set a good distance from the nearest town and other territories. The Order had ensured adequate seclusion and privacy by owning all of the surrounding lands. The lands were lush and green with a fruitful forest on their outer reaches.

Within its walls, the monastery grounds themselves had a main castle-like structure built out of grey stone cut from a local quarry. It too was owned by the Order. It was the only stone of its kind in the world. The builders had used the same unique stone for the several modest structures that flanked the main building, and for the high wall that surrounded the main grounds.

Within the monastery, the exquisite architecture comprised beautiful high ceilings and magnificent archways made from exotic dark woods and stone from the quarry. Accented by floors of polished stone with large granite inlays, it had an almost regal feel. At any given time, the Order housed between 250 and 300 monks of every ethnicity, and from an array of religious denominations. The dorter of the monastery housed the monks' sleeping quarters, or cells. Rows of doors, set very close to one another, lined each side of the dorter's lengthy halls, a clear example of the modesty of a monk's communal life.

Dressing in the brown hooded wool garb was where tradition ended for these monks. Wearing their hair in a ponytail bound in a white sleeve embroidered in gold had replaced tonsuring, the European tradition of shaving the crown of a monk's head. It not only distinguished members of this order from all others, but it was neat and eased the grooming needs of a busy and dutiful monk.

Most days at the monastery were numbingly routine, but this warm summer day was a special one for Solis, one of the Elders and Headmaster. An intellectual in his mid-fifties with a distinctive scar across his left eye, Solis was the youngest of the Elders. Considered too young yet to ascend to the Court of Seven, he was nonetheless next in line should one of its current members die. Solis had been with the Order since he was very young, elevated to the position of Headmaster at a very young age with the sudden passing of his predecessor. As Headmaster, his job was to oversee the monks' education and training. When the Headmaster decided that a monk's training was complete, he sent the monk into the world to share and teach all that he had learned. On this day, a monk was leaving.

One of the benefits of being Headmaster was that the Order provided Solis an abbacy where he could execute the duties of his position. His abbacy was more like a library than an office. With a huge desk and sturdy chair, he had more than ample space for research and study. Wall cabinetry and shelves, which had lasted centuries, were filled with an abundance of old books, scrolls and parchments. As he prepared for the monk's departure, Solis pushed aside a rare and beautiful tapestry on his wall, revealing a large old wooden wall cabinet. Carefully, he used a key, tethered to him by a leather cord, to unlock it. Inside were precious papers, maps and religious artifacts, among other items. Most precious to him was a long, tube-shaped case containing a precious scroll. He felt the aging texture of the case. Tooled into its dark tanned leather was the Arc-Pen Symbol. So important was this scroll. Solis paused to think about what he was doing. Should he? This particular treasure had never been outside the walls of the monastery. Yes. Solis knew this monk well. He was the right one to have it.

Solis slowly moved over to his desk, which sat in the middle of the room, and untied the leather rope binding of the case. Ever so carefully, he removed the end cover and slid the scroll from its case. He handled the scroll with exceptional care, unrolling it carefully to confirm its contents. His eyes sparkled as he beheld this precious item. The scroll's pungent odor struck his senses like nothing else he'd ever experienced. Then Solis carefully re-rolled the treasure and returned it to its case, securing it with its leather binding. After tenderly kissing the case, Solis quickly exited his abbacy.

The main entrance to the monastery grounds was grand indeed, with a lush combination of green manicured lawn, trees and shrubs. Its wide, exquisitely laid stone pathway led from the wall's main gate to the massive granite staircase, which led to the huge, thick, solid wood front door. Hanging lanterns adorned the pathway as well as the two walkways coursing to either side of the main building. Midway between the main gate and the staircase was a large and beautiful stone fountain. Surrounding it, a superbly manicured garden, itself encircled by hand-crafted stone benches. The pathway beautifully encircled the fountain and garden in all of its splendor. Its grandness and beauty were things of pride for Solis, so much so that he traditionally received and sent each monk off into the world from here.

On this day, the fountain hosted Tan, a handsome young Asian monk. After tightening the last of his supplies to his horse, Tan paused for a moment to look up at the monastery and take in the grandness of its main entrance. Almost twenty years of his life had been spent within the hallowed walls of this place. The Order bought his family out of indentured servitude those many years ago. In exchange, the Order wanted a life for God's work — the life of young Tan.

Feeling both grateful and indebted, Tan's family allowed him to come to the monastery to learn the ways of a holy missionary. In Solis's eyes, Tan was the model monk during his time with the Holy Order, a truly fine example of his personal mentoring and leadership.

After checking to ensure all was secure, Tan mounted up. He steadied his horse, which moved about, anxious to begin the journey.

Solis rushed from the monastery front door, yelling "Tan! One last thing!" Solis hurried over and handed Tan the scroll. "Something very special."

Tan's eyes widened with disbelief. He ran his fingers across the Arc-Pen Symbol as he scanned the case. He gave Solis a stunned look. Tan knew not what the contents of the case were, only that they were very important. Solis told him that the scroll contained within was given by God, and that if he should ever find himself charged with its protection, he should protect it by whatever means necessary.

"I do not have the words, Headmaster," said Tan, in total awe.

"Do you have them with you, Tan?" Tan turned his eyes to Solis. Although startled by Solis's sudden seriousness, he knew what he referred to.

"Yes, Headmaster."

"Are you sure?" Solis asked.

"Yes."

"Do you remember everything I've told you?" Solis asked.

"I do, Headmaster."

"Everything, Tan?! Everything I've taught you?! Everything about them?!" Solis asked with more intensity.

By now, Tan's expression changed to one of deep concern. "Yes, Headmaster. Everything."

Solis smiled. "I know you will keep it close to your heart." Tan immediately raised the strap of the scroll case above his head and across his shoulder.

"It will never leave my side, Headmaster," said Tan as he pressed the scroll case firmly to his chest.

"You are one of good heart, Tan. The Shao-Tan monks are fortunate to get such a dedicated missionary. You will bring much to the people and land of your birth," Solis told him.

"I look forward to seeing my family again, Headmaster."

"The weeks ahead may challenge you. Make your journey home direct and swift. Be fearless, for you go with God."

"I will never forget you, Headmaster," said Tan, smiling proudly.

Solis nodded his head with pride as Tan adjusted his outer garment to more tightly secure the scroll case.

"And Tan… give my best to your mother and father. Tell them The Order says, 'Thank you.'" Tan smiled as Solis, holding back his emotions, lightly smacked Tan's horse on the rear. Tan rode off, leaving Solis looking on with great satisfaction. Solis then turned and walked back to the front door of the monastery. He turned for one final look at Tan riding off towards the main gate which had already been opened in anticipation of his departure. He then turned his eyes to the sky and paused a moment with a concerned look. Solis had prayed for good weather, but his greatest hope was that his prayers for Tan's safe passage would be answered. After another moment of thought, Solis entered the monastery.

Having made his way past the monastery gates and into the forest beyond, Tan struck a modest pace, knowing there would be a long journey. Focused on the road ahead, Tan had not noticed the lone figure observing his every move from behind a nearby tree. Licronus. Watching. His face reflected his high level of suspicion of what he was seeing. This arrogant monk riding with his false confidence.

"They think they know God," Licronus said to himself. "I know Him far better."

Just as Tan passed, a Kraylen man named Barejis and a Kraylen woman named Jirsa flew in, transforming themselves to their human form and tucking their wings as they landed. Barejis was tall, thin and lanky with dark hair. Hardly the warrior type, Barejis appeared more like a creepy spy of sorts, complete with the scraggly voice. In complete contrast, Jirsa was tall, dark and beautiful. While her dark brown flowing locks complimented her piercing eyes and her lovely olive toned features, they stood out in stark contrast to her warrior form. She looked to be someone who would not stand aside at a time of battle. They approached Licronus as he stared off through the trees.

"He gave him something, Licronus," Barejis said. "I knew there was something different about this one. My spies are never wrong."

Licronus furrowed his brow in anger. "Take as many as you need and follow him. Get whatever he has and bring it to me," Licronus said to Barejis.

Jirsa stepped closer to Licronus. "Licronus. Why do you send a spy to do a warrior's job? Why not allow me to handle this monk?" Barejis bristled at Jirsa's insult.

"Patience, Jirsa. I have something a bit more interesting for you. Besides, this monk is not chosen. It should be a simple task. Am I correct, Barejis?"

Barejis replied, glaring at Jirsa, "Yes, Licronus. You make the right choice, I assure you."

"Then you will not disappoint me," Licronus said.

Immediately, Barejis transformed into a winged Kraylen and took flight above the trees. Licronus continued to stare into the forest.

"Why not handle the monk yourself, Licronus?" Jirsa asked.

Licronus took a deep breath. "I have a much more important task at hand, Jirsa." After a moment, Jirsa rolled her eyes, shook her head, and began walking away.

"Jirsa!" Jirsa stopped and turned to Licronus. "One of the chosen will be yours. So that you may finish what you started." Jirsa gave Licronus an evil smile. She then turned, transformed into her winged Kraylen form and flew from the forest, leaving Licronus staring with a sinister look.

⌘

Solis entered his abbacy, pausing with a look of deep concern as he reflected upon what he had just done. Then, his concern began to mitigate as he smiled with pride about what he had given mankind in Tan. So long had he wanted a scholar like him. In all things, Tan had excelled. Especially at things which Solis knew he could never share with anyone, but somehow knew would someday come of use. Perhaps much sooner than later, Solis feared.

Solis had begun to arrange an assortment of books and scrolls on his desk when a familiar noise from just outside his window caught his attention. Being one of the Elders of the Order, Solis had the distinct pleasure of having a window which looked out onto the monastery square. Solis crossed to his window to spy on the activities.

Reflecting, Solis smiled again. His pride in Tan as a student extended far beyond his studies. Tan was a brilliant marksman at the only sport deemed mandatory for all monks by the Order: Archery.

In the square, a couple of dozen monks were fulfilling their required archery training. Although touted as sport for the improvement of focus and sharpening of the senses, the Elders had always known that the Order would need some way of defending itself against an enemy, should the need ever arise. As such, a monk's commitment to study was equaled only by his commitment to archery. As Headmaster, Solis made sure that this requirement was fulfilled - often giving personal instruction to the best students. The monks of the Order were the finest marksmen in the world. However, this was not what captured Solis's attention.

While some of the monks practiced their aim with a bow, others were engaged in a fierce battle of Cuju, the ancient kick-ball game Solis had played and loved all of his young life. Many a time Solis considered breaking a principal rule and entering a team in one of the local tournaments. He had always considered himself an excellent player and felt a team of his monks could meet the challenge of any in Europe. Alas, this could not be. A monk's life was a modest one. Studious and obedient. To break this rule would be unforgivable.

Solis was not the only one with a hearty interest in Cuju. Master Naji loved the sport as well. Chinese and in his mid-seventies with a lengthy silver beard, Naji looked as old as his years but was wise beyond them. He was smart and spiritual and had all of his wits about him. He was an Elder of the Order, and the Master Teacher of the

Hamen Art: the fighting art of the Sitcian Angel Warriors. The warrior forces of God.

Although Master Naji had lived at the monastery for many years now, his place was once out in the world as a holy missionary of the Order. It was believed that during this time he received and mastered the Hamen Art. His activities during the many years that followed were a well-kept secret by the Elders of the Order. Along his extensive travels, he picked up many a rare item for his weapons collection, in addition to his love for Cuju.

Master Naji sat almost floating in a meditative state on his balcony which looked out over the Square and the Cuju field. The expansive, well-manicured playing field was enclosed entirely within the walls of the monastery grounds. It was set up with netted goals on each end specifically for this game. Other than the occasional challenge on the archery range, it was the only truly competitive activity in a monk's life during his time with the Order.

Master Naji broke his meditation to spy on the game. He began to smile when suddenly, off in the distance beyond the walls of the monastery, an all-too-familiar sound of wings — heavy flapping wings — got his attention. His facial expression slowly changed as the steady beat invaded his senses. No matter how many times he heard this sound, it always struck a sense of horror in every inch of his being. He slowly looked up and saw the dark winged creature he had seen many times before, flying in the distance. This creature knew that Master Naji had seen him. He wanted to be seen.

"Our time will soon come, my enemy. You will pay for your misdeeds," Master Naji said, glaring at his unwanted visitor.

The creature then soared off. Master Naji continued to stare as the creature disappeared into the distance. He then began to reflect on the past, recalling the time when this creature first showed itself. It was not long after the arrival of his current Hamen student. One who, even at such a young age, made him aware that there was an enemy in their midst... that evil had invaded the hallowed ground on which the monastery stood. One whom Naji had trained since his childhood, and had loved like a son. The sound of the Cuju game filtered in, and once again Naji's attention turned to the group of monks being quite competitive just below his balcony. There he spotted his ward, the young monk called Agean.

Young, dark and handsome, Agean lay face up with his eyes closed on a stone bench just off the Cuju field. Sunlight trickled through the slight cloud cover and danced off his oily dark hair. He would often lie there, soaking up as much of the bright sun as his monk's garb would allow. Master Naji knew how special he was. He also knew his pain. He knew it as if it were his own.

Suddenly, a kick sent an errant Cuju ball bouncing Agean's way. Just as it was about to land directly on his face, he raised his hands and caught it as if somehow he could see it coming. Master Naji smiled at Agean's use of his razor sharp senses. He had always been impressed with this one. Jorgan, one of the Cuju players, jogged over to retrieve the ball.

"Agean, why don't you join us?" he asked, expecting the usual.

"No, Jorgan. Perhaps another time."

"You always say that," Jorgan huffed. "Come on, just one game."

"No, Jorgan."

"You are so stubborn. I'm just trying to be a friend."

Agean replied, "Sorry, Jorgan, I have other, less dangerous things to think about."

"Oh, yeah. Big warrior," said Jorgan sarcastically. "All you ever want to do is play with your swords. Well, in case you hadn't noticed, there aren't many battles going on around here."

Meanwhile, the monks, muttering from a distance, grew impatient waiting for the ball. Briton, one of the young monks, spoke up. "Jorgan, come on! His Preciousness won't play!" The other monks laughed. "Besides, all he is, is trouble."

Briton turned away and walked farther onto the field.

Jorgan gave Agean a look as if he knew what was coming.

Agean sucked his teeth, and then stood with the ball.

"Agean…" Jorgan said.

"He's right, you know."

"No, no. Agean, don't!" Jorgan begged.

Agean tossed the ball into the air and executed a masterful spinning kick, sending the ball rocketing top speed at Briton.

Jorgan yelled, "Briton! Look Out!" As Briton turned to the sound of Jorgan's voice, the ball struck him directly in the face, flipping him over backwards onto the ground. Briton, furious and holding his eye, got up and tried to storm his way over to Agean. His teammates rushed in to hold him off as the ball bounced its way back, stopping at Jorgan's feet. Fighting, at least out in the open, was strictly forbidden.

Agean, eyeing the ball said smugly, "Hmm. A rather dangerous game, wouldn't you say, Jorgan?" Agean then flipped the ball up to Jorgan with his foot. "One really ought to wear protection."

"Why did you have to do that?" Jorgan asked, gripping the ball angrily. "You're nothing but an ass! The only reason I came over here was because Headmaster asked me to!" Agean cut Jorgan an inquisitive look. "So, you know… when the next opportunity comes about, to try and maybe… be your friend." Agean turned directly towards Solis's window across the square and gazed at him. Solis, peering intently from his window was not at all surprised by Agean's actions. He shook his head and retreated into his abbacy.

"Sorry, Jorgan, never had much use for friends, and definitely not for Cuju," Agean said. "Besides, I need my rest." Agean resumed his position lying on the bench, stretched, and then closed his eyes. "Almost time to go play with my swords."

Jorgan slammed the Cuju ball onto the ground in anger and caught it off the bounce. He huffed and then began to hustle back onto the field. He turned to Agean. "I hope you get fat, just lying there!"

Agean replied, "Not as fat as you, my brother." Jorgan self-consciously paused for a moment to inspect himself, shook his head, then continued on to the Cuju field. Agean continued to lie with his eyes closed. A light breeze and the sound of the Cuju game in the distance relaxed him. Moments like these were a Godsend. Rare moments of peaceful thought. As he began to drift off into a light slumber, suddenly it began… again.

It started like it always had. Flashes of light through darkness intertwined with flashes of a scene Agean had never been able to understand, forced their way into his mind. Again and again, over and over, for as long as he could remember, the visions assaulted him. Blurred visions of flames, then darkness. Horrible screams, then darkness. Then, the very worst of it. The scene became more focused, more vivid: two unrecognizable women, their bodies bound to a post, were struggling, screaming out in horrible pain as flames engulfed their bodies. Then, the dark and morbid hand of a horrid creature, its thick leathery fingers bearing an unusual ring, crushing a man's throat in its grip as he chokes for air. Agean had never been able to see the face of this creature, nor that of the man whose throat collapsed in its grip, choking, trying to cry out. Then, sweating, Agean popped up, yelling "No!"

Breathing heavily, Agean tried to shake it off. This thing — this horrid thing will not let loose of me. Why? Why must I be tortured by this? Agean loosened the garb around his neck, gasping for air, revealing the Sitcian Mark of Hamen. It was as if he were the one being choked. By this point the Cuju game had stopped, with everyone looking at Agean.

Still gasping for air, Agean looked out at the monks. A few more deep breaths and he began to settle. Agean swallowed hard then struggled to get up. He gathered himself and walked to a nearby entrance of the monastery. The

Cuju players resumed play as Briton stared at the door Agean entered, watching it close. From his balcony, Master Naji had been watching, hoping the nightmare would not visit his student this time, hoping Agean could find some peaceful rest before today's Hamen training session. Naji turned back to the sky where he last saw the winged creature. Something within him told him that this demon and Agean would soon meet. Of this he felt certain.

Master Naji's training room was a virtual museum of weaponry from around the world; some arranged as ornamentation, some for training. On the walls and in display racks, weapons from ancient dynasties and realms past were presented for both their cultural beauty and their deadly purpose. Neatly arranged in open racks around the training room were warriors' weapons of choice. Spanning continents and kingdoms, all were necessary to properly train a Hamen Warrior. The floor was covered with a thin mat of interwoven reeds and straw. There were no chairs from which an observer could watch, no space for multiple students to train. There was just one wooden kneeling block mounted in the floor at one end of the room. In this training room there was only one Master, one student. A few well-placed oil lanterns provided modest yet adequate lighting. It was a place for intense training and, as well, it was a spiritual place.

Master Naji stood in a meditative state near the center of the room wearing his usual blood-red satin training garb. Agean entered dressed in comfortable training garb matching Master Naji's, but white in color. Master Naji explained to Agean early on that white stood for the purity of his heart, the flawlessness of his movement, and the perfection of his art. He would wear this color until he completed his training.

Upon his waist, Agean carried the Swords of Hamen that Master Naji bestowed upon him as a teenager. Formed from Hamen Living Metal, these weapons were light, razor sharp and unbreakable. Unlike the heavier swords used by the warring masses of conquerors and pillagers alike, the Hamen Swords were made to be fast and highly maneuverable. They slid like silk from their beautiful black and silver sheaths. Upon both sword and sheath, beautiful crests bearing the Arc-Pen Symbol.

Agean entered hesitantly, knowing he was late for his session. Master Naji seldom mentioned Agean's tardiness upon his arrival; nevertheless Agean knew he would pay the price for it eventually. He presented himself to Master Naji and bowed respectfully. Master Naji remained silent and still. Agean removed his Hamen Swords and laid them on a table next to the door. As he turned, he bumped into one of Master Naji's sword relics, making a noise.

Master Naji reacted instantly. "Shh!"

Agean clenched his teeth, then scurried to take his usual position on the wooden kneeling block. They remained still in silence for a few moments until finally Agean's curiosity got the better of him.

"Master, if I may ask. Why do you stand?"

Master Naji replied, "My boy, many a battle has been lost because someone was sitting when it began."

At that very moment, with the quick movement of only one arm, Master Naji hurled a dart from his robe at Agean. With his keen Hamen senses, Agean heard the needle-sharp dart and caught it without looking, before it penetrated his head.

Impressed, Master Naji told him, "Your Hamen skills are nearly perfect."

"If I may say, Master," Agean said as he eyed a fly buzzing about near a post close to Master Naji. He also saw that another fly had already landed on the post. Agean focused and hurled the dart, piercing the fly in the air, and pinning it to the one on the post. "It is not my skill that worries me."

Master Naji looked at the dart and then turned to Agean. "What is it, Agean?"

"The visions, Master."

"You have not mentioned these visions for some time, Agean."

"Yes, Master. I try not to burden you with such things. But they haunt me now more than ever. I can still see it so clearly, yet I cannot see who or what it is... what it means."

Master Naji removed the dart with the impaled flies and then turned, holding it up for Agean to see. "Mysteries are many in a young warrior's life, but it is mystery that allows one a chance to learn... to achieve clarity. Along the path to clarity, what is revealed for a Hamen Master is that a life taken, even if taking it serves the purpose of goodness, is still a life taken. A Hamen Master must preserve life whenever possible. One must be patient and understand that the lesson we learn from this is at times a painful one." Master Naji held up the dart. "Even for the lowly fly." Agean got the message. He was now embarrassed by his needless display of skill.

Then suddenly, lecture over, Master Naji spun, discarded the dart back into the post, and froze in a Hamen fighting stance. With his head, he beckoned Agean to join him. Agean jumped up into a Hamen stance and then quickly responded as Master Naji hurled six small razor sharp disks directly at Agean. Agean snatched the satin sash from his waist like a whip and spun, masterfully targeting each spinning disk as it nearly penetrated his flesh, stopping each dead in its path. The Hamen training for the day had commenced.

Both Master Naji and Agean flipped backwards to remove swords from weapons racks. Master Naji displayed a level of sword weaponry unmatched by any. Agean met his challenge masterfully — that is, until the great Naji, as he had always done, reminded Agean just who was indeed Master. With a move that landed Agean face down on the floor, Naji placed the tip of his sword to the base of Agean's skull. A mere inch of penetration would have taken Agean's life.

"You were late today," Master Naji said. Agean rolled his eyes, took a deep breath and executed a rolling maneuver that sent Master Naji flipping through the air, allowing Agean to escape. The Hamen training continued for the next hour, weapon after weapon, until Master Naji decided to end it.

Once the training was complete, Master Naji bowed to Agean, who respectfully returned the gesture. Naji then, as he had always done, crossed to a small dark wooden cabinet near the far wall of the training room. He grasped the small brass knobs of the cabinet doors and opened it, revealing a human hand sealed in a clear square glass container.

Master Naji then turned to Agean and asked, "Agean. What is it you see here?"

Agean walked over to the container, just as he had done so many times before, peered through the glass, and replied, "I see what I have always seen, Master. The hand of a man." Master Naji nodded, acknowledging Agean's answer.

"Master. When shall I know the reason for this question?" Agean asked.

Master Naji replied, gazing into Agean's eyes, "As I have always said. It is not for you to know, until it is time to be known."

Just as he had done so many times before, Agean accepted the Master's answer, then bowed. Master Naji returned the bow, then watched as Agean crossed to the door, retrieved his Hamen Swords and exited. Master Naji then closed the cabinet, saying to himself, "I fear, however… it will be soon."

Agean always felt exhilarated and renewed after his training. Master Naji had trained him since his awakening at the monastery. Agean usually referred to his arrival as an awakening because he had little recollection of his life beforehand. Although he had never been sure why only he had received the honor of training in the Hamen art, it was his Hamen training that allowed him to survive his life as a monk. Questioning Master Naji about this only subjected him to an onslaught of proverbs instead of answers. He had given up asking many years ago.

From the moment Agean set eyes upon him as a child, Master Naji filled the void of family and friendship for him. This was fortunate for Agean as his reputation for rebelling against his dutiful studies and lengthy prayer, as well as his negligence of charitable works and chores, had gained him little in terms of friendship or regard. Rather than be continually punished for his disobedience, Agean learned to stick somewhat to the regimental schedule — at least until he decided to break the rules.

For now, Agean sat in a large dusty room in the cloister of the monastery with a dozen other monks, each with an assortment of old books and scrolls. Some of the monks were reading, some were scribing with quills. The study rooms were the most uncomfortable of any place in the monastery. Drab curtains covered the walls and doorways. There was no sunlight, only oil lamps that burned with a stale odor. Hard, flat wooden chairs had no padding but did have the occasional splinter. Agean was sure the Elders decided that discomfort might just prevent the young monks from nodding off. Besides, suffering was part of the deal for a monk.

Gastus, a burly old monk instructor who had surely

eaten more than his share of the morning meal, sat at the front of the room napping and lightly snoring. Agean noticed years ago that the instructors were the only ones provided padding for their chairs in the study rooms. This would certainly explain Gastus's ability to slumber with such ease. Bringing one's own pad was expressly forbidden, so some of the monks had taken to hiding small pads under their robes for themselves and others. Aside from Cuju, this camaraderie had become the basis of fraternity among many of the monks. A fraternity Agean elected not to be part of.

Agean sat in back at a far corner desk, appearing to read but constantly nodding, fighting sleep. The discomfort of the study room had never been a match for Agean's need for sleep. He was never sure whether it was the interminably boring scripture, the late nights practicing his Hamen skills, or the dark, gloomy light of the study room that brought on the insatiable need. Nevertheless, the fight continued — not only because sleeping during study broke a fundamental rule, but because of the troubling visions.

As most often occurred, Agean lost the battle, and the haunting visions took over. The horrid images and terrifying screams raced through his mind, intensifying and torturing him, until finally, they jarred him awake, causing him to make a loud noise as he was ripped from his slumber. This got the attention of the monks around him and awakened Gastus mid-snore.

Gastus yelled out while slamming an old text on the desk, "Quiet! Or I'll take your Cuju privileges away!" He then snorted, repositioned himself in his chair and resumed his nap. Harsh stares cut through Agean like a knife through soft bread. Once the stares subsided, Agean quietly gathered his books and things and slipped through the curtain and out the rear entrance.

Monks walked briskly back and forth through the halls of the monastery, much like ants circulating throughout their nest. Agean, with books in hand, made his way towards the Great Foyer. His mind still recovering from the episode in the study room, he bumped into a monk headed in the opposite direction, causing an avalanche of books to the floor.

"I am so sorry. Forgive me," Agean said as he and the monk scampered to pick up and sort out the books. The monk gestured his appreciation as he gathered his last item and quickly continued down the hall. Agean watched as the monk disappeared around a corner. He took a deep breath and blew it out. He then turned and continued down the hall.

Agean entered the Great Foyer, the expansive main entry

hall of the monastery adorned on both sides with huge white marble statues of various warriors, all bearing real swords. Agean paused as he entered the corridor. There had always been something about this place that had given Agean a strange feeling; almost as if the statues were reaching out to him each time he passed through. Agean's usual choice was to walk quickly, dead center through this corridor, to lessen these effects. If it weren't for the fact that this path was the quickest to the front garden and main gate, where Agean often sought solitude, he would seldom pass this way.

Agean noticed that the massive front door at the other end of the foyer stood open. He hadn't expected it this soon after Tan's departure, but this usually meant only one thing. Fresh meat to fill the empty slot.

"Agean," a familiar voice rang out, startling Agean as Solis approached from behind.

Agean turned, "Headmaster."

"Shouldn't you be in the study room or something right now?" Solis asked.

"On my way, Headmaster," Agean replied.

"Well, loitering in the halls will certainly not get you there, my boy," Solis said as he started walking towards the front door. "Move along now."

Solis quickly made his way down the hall as Agean

watched for a moment. Once Solis was at a good distance, Agean too began walking quickly, following Solis's path. Solis exited through the front door and disappeared from view. After a few moments, Agean reached the front, but instead of exiting, he veered over to a window just to the left of the door and peered out.

Solis stood at the bottom of the granite staircase, graciously welcoming a young wide-eyed teenage boy to the Order. A Norse, Agean guessed by his appearance, about thirteen years of age. The boy's parents huddled together a few paces to his left. Although they appeared to be of modest means, in their eyes there was no shortage of love for their son. They failed miserably at masking their looks of sadness with that of pride as they gave their child over to what they hoped would be a better life — an honorable life in service to God.

Agean had always imagined this to be the way it was for him; his parents making the ultimate sacrifice so that he could have a life that they could not give him. Loving parents who would hope to see him again someday, but knowing that giving their son to the Order might make that impossible. Parents whose faces he cannot remember. Perhaps he was simply too young. It wasn't long after his arrival that Agean learned one of the most important directives of the Order: Free your minds of that which brought you to this place, for this is your rebirth as a servant of God. Yes, Agean supposed that he too was once fresh meat.

The teenager's grip on his travel sack, all that remained of what would soon be his former life, tightened as he looked over at his parents for the last time. Tears began to well up in his eyes as he scanned the front of the massive main monastery building, trying to soak it all in. In contrast, Solis displayed a very proud demeanor, happy to add another fine young monk to the ranks. He would soon receive the directive. "Fresh meat," Agean said to himself. "Good luck."

❧

As the sun retreated beyond the forest on the horizon, evening routines set in at the monastery. Daily tasks were complete for most monks. Those who chose to participate in the evening chants were already gathered in the chapel. While the Order considered chanting a higher form of meditation, it was also a source of pride for the monks and particularly the Elders. Some felt the chants were like the sound of an angel's harp, somehow bringing them closer to God.

For now, the monastery halls were quiet with the exception of a subtle ambiance that seemed to occupy every inch of the place, almost like a low hum resonating just south of the senses. Then, footsteps: piercing, familiar footsteps that permeated the halls in a manner in which their purpose could not be mistaken. Solis's angry footsteps.

Solis walked hurriedly down the hall to Agean's cell door and knocked.

"Agean!" Solis called out in a stern voice. No answer. Solis knocked harder. "Agean, if you are in there, open this door!"

The door directly across the hall slowly opened. Briton looked out sporting a black eye from his earlier confrontation with Agean. Solis heard the door open and turned to him.

"Where is he?" Solis asked.

"I do not know, Headmaster. Perhaps the chapel," replied Briton.

Solis cut a stern look to Briton. Everyone knew Agean would not be caught dead in the chapel unless it was mandatory. "Briton, someone mentioned seeing him leaving the grounds. Now if you know where he is-"

"Truly, Headmaster, I have no idea," said Briton, interrupting. "Even if I did, I'm not sure it would matter."

Solis asked, "What do you mean, Briton? And this had better be good."

Briton swallowed. "I intend no disrespect, Headmaster, but for some reason our brother appears to have privilege, as you allow him to do as he pleases. As if he's royalty. We all see it. He runs off at night to God knows where. Dare I say, Headmaster, if no reason exists for such privilege, then none of us understand why you keep him here."

Solis paused, considering Briton's words, then said to him, "Get some sleep." Briton gave Solis a confused look, took a deep breath and then turned to go back into his cell. "And Briton!"

Briton turned back to Solis. "Yes, Headmaster?"

"Have that eye looked at."

Briton smirked and then turned and shut the door, leaving Solis with a concerned look.

chapter three
A Warrior's True Self

The Dancing Swine. In the nearby town of Dearby, The Swine, as it was affectionately called, had for decades been the local watering hole for travelers, vagrants, traders and anyone wanting a pint at the end of a long day. Tonight was no different.

It bore a somewhat rundown appearance as it could have used a few repairs, but its creaking sign and scratched door fit well with the surroundings. Inside, The Swine's walls were lined with trophies of the hunt, relics from adventures abroad donated by grateful patrons. There were dents, cracks and deep slits from the many drunken brawls of the past. The old chairs were comfortable enough, and the place had enough light for those who wished to see with whom they were drinking, and dark enough for those who lurked in the corners discussing less than honorable things.

This night, The Swine was abuzz with laughter, merriment and spirits. Both men and women, grungy from the trail and fresh from the hunt, told their embellished tales of victory, and excused their failures in good cheer. Sally, a waitress of Scottish descent, whose face showed the effects of a long hard life, took an order from an unruly bunch at a table. She smacked away the hand of one who had gotten the courage to touch her backside. After the collective "boos" of disappointment for her actions, she crossed to the bar where Jacob, a greying Scottish bartender, handed off a foamy brew to a patron.

In their youth, Jacob and Sally had each made the long trip from Scotland with their families, as many did, seeking a better life mining in the ore-rich areas of Eastern Europe. While precious ores of gold or silver were the ultimate goal, most often mines yielded ores more suitable for armor and swords. It was a filthy job bringing no great amount of wealth to those seeking more.

Now, having served patrons at The Swine for many years, Jacob and Sally knew almost everyone and everything, including that of which they preferred not to speak.

Jacob, leaning in and speaking softly asked, "Now Sally, what damage will those cretins be doin' tonight?"

"Well, let's see now. We'll need a couple of Brown Ales, a shot of Burgess and, oh, this one on me left here wants to try the house special," Sally replied. Jacob eyed the drunken man sitting at the bar to Sally's left.

"Well, does he now? And not a smarter gent in the place, I'd say," said Jacob standing tall and full of pride. "T'was me Granddad's recipe, don't ya know."

"Yes, Jacob, I know. We all know," Sally responded, rolling her eyes.

Jacob turned and reached into a cabinet behind him to grab an unlabeled jug of the house special. Just as he lifted the jug from its place, the drunken man fell off his stool and loudly crashed to the floor. Out cold. Jacob, hearing him fall, simply placed the jug back into the cabinet. He leaned over the bar to have a look at the gent.

"You, my friend, are missing out. That was a fresh batch made just this mornin'," Jacob said to him.

Then the front door swung open and Agean entered. Agean's popularity was apparent as the regulars showed their happiness to see him. Agean waved to some of the ladies and gents and then walked over to the bar. He saw the drunken man sprawled out on the floor.

"Another good night, aye Sally?" Agean asked.

Sally replied, "Ah, never mind him. He doesn't like me prices." They all laughed.

"Well, well. Good to see ya, Agean," Jacob said. "Come by to pay us a quick visit? Or will ya be stayin'?"

Agean replied, "Definitely stayin', my friend."

Sally happily responded, "Well. Then a bit of an honor for us it is. Pour him up, Jacob. Ya don't want to keep the gentleman waitin'."

Jacob bowed to Sally. "As you wish, me lady." He then turned to Agean, "So what'll it be, Agean, the usual?"

"Well I definitely don't want what he's havin'," Agean said referring to the drunken man still sprawled out on the floor.

"Well then, say no more, my friend," Jacob replied.

Jacob poured up a dark ale for Agean as Sally took her drinks to the now impatient, unruly bunch.

Sally yelled, "Keep ya breeches on, Gents! I'm comin'!" Agean smiled at Sally's antics.

Jacob said, "Good to have ya here tonight, Agean. Not sleepin' much, eh?"

"Not much, my friend," Agean replied.

Jacob said whispering, "Ya know. There's a friendly game of sin goin' in the back room there. Might be room for one more." Jacob winked at Agean.

Agean leaned in and replied, "Now Jacob. Being as how I'm a holy man, it goes against all that I stand for." Agean proceeded to slam a pouch of coins onto the counter. "But seein' as how I'll be sittin', I don't think the Big Fella upstairs will notice."

Jacob laughed. "That's me boy."

They both laughed as Agean picked up his drink and slyly went around the bar to the door of the back room. He heard a ruckus coming from the room as he neared the door. Then, he heard a glass explode against the door. Agean turned to Jacob, "Friendly, ya say?"

Agean opened the door and entered the back room. Jacob smiled, poured up a shot and took it down in a single gulp.

"Ahh. Looks as if it's gonna be a good long night," said Jacob to the empty shot glass.

Outside The Swine, the flickering light from oil lanterns and shadows of movement within filtered through the strange eerie darkness of the moonlit road just beyond its front door. The road was empty and silent but for the faint sound of activity inside. Then, the distinctive sound of crunching footsteps emanating from the dark passages in the distance soon broke the emptiness. Suddenly, three dark figures slowly appeared from different directions and approached the pub. As they approached, the moonlight slowly revealed… they were Kraylen — weapons drawn — their evilness piercing the darkness. Then, they all stopped and stared with menacing looks at The Dancing Swine.

❧

By the early afternoon, the skies had opened up to a torrential downpour that continued long into the night. Through the darkness, rain poured onto the forest canopy with a fierce intensity. Lightning streaked across the sky, piercing the stillness of dark clouds as they loomed frozen in place, coursing through the grey fluff like veins through flesh. The onslaught of pounding rain weighed down the canopy top, partnering with the harsh wind to bring down the occasional tree branch.

Tan knew that the harsh wind whipping through the trees could hurl one of those deadly branches his or his horse's way. It would prove an odd demise, but demise nevertheless. Then again, perhaps this was just an excuse. He recalled the seriousness of Solis's last words to him. It replayed over and over in his mind countless times since his departure from the monastery. This, along with the strange unshakable feeling that he was being followed, fed both his suspicions and his actions. It kept him sharply alert at all times, allowing him little sleep in the week since his journey began. So in a small clearing among the trees, Tan and his horse waited. Tan, his hood completely covering his head, knelt in the mud next to his horse, getting drenched. Tan needed the space provided by the clearing so he could defend himself against any approaching enemy or airborne weapons. The rain was of no consequence.

Tan was smart and he had learned long ago that the rain was no enemy. It had been some time but he remembered much about his life before the Order. While his parents and others in his small province rushed indoors to get out of the rain, he and his grandfather would make their way to a nearby lake – to the usual spot where, just at its edge, sat two perfectly situated smooth stones that provided enough comfort to sit and meditate for hours if they chose. Once there, he and his grandfather would allow themselves to be drenched and become one with nature. "One must never run from that which gives life," his grandfather would tell him in his native Mandarin. Stories about his family would soon follow - of times before they were forced out of his homeland by a territorial conflict with the Ming almost forty years prior. Left no choice but to flee the country with his family, he eventually settled into servitude so that his wife and young children could have food and shelter. Shelter. Today, Tan would have none. But neither his gut feelings nor his desire for shelter would deter him from his task. He must make it to the Shao-Tan province: the place of his youth. Although most monks from the Holy Order never saw home again, this was part of the deal Tan's parents negotiated. The Order only agreed because of the Shao-Tan Temple. Tan would be the first holy missionary from the Order to be placed there. But for now, this was secondary. His primary task was to make it safely to the Temple – Solis's precious package intact.

The light of a fresh morning day shone upon the Holy Order of God monastery. However, a vow of poverty for a monk not only means no windows through which to receive the warmth of the morning sun, but also very modest accommodations. A small bed with a thinly stuffed mattress, a bowl filled daily with fresh water for washing, a desk for studying, a rack to hang one's clothing, and a rag. Unlike that of his brethren, Agean's cell had a square wall mirror hung with chord above his washing bowl. Master Naji saw to it that his young student was provided this mirror soon after his arrival. He felt it necessary for Agean to connect with his soul by looking deeply into his own eyes – to see within himself. He assured Agean that it was an essential part of his training as a warrior.

Suddenly, the door to Agean's cell burst open, revealing an angry Solis holding a stumbling, drunken Agean tightly by the arm. Solis stumbled with Agean into the room and shoved him onto his bed. Agean grimaced and moaned. His head ached from a night of spirits and gambling.

Solis yelled angrily, "You set an awful example for the others, Agean! Just look at you!"

"You should see the other fella. No wait… wait. Was it you? Are you the other fella, Headmaster?" Agean replied, laughing, sarcastic and drunk. Agean then removed three sacks of coins tied together from his pocket. He'd had a very successful evening at the card table.

"How dare you bring your ill-gotten gains into a house of God?" Solis said angrily. Agean then quickly held up one finger as he began to gag.

"Um. Excuse me," Agean said as his cheeks began to puff out. Then, suddenly and violently, Agean leaned forward and hurled vomit all over the floor in front of Solis. Solis jumped to avoid getting hit, looking at Agean with sheer disgust. Agean leaned up and proclaimed, "Sorry, Other Fella."

Solis began to fume. He pointed, yelling at Agean, "You have no respect for our rules and think only of yourself! We shall see what the Court has to say about this one!" Agean let out a huge, loud belch, then began fanning his mouth. Solis frowned from the putrid odor. Suddenly, Agean plopped backwards onto the bed and lay there, trying to shield his eyes from the light coming in from the hall.

"And you will clean this up!" Solis said sternly. Getting no response, Solis huffed then marched out of Agean's cell and slammed the door. Agean reacted with pain to the door slam.

"Oh! Oh, that hurt," Agean said grimacing. Agean then lifted his arm and waved to the door. "Good night." His arm flopped back onto the bed, and almost immediately Agean began snoring as he passed out asleep.

Once again, Solis found himself in the hallway outside

of Agean's cell, this time just glaring at Agean's door. The flames from the lanterns that lined the halls flickered as monks passed back and forth. Solis breathed a heavy sigh. As he pondered the situation, Iorbus, a very wise looking Elder of the Order, approached from down the hall. He was in a fine mood that morning and saw Solis at Agean's door.

"Ah, Solis," Iorbus said, patting him on the shoulder. "And how is our young Agean doing this fine morning?"

Solis said reluctantly, "Oh, fine, Iorbus. Fine. Just tired from another late night of… study."

Iorbus responded, "Solis, you push the young man too hard. You should tell Agean to take time out and have some fun."

Solis, accepting Iorbus's advice, bowed respectfully and said calmly, "Yes Great Elder."

Iorbus softly patted Solis's shoulder then continued down the hall.

Solis quickly turned to catch him. "Iorbus!" Iorbus stopped and turned back to Solis. Solis took him aside and spoke softly to him. "Great Elder, I must speak with you about Agean's behavior. It only gets worse, and I fear the others are noticing that we do nothing to control him."

"Solis, we have spoken on this topic before. Agean will be fine," Iorbus said. Iorbus turned to continue down the hall, only to be stopped by Solis again.

"But Great Elder, should we not do something?" Solis asked.

Iorbus replied, "Solis. If you recall, this was your decision. So you, if anyone, should know why we choose to allow him the room we have. If he were to discover what we know, what we keep from him, we might lose him forever and that cannot happen. You yourself have admitted that the guilt tears at you. We've already lost one, Solis, and you do understand how disastrous that could have been. And the Court agrees."

"But Great Elder…"

"Let him be, Solis," Iorbus interrupted. "He will be fine." He again placed a hand on Solis's shoulder, then turned and continued down the hall. Solis watched as Iorbus walked away.

Solis turned and walked back to Agean's door. Suddenly, something out the corner of his eye caught his attention. Briton had cracked his door and stared out at Solis. As Solis turned to look directly at him, the door quickly closed.

"You are all responsible for each other around here, Briton!" Solis exclaimed, staring at Briton's door. "As such, you and your brothers can expect the usual extra chores and study to pay for Agean's transgressions!" A frustrated Solis huffed, then turned and marched off in the other direction.

Almost pitch black darkness, except for a thin beam of light which penetrated from underneath the door. It had only been several hours since Agean met Solis's wrath head-on for his drunkenness and sinful gambling so he was still asleep. The sounds of hustle and bustle which normally emanated from the halls were all but gone. The only sound to be heard was that of Agean's deep loud snoring as he lay in the same spot on the bed where Solis left him earlier. Then suddenly, there was another sound. The door latch to Agean's room began to slowly click as if someone wished to enter unnoticed. The door creaked and whined from a lack of grease as it slowly opened. The light from the hall slowly penetrated the room until it reached Agean's face. Never capable of deep sleep, Agean's slumber was immediately disrupted by the light. His snoring ceased as he struggled to part his eyelids while using his arm to block the light shining in his face. When he managed to do so, he saw a blurry yet familiar sight: several figures, some holding candles, approaching him. Leading the rebels was Briton who bent down and stared at Agean with disdain as he began to awaken. Briton fanned his nose from the putrid odor of vomit and drink on Agean's breath. Suddenly Agean realized what was happening.

"Oh, come on… not again!" Agean blurted out as several arms reached out and grabbed him from his bed. The added chores and study brought on by Agean's antics had once again raised the ire of his monk brothers. "Remember what happened last time!" Agean garbled, still feeling the effects of last night's spirits. Briton lagged behind as the monks struggled with Agean, forcing him from his room.

Briton said, "I think we can handle you this time, Agean." As he took a step towards the door, Briton slipped and landed flat on his back. After a moment of moaning, Briton's attention was diverted from the pain, to the retched odor which seemed to surround him. He sniffed and frowned in disgust and confusion. Then he realized that he had landed in a thick puddle of vomit, the very same which Agean heaved during his scolding by Solis. Briton did all he could not to lose his stomach as he quickly peeled himself from the floor. Still struggling to keep his stomach, Briton exited the room, shutting the door behind him.

PART THREE

The Time Is Now

chapter four
Death Is Captured

Kraylen do not die. They age to adulthood, and then at some point, stop. Living on earth among the humans has been their Hell for thousands of years. Hidden. Transformed so as to go unnoticed by these beloved children of God. The Kraylen considered humans filth. They should have been able to crush the Sitcian Angels and defeat God. But they failed and now they were here.

The Kraylen dared not rise up against the humans. Besides, they had no real interest in what the humans possessed, and the Kraylen were outnumbered. So they waited, secretly coexisting deep within the fabric of the human world. Eating as humans did, working their lands, fighting their wars, patiently planning while increasing their numbers. Yes, it wasn't long before the Kraylen discovered that the humans were suitable for but one thing: breeding.

When a Kraylen bred with a human, their offspring were born of the great evil. They were half-breed, but they were Kraylen. The newly born were raised to keep their evil secret from their human parent. This deception served as the first training of a young Kraylen's existence. If the deception did not hold, they simply ended the life of the human parent. In time, the Kraylen were in every corner of the globe. After many centuries of hiding in the darkness and carefully plotting, their leader, Licronus decided. It was time.

Licronus and his two young Kraylen Generals, Poragon and Bralorg, all in their human form, rode top speed on horseback through the forest. Poragon and Bralorg were big and strong, and among the most highly skilled of the Kraylen warriors. Once successfully embedded deep into the workings of human life, the Kraylen forces formed a secret training network. They had been preparing their forces for battle for centuries. Poragon and Bralorg had trained thousands of Kraylen. While Poragon was dark haired and Bralorg fair, a morbid similarity to Archangels Michael and Gabriel, Licronus had one distinguishing characteristic that continually fueled his anger against the humans. He was missing his left hand.

The sun entered the beginnings of a full eclipse, an event so rare that most considered it a thing of myth and folklore. Some called it God's work, while others called it evil and a sign of imminent doom. To Licronus, it served as the ticking clock by which they must reach their destination. As they rode, Licronus looked up to check the status of the eclipse. They thundered on and soon reached a clearing at the outer edge of the forest. At the other end of the clearing, a cliff with an immense drop onto the flatlands below; an unfortunate circumstance for a mere human, but proving little more than an everyday challenge for a superior Kraylen.

Instead of slowing as they approached the deadly cliff, the Kraylen rode harder and faster. Reaching the edge, they quickly transformed into their winged form and grabbed tight to their saddles. Having done this many times before, their steeds blindly stayed the course. The horses neighed loudly as all three leapt from the cliff and glided to the ground below. As they touched down they did not slow one bit. The Kraylen tucked their wings and continued thundering on. As they approached a marketplace in the distance, they transformed back to human form. The eclipse was now more than half complete as they raced against time.

It had been close to an hour more of non-stop riding for Licronus and his Kraylen Generals. The eclipse was not yet complete. They made it to their destination in time.

The marketplace consisted of a main street lined on both sides by tent-like shops of all sorts. Like a small town, it popped up out of nowhere many years ago. Like so many of these makeshift towns, its inhabitants were mostly transient. And like its inhabitants, it too would vanish when the time came.

As the sun was now almost completely eclipsed, the people of the town shielded their eyes as they tried to see. Some scampered for cover from the evil setting upon them, some welcomed the marvel from God's hands. Licronus and his Kraylen quickly rode in, dismounted, and tied off their horses. They hurried down the street.

Drokus, an ill-dressed older man with bad teeth, and breath to match, hurried to meet them as they approached.

"I did not think you were coming," Drokus said.

Licronus quickly responded, "We haven't much time. Where is he?"

"In the shop over there," replied Drokus, pointing the way. Licronus eyed the small artifacts shop a short distance away.

"Did you get what I asked for?" Licronus asked.

"Yes," Drokus replied, as he directed Licronus's attention to a horse-drawn wagon with a coffin-like box and locking chest in it. "Do you have the gold?"

Licronus replied, "You will get it when we have what we came for." Licronus then turned to his Generals. "Prepare." The Generals headed for the wagon.

"Come with me," Licronus told Drokus as they headed for the entrance of the artifacts shop.

Licronus and Drokus quickly entered the shop, a tent filled wall to ceiling with items from various places around the world. They weaved their way through various pottery items and religious and pagan artifacts till they reached a black curtain covering the entrance to a back room. Drokus entered first, followed by Licronus. Many more ancient cultural artifacts filled the dimly lit room.

Seated in the middle of the room before a fire warming a small bowl, was Gabris, an old bearded gentleman looking both enlightened and weary of the world. He knew things few others dared to know, and had been places few others had ever heard of. He had surrounded himself with glaring proof of this in the form of artifacts from hidden tribes and cultures. Robes, books, crosses, rugs, tapestries and other items filled every inch of space.

The strong aroma of burning bark and petals filled the air. Gabris peered into a half empty bottle of yellow liquid, caressing it as if it were gold. Drokus and Licronus approached. Drokus gestured for Licronus to sit on the pillows in front of the warming bowl.

"So. Our time has come," Gabris said.

Licronus took a deep breath. "It has." Licronus removed two small bags of gold from his waist and tossed it on the ground beside Gabris. "Two bags of gold coin and the sparing of your pathetic life, old man."

Gabris responded, "Beware, Licronus. He will not like what we are about to do. Inquire of him quickly. You will not have much time." Gabris reached down to a group of bottles and small plates near him and began placing exact amounts of ingredients into the warming bowl. A foul odor filled the air as the items bubbled and mixed together. "There. Were you able to find it?"

"After many years, it has finally come to me," Licronus replied. Licronus reached into his pocket and removed a folded piece of old cloth. He unfolded it to reveal a small lock of grey hair tied together by the stem of a small thin plant. He carefully handed it to Gabris.

"From the only being to which he has ever revealed himself," Licronus said.

Gabris, in total awe of the delicate lock, took it and admired it for a moment. He then untied the lock of hair and laid it gently into the bowl. It made a crackling sound as it burned from the heat. Gabris then gathered some additional powders and other items from around him and placed them into the bowl. The hair began to cook in the mixture. Gabris closed his eyes tight and bowed his head. He began uttering an incantation in an ancient dead language. A look of fear and dread began forming on Drokus's face. Licronus, on the other hand, displayed an evil look of growing anticipation. Suddenly, the room filled with a thin white smoke. Gabris opened his eyes and marveled at the sight of it.

He turned to Drokus and asked, "Now. Are you ready to go?"

Drokus, looking confused, replied, "Go? Go where?"

In a swift and violent move, Licronus pulled a dagger from his sleeve.

"To Hell!" Licronus said as he plunged the dagger into Drokus's neck. Drokus screamed out in pain, gurgled and collapsed to the floor, convulsing as the blood poured from his neck. Suddenly, with a swirling of the smoke, the Angel of Death appeared, leaning over Drokus's twitching body. Death's limbs were that of a human skeleton, pure white in color. He wore a black robe with a hood large enough so that his skull was not visible. All that could be seen was a deep black darkness. His skeletal hand reached out and his extended white bony finger touched Drokus. Drokus was now dead. Licronus immediately stood.

"Finally, Angel, you are mine!" Licronus proclaimed.

Death heard Licronus and immediately spun around and pointed his long bony finger directly at him. Then, immediately, Death realized that something was not right. He saw his own skeletal hand. He looked at it, clenching his fist for a few seconds, realizing the impossible... he had been revealed. Death scowled at Licronus. He then jumped up, reached into one of his sleeves and removed an item that Licronus had known only as myth over the centuries. He had first learned of its actual existence from Master Naji during his time with the Order. There was only one, and it belonged to the Angel of Death. The

Scytheren: a glistening, metallic, arm's-length silver bar. Crested upon one end was the Arc-Pen Symbol. Death held the Scytheren out towards Licronus. Licronus placed his hand on his sword, not knowing what to expect. Then suddenly, the Scytheren transformed into one of the deadliest of Hamen weapons. The Hamen Scythe. With a length as long as Death stood tall, this weapon, flawlessly formed from the Hamen Living Metal, was razor sharp and perfectly balanced for battle. Death then used his scythe to rip through the tent wall and make his escape. Licronus quickly followed.

Gabris yelled out, "Wait! You said you only wanted to see him - to speak with him!"

Licronus exited through the rip in the tent, then immediately transformed into his winged Kraylen form. He took to the air and flew over Death's head, landing ahead of him, cutting off his path. Death stopped, then turned to go another direction, only to find himself trapped. The Kraylen Generals had cut off his exit on both sides. Licronus checked the status of the eclipse.

"It would be much simpler if you would just come quietly, Angel," said Licronus.

Realizing his circumstance, Death swung his Hamen Scythe masterfully into a Hamen fighting position. Death's willingness to fight, as well as his obvious preparedness to do battle, surprised Licronus. He was unaware that he too was a Hamen Warrior. As Licronus slowly drew his sword, it became Death's turn to be surprised. Death immediately recognized Licronus's weapon as a Sitcian's sword. A Sword of Hamen. Why would a Kraylen be wielding the weapon of God's warrior?

"Ah, I see you recognize it," Licronus said. Licronus showed off the sword by holding it up and admiring it. "I had to kill one of your fellow warriors to get it. I must admit however that I find this weapon to be a little weak. A weak blade forged by a weak God." Death immediately spun his scythe and attacked Licronus. Death demonstrated that he was indeed a Master of his Hamen Scythe as he delivered skillful blows towards Licronus. The sound of the silver scythe cutting through the air was both frightening and intimidating. However, much to Death's surprise, Licronus, even with just one hand, showed the masterful skill of a Hamen Warrior.

They battled briefly yet brilliantly until Licronus showed his superiority by catching the Hamen Scythe with his sword and snatching it from Death's hands. His movement flung the scythe through the air. It landed on the ground next to Poragon and instantly transformed back into its original Scytheren form. Then, with an even quicker move, Licronus caught the top edge of the hood of Death's robe with his sword and snatched it off of him entirely. As the robe floated through the air like the petal of a flower, Death's skeletal appearance became fully revealed. It then began to slowly change to that of a man, bald and pale white. Once fully transformed, Death collapsed. Licronus directed his focus skyward and peered at the eclipse with a look of accomplishment in his eyes.

"He is ready! Bring him!" Licronus demanded.

The Kraylen Generals moved in, picked Death up and dragged him back towards the rip in Gabris's tent. Gabris, who had been watching, scurried out of the way. Licronus picked up the robe and Scytheren and followed as the eclipse continued to reverse.

The Generals carried a subdued Death through the rip and into the back room. Gabris stepped back in horrible shock at what was happening.

"No, please!" Gabris begged, with no success. The Kraylen carried Death through the room and exited through the black curtain. Licronus, entering through the rip, only intensified the stunned look of terror on Gabris's face. Gabris stopped Licronus as he began to follow the Generals.

"No!" Gabris pleaded. "You cannot do this! Please don't…" Licronus quickly grabbed Gabris, removed a dagger from his waist and plunged it into Gabris's stomach. His eyes bulged as the knife pierced his flesh and sliced through his vital organs.

"In the future, never make deals with the Devil," Licronus advised. Licronus then forced the dagger deeper into Gabris's stomach. Licronus laid Gabris's quivering wounded body onto the floor. "As you well know, as long as I have him, you cannot die. Find a way to enjoy your pain." Licronus then looked over and spotted the two bags of gold next to Drokus, who lay dead on the floor. He picked them up and turned his gaze to Drokus's dead body. "You were very fortunate."

Licronus then forcefully removed his dagger from Gabris's stomach, leaving blood spewing from the gaping knife wound. He wiped the blade on Gabris's clothes and then gathered up Death's robe and the Scytheren. Licronus exited the room, leaving Gabris suffering horribly next to Drokus's corpse.

The Kraylen Generals laid Death into the open coffin-like box which was now sitting on the ground by the wagon. Bralorg positioned Death's hands on his chest then closed and locked the lid. There was a small window with bars fashioned in the lid at face level. Death lay still in a trance, unable to move, staring straight ahead. As Licronus approached from the artifacts shop, the Generals loaded Death onto the wagon with the empty chest. Licronus opened the chest, placed the robe and Scytheren inside, slammed and locked it. With the sunlight still fully hidden by the eclipse, Bralorg quickly boarded the wagon, snapped the reins, and off they rode with Death in tow.

☙❧

A rare darkness had covered the expanse of the dry landscape for some time now. The mountain range in the distance, moments ago barely visible, began to show itself as the rare solar eclipse continued to reverse. Such an event would be once in a lifetime for Tan so he paused atop his horse to meditate in the glory of God's work. Eventually, the unveiling of the landscape by the sun's return reached Tan and his horse and then continued on into the distance. The rebirth and warmth of the sun reminded Tan of his journey – of his own rebirth. Once he reached the Shao-Tan Temple, his new life would begin. Monks of the Holy Order were greatly revered among even the holiest of orders. The rest of his life would be meaningful and fulfilling in service to God. Then, Tan's thoughts were interrupted. His horse shifted and snorted as if disturbed by something. Tan ended his meditation. The bright sun stung his eyes as he focused to take in his surroundings. Tan's senses were still on high alert since departing the Holy Order to Solis's words of warning. Tan's horse shifted again, snorting and grunting more loudly this time. As Tan's eyes adjusted to the sun's rays, he found himself staring straight ahead. Before him in the distance was a strange flash of bright light. Like a star in the distance. Could it be a fire? Tan placed his hand on his coat at the waist then visually scanned the area for thieves or others that might do him harm. Nothing. Flat dry empty land as far as the eye could see. Nothing but that strange bright light ahead.

Tan snapped his reins and he and his horse slowly moved forward towards the light. As he got closer, he saw that the light was not fire, but a reflection of the sun. As he strained to focus, moving even closer, he saw what it was that caused the reflection. A long knife: half the length of a sword, but just as deadly, driven into the dirt — in the middle of nowhere. Tan's senses sharpened as he halted his horse and again scanned the area. Seeing nothing, Tan slowly dismounted. After another quick scan, he moved forward, hand on his waist, towards the knife. Tan was instantly stopped in his tracks by a strange and unfamiliar sound. The sound of heavy flapping wings. Suddenly from nowhere, a dark winged creature approached in the sky from behind him. Tan spun around as the creature flew towards him. Tan executed a magnificent flip and roll in order to avoid being struck.

Tan's education at the Holy Order Monastery had gone further than that of the other monks; undoubtedly the result of his "special student" status with Solis. Unbeknownst to Agean and all but the Court of Seven, Tan had been secretly taught the Hamen fighting art. Although Tan was not one of the Chosen, he had been provided everything he needed to defend himself: most notably, the deadly skills of a Hamen Warrior.

As Tan positioned himself in a Hamen stance, the dark winged creature landed next to the knife. For the first time, Tan laid eyes upon the greatest evil to walk the earth: a Kraylen in its full winged form. The Kraylen spy, Barejis. Tan quickly reflected back to Solis's teachings, knowing that what stood before him was the great evil he had spoken of for years – and taught Tan to defend against. How could Solis know that Tan might encounter them? Tan placed his hands at his waist inside his coat, poised for battle.

"Well, Young Monk, finally we meet," said Barejis.

"I do not know who you are, but I do know what you are," Tan said. "I know who you follow. Lucifer himself." Tan's words caused Barejis to begin laughing.

"What is it you want with me?" Tan asked.

"You, Young Monk – putrid human filth — have something I want and I mean to have it." Barejis then took a few steps past the half buried knife and closer to Tan. Tan flung open his coat, revealing the scroll case and stopping Barejis in his tracks.

"Is this what you speak of, Kraylen?" Tan again scanned the immediate area. "Is it you, alone, who plan to take this from me?"

"You are no Hamen Warrior, monk! You are not chosen. I need no help taking what I want from you." Barejis revealed a row of crudely fashioned razor sharp long knives adorning his waist. Barejis was a "knifer" – a long knifer; known to be particularly challenging because of their deadly accuracy. Tan's senses began to focus, his eyes locked on each of the deadly weapons along the Kraylen's waist. Tan moved away from the direction of his horse to avoid it being injured during what now appeared to be certain confrontation. Then, with a quick sudden movement, Barejis removed and threw the first two of his knives. They whistled as they cut the air towards Tan. Tan zeroed in on the projectiles and removed his weapons; in each hand, a precision crafted Bouma. Known in parts of the world as the boomerang, these weapons were perfectly balanced, fast and deadly. With a quick Hamen move, Tan used the Bouma to deflect both of the knives away. Barejis spun and hurled two more of the razor sharp weapons towards Tan. Tan quickly executed a Hamen spinning move and knocked both of the knives off their path and into the dirt. Barejis huffed with frustration as Tan stood poised for his next move. Just as Barejis made his move to grab another knife, Tan hurled his Bouma, striking him directly on the hand. Barejis grimaced as the knife flew from his hand and into the dirt with the Bouma. Then, with a single precise movement, Tan launched his second Bouma, striking Barejis directly in the forehead with such force that it lifted him into the air and landed him flat on his wings. The second Bouma whirled around and returned to Tan who caught it, still poised for battle. Tan took a moment of pause to again scan the area for more of the Kraylen as Barejis moaned in agony on his back in the dirt. Tan then eased his battle pose and walked over to Barejis. He grasped the scroll case which still hung securely across his chest.

"As God is my witness, you shall never have this, Kraylen." Tan picked up his other Bouma and secured them both to his waist. He then quickly made his way to his horse, mounted up and trotted over to Barejis who still moaned, holding his injured hand. Tan stared into the injured Kraylen's eyes for a moment before snapping his reins and galloping off full speed into the distance. After a few moments, the sound of flapping wings returned as several of Barejis's Kraylen cohorts landed near him.

"I see one of us is no match for this mere monk, Barejis," said one of the Kraylen. Barejis bristled as he struggled against the pain in his hand and head to sit up. "But he will be no match for all of us."

"No. Someone has taught him the Art. Let's see where he goes first. Perhaps we can learn more of their secrets," Barejis said.

"Always the spy, aye Barejis?" the Kraylen added.

Barejis replied, "This time he will not see us coming." The Kraylen stood looking into the distance, seeing only the dust trail from Tan's horse as he raced through the open landscape.

chapter five
The Passing of a Godly Torch

Gradore's farm was quaint yet lush, with beautiful fields bordered by green landscape. In the center was a modest farm house with a stable, barn and an assortment of corrals and coops for a modest variety of animals. The adjacent crop fields were just large enough to feed his family and sell the rest to traders at market in the nearby town. It was a beautiful place bordered by a small mountain range on the North, forests to the East and West, and an ample stream to the South where Gradore and his teenage son Brand tried their hand, often unsuccessfully, at fishing.

Gradore was a handsome, hardworking, middle-aged family man whose farm had been handed down through many generations. It was a bright summer day and Gradore was near the stable brushing and tending his horse Shayna with great care. A warm summer breeze blew through his thick black hair, while at the same time tossing Shayna's dark mane and tail. His beautiful brown-haired wife, Zeta, tended to laundry while Brand was busy sweeping the front porch. Brand, who shared his father's strength and his mother's good looks and brown hair, had grown into a handsome, strong and capable young man. If Brand had his choice, he would be tending the crops with his father. Unfortunately, recent heavy rains had left the crops needing no attention today.

Brand took a moment from the boredom of sweeping to watch as the hawk, the one that had always been there, screeched and circled overhead. This hawk remained a source of confusion for Brand, although less so in recent years. He had gotten used to the majestic bird watching over his family. He had accepted its presence as a sort of guardianship from above. Especially since his mother and father were not forthcoming with answers to his inquiries about the hawk. The most curious answer he had received pertained to the beautiful pendant with the odd symbol he had seen around the hawk's neck. Gradore would simply tell him, "He is a blessing. Someday you will understand." Brand loved his father and trusted his words.

Deciding to take a break, Brand walked over to where his father was grooming his horse. "A lucky one, she is, the way you toil and care for her. It's enough to make a son jealous."

Gradore replied, "Ah, no need for that now, Brand.

You will always be at the top of the list - right after your Mom and Shayna here."

Brand playfully snuck around and tackled his father to the ground, laughing. They wrestled around for a bit until Zeta spotted them.

"You two! Stop your playin' and hurry now. Supper is almost ready," Zeta yelled.

Gradore and Brand replied in unison, "Okay!"

"You see. You've gone and gotten us into trouble," Gradore said.

After a final laugh and tug, Brand returned to the front porch to finish his sweeping and Gradore resumed brushing Shayna. Gradore smiled at his son with pride.

Dusk had settled onto the farm as Gradore, exhausted, carried a saddle up the stairs of the front porch. As he often did each evening, he turned to look out at the expanse of his land and beyond. The hawk circled above, screeching to wish Gradore a good evening, and to let him know he was still there.

Gradore looked to the sky. "Good night, Brave One." Gradore hung the saddle over the railing of the porch and then went inside.

The small, modest farmhouse, built from the strong timbre of the surrounding forest, was a perfect dwelling for Gradore and his family. His life and the lives of those ancestors who had lived on this farm before him had always been simple. Gradore's greatest treasure had always been his family. As Gradore entered, Zeta lovingly met him at the door.

"Aww... What better for a woman than to see her man after a hard day of playing with his son," Zeta said.

"Hey, you never complain when I play with you, my queen," Gradore said as he tickled Zeta. "Besides, he started it."

Zeta laughed. "Ooohh, he started it. Both you boys just need a good strappin'."

"Now now... Don't cha go makin' threats," Gradore said.

"Well, they'll be more than threats if ya don't set yourself at the table," she replied.

"Now ya get no fuss from me on that one," Gradore said, love in his eyes.

Zeta kissed him and exited to the kitchen. Gradore took off his coat, hung it on a hook by the door, and began making his way towards the dinner table. On the way, he passed his study and noticed that Brand's attention had once again been stolen by the unusual urn that sat on the mantel. The Credara. Gradore leaned against the doorway to observe. Gradore's mind traveled back to when he first entrusted the 13 year-old Brand with the family secret. Just as today, Gradore watched as Brand stood staring at the mysterious object on the mantel. Questions swirled around in Brand's mind as he stared, fascinated by the beautiful object. What was it? Why was it here? Why has it always been here? Just as with the hawk, his questions were always answered the same. "It is a blessing. Someday you will understand."

Like the hawk, the Credara had been an object of unending fascination for Brand. Brand reached up to touch it. As had been true each and every time Brand had reached for it, when his fingers got close, the Credara emitted a faint glow — an odd glow that made it seem as if it had its own sun inside. Brand moved his fingers up and down, watching the Credara glow.

"Brand," Gradore said. Brand snatched his hand back, startled and embarrassed. Gradore entered the room. "Now, Son, how many times have we talked about this?"

Brand replied, "I know, Father. I'm sorry."

"How old are you now, Son?"

Proudly, Brand answered, "Thirteen, Father."

Gradore paused a moment to think, then grabbed a chair near his desk and moved it over to the mantel.

"That's right, isn't it? Thirteen," Gradore said as he grabbed a second chair from near the door and placed it near the mantel. "You know Son, perhaps it is time I told you the story. But Brand, this that I tell you means you are now a man; a man who will carry on a great family trust with God."

Excited, Brand said, "Yes, Father. I understand."

They both sat in the chairs in front of the mantel, facing each other in front of a warm fire as Gradore proceeded to tell Brand the story.

Zeta entered and leaned against the doorway smiling proudly as she listened to what Gradore was about to share with his son. Brand's piercing eyes were all aglow as he listened to his father's words.

"This, Son, is the story of the Sitcian," Gradore began.

"Sitcian, Father?"

"Yes. God's bravest warriors," Gradore replied. "The first was named Fitaris. He was a truly dedicated man of God who spent many hours praying and honoring Him. Through his prayers he knew that God had a special purpose for his life. So patiently he waited and prayed for a sign. Till one day, Brand, the hawk came to him."

"The hawk? Like the one outside?" Brand asked.

"The very same. Sent from God to lead him to his destiny."

Gradore's words took him and Brand back to a time thousands of years ago. "Fitaris was a little-known priest of a small parish in a small port town. Travelers came and went. He tried his best to bring the word of God to the people but, much to Fitaris's dismay, he received only ridicule and rejection. You see, Brand, it seemed that debauchery, gambling and drink were all that the people cared about in this town. But Fitaris remained faithful and vigilant. He kept praying to God for guidance and purpose — for a sign.

Then one day, there it was. The hawk - perched on the altar of Fitaris's parish. Fitaris saw the sacred pendant the hawk wore upon his heart and knew that the time had come. So he gathered what he could carry and he rode out of the town on horseback, full gallop, following the hawk as onlookers stared at him. Fitaris followed the hawk for many weeks and for many miles, vowing to follow it wherever it would lead him." Brand's face lit up as he listened studiously to his father's story.

Gradore smiled and continued. "Through the scorching desert, treacherous mountain passes, exhausted and hungry, Fitaris followed the hawk, no matter how dangerous. After a long painful journey, it was in the thick Badril Forest that he felt he could go no further."

Brand asked, "Did he die, Father?"

"No, Brand. But he was in an awful state. Fitaris lay on the forest floor, horribly defeated, in both body and spirit, when suddenly he again heard the call of the hawk. Fitaris looked up to God and asked, 'Why hast thou led me to my death?' Fitaris then mustered his last bit of strength to rise up and make his way towards the screeching sounds, until suddenly he found himself in a strange clearing. Just ahead was a small mountain with a strange symbol at its peak: The Arc-Pen Symbol."

"Arc-Pen? Is that the symbol on our hawk's pendant?" Brand asked.

"Yes, Brand. The same as on the urn there," Gradore said, pointing to the mantel.

Brand's eyes burned with curiosity as Gradore continued. "Fitaris crept over to investigate. Meanwhile the hawk perched on a rocky ledge nearby. As Fitaris got nearer, an old man with a staff suddenly appeared out of nowhere carrying a large sack. His appearance startled Fitaris. Then the old man began to speak, saying to him, 'You have come a great distance, Fitaris. I have awaited your arrival.'

'Who are you? What is this place?' Fitaris asked.

The old man said to him, 'Who I am is not as important as who you are; who you will be.' Then, Fitaris tells the old man that it was the hawk that brought him there. The old man smiled, looked at the hawk, and this is what he said, Brand: 'Flittorin.' That is his name, Brand. Flittorin."

"After all these years. Flittorin," Brand said.

"The old man told Fitaris that he had hoped he would trust Flittorin to lead him there, and that he should trust Flittorin from then on," Gradore told him. "Then, Fitaris and the old man sat. The old man gave Fitaris food and water and told him all that God wanted him to know. Then, he gave him his gifts."

Brand asked, "Gifts?"

"Now listen carefully, Son," Gradore said firmly. "This is very important." Gradore stared into Brand's eyes. "He gave him the Box of Hamen Living Metal, with which to forge God's weapons. He gave him a great holy book called the Bisalis. Then finally, Brand, he gave him the holy urn. The Credara."

Brand looked at the urn on the mantel. "The Credara."

"Yes, Brand. God's key to Lucifer's Lair."

"Lucifer's Lair, Father?" Brand asked, worried.

"Yes, Son. Lucifer." Gradore put a reassuring hand on Brand's shoulder. "This is our family's charge, Brand. This is why it is so important for you to understand everything I say."

Brand paused, taking it all in. He could not believe what he was hearing.

"Yes, Father."

"Good, Son." Gradore looked Brand in the eye and continued. "He handed Fitaris the Credara. A tear ran down his cheek when he realized the great responsibility God had bestowed upon him. He told Fitaris of the Mark of Hamen. How God's Army would bear this Mark. And that it was he, with Flittorin's help, who must find them and tell them who they are, and teach each of them to master the sacred Hamen Fighting Art. Then, he told Fitaris the most important thing of all: that the one born bearing the Sitcian Mark of Hamen must also be found, protected and trained to master the sacred Hamen Art: the fighting art of the angel warriors of God. Then the old man took his staff and touched it to Fitaris's neck, painlessly placing the Sitcian Mark of Hamen upon it. Fitaris was to be the first. Fitaris touched his neck. As he did, his new Sitcian Mark and the symbol on the Credara began to tingle and glow. Fitaris felt a surge of energy coursing through his entire being. It was an energy he had never felt before. He and the Credara… he and the Hamen Fighting Art… all three, now as one."

Brand sat looking stunned at what he was being told.

Gradore continued, "Fitaris swore he would do as God commanded. On his journey, Fitaris studied the Bisalis while Flittorin led him to those bearing the Mark of Hamen. For them he forged God's weapons using the Hamen Living

Metal. He then formed God's Holy Order, to find, protect and teach every generation of Sitcian. But the important part for us, Son, is that God also led him here."

"Here? Are you one of God's warriors, Father?"

Gradore responded, "No no, son. Just a simple farmer. But the Credara and its protector, Flittorin, have been with our family for centuries. And for centuries our family has kept our promise. So now, Brand, it is your time."

Brand asked, "What must I do?"

"You must watch over it, but tell no one about it," Gradore told him. "Make sure it is always safe and if anything about it ever changes, you must let me know. Then and only then must we take it away from here, to God's Holy Order. They will know what to do. Okay, Son?"

Brand responded with a new sense of responsibility, "Yes, Father."

Gradore smiled, stood and gave Brand a hug. "I'm proud of you, Son." Brand smiled while his father embraced him, knowing the importance of what his father had placed upon him.

Brand took one last glance at the magnificent urn. As Gradore's mind returned to the present, Zeta entered the doorway. "All right, men of the house, time for supper." Brand turned to find his father watching him. He smiled, navigated around both Gradore and Zeta, and then exited the room. Zeta gazed at Gradore, and then crossed over and wrapped her arms around him. "I'm a pretty lucky girl to have such wonderful and brave men."

Gradore told her, "Well, you'll need to be pretty brave yourself if our dinner is cold." Gradore and Zeta began to exit.

Zeta replied, "Oh, you. Many a brave man has eaten a cold meal."

"Yes, but I promise they did not like it," Gradore responded as they left the room.

chapter six
The Greatest Fear
Comes To Pass

A warm brisk morning had a few monks out kicking a Cuju ball around the field. Agean, strolling along the stone path near the square, stopped to observe the day's archery training. Solis watched as one monk drew back and fired at a target one hundred yards away, missing dead center by a mere pittance. The monk shrank in disappointment.

Solis said, "No, no! Remember, wind is not your enemy! Briton, if you would please!"

The group of monks stood staring at Solis as Briton failed to appear. Solis gave a confused, yet suspicious look. Briton was scheduled for today's training and not only was it rare, but it was a punishable offense for a student to miss archery training.

"Briton, step forward!" Solis demanded. Slowly out of the gathering of students, Briton appeared. He looked as if he had been in a brawl with bruises and lacerations on his face and head and his eye still blackened. He tried to act as if nothing was wrong.

Solis looked stunned. "And may I ask what happened

to you, young monk?" Briton frowned in a manner that said it all. Solis quickly got it.

"I see. How many others were involved in this little incident?" Solis asked.

At that moment, several more monks appeared out of the crowd, all looking battered and bruised. Again, Solis displayed a stunned look, which he quickly turned to Agean who was still standing nearby observing. Agean shrugged his shoulders as if he had no idea what happened. Solis cut Agean a raised eyebrow then moved closer to Briton and the others to inspect. That is when it hit his senses. The stench.

Solis frowned. "What in Heaven's name is that retched odor?" After a quick moment, his senses dialed in on the reeking culprit. Briton. Solis took a sniff to make sure and snapped his head back in disgust.

"After your training, you young monk may request another garb," Solis said, trying not to gag. "Meanwhile, grab a bow."

Briton took the bow of the monk who missed the target. He then pulled an arrow from the monk's quiver, set it upon the bow and aimed directly upward into the sky.

Solis stood a good distance from Briton and continued, "As I was saying… the wind is not your enemy." Solis then began fanning his nose having realized that he was down wind of Briton. "Although, perhaps in this case…"

Briton held his position but turned his head to see Solis fanning and frowning. Embarrassed, he returned his focus to the sky. "It is your friend. Use it!" Briton drew back the bow and let loose its arrow. All monks' eyes turned to the sky as the arrow soared upward and vanished from sight.

"Remember your angles!" Solis said as Briton pulled another arrow from the monk's quiver. "You must execute smoothly! Your timing must be perfect!" Briton drew back and released the arrow towards the target just as the arrow he launched into the sky dropped into its path. His arrow snapped the first in half, then struck the target dead center. "You must also be quick! Exceptional, Briton!" The monks were awed by Briton's demonstration of skill with a bow. Briton then looked over at Agean with pride.

Agean began slowly clapping sarcastically at Briton's demonstration. "Impressive, Briton! Even with that eye thing… very impressive indeed!" The group of beaten and bruised monks began to move towards Agean in anger but Briton extended his arms to restrain them. He then shot an angry look to Agean. Not only Briton's cohorts, but the other monks as well shared the sentiment. Agean, much to the chagrin of his fellow monks, had been excused from this training. At a very early age, Master Naji taught Agean to master the archer's bow. His skills were so refined that Master Naji felt there was no more he could learn. But it was not always this way.

Agean recalled on one occasion in the forest beyond the monastery, pulling his bow taut, his focus dead center of his target. Then, without warning, from behind him, a whirring sound penetrated the air. Something moving so fast he could not see it, tore past his head, coming so close he could feel the loose strands of hair on his head blowing in its wake. Then suddenly, with a low thud, embedded at the center of his target was a bouma. Agean realized that this was no ordinary bouma. This one was made of the finest polished ebony he had ever seen. Precision balanced, deadly, and with the Arc-Pen Symbol intricately carved on each side. In the hands of a Hamen Warrior, it would be fast, accurate, and able to render even the most skilled warrior defenseless against it. The Hamen Bouma was a weapon Agean had become very familiar with under Master Naji's tutelage. Agean immediately pulled his bow tight and turned, searching the area around him. Seeing no one, he whirled around, back to the target, and there stood Solis, holding the Bouma.

"Someone is neglecting their studies again," Solis said.

Agean eased his bow. "My apologies, Headmaster. I was just finishing some extra training."

"I see. Your commitment to training is commendable, Agean. This makes Master Naji very happy. But your duties as a monk are my responsibility. Might I suggest you get back to them," Solis said.

"Yes Headmaster." Agean then stowed his arrow, bowed to Solis, and turned to begin making his way back to the monastery.

"And Agean," Solis said. Agean stopped and turned back to Solis. "Keep your senses razor sharp at all times. In the wrong hands, a weapon like this would have surely taken your head." Agean gave Solis a confused look. In the past, Solis not only seemed unconcerned with Agean's training, but had never spoken to him of anything Hamen, and had certainly never given him advice. What did Solis know of the Hamen Bouma? How did he get his hands on one? How could he have thrown the weapon so accurately without Hamen training? And more importantly, how could one man throw the weapon from behind Agean, then appear at the target within a matter of seconds? Agean had pondered this all the way back to the monastery.

As Agean's thoughts returned to Briton's demonstration, Agean continued his stroll near the Cuju field, taking in the sun's warmth, trying to draw its energy.

Despite the activity below, Master Naji had been performing his ritual Tai-Chi on his balcony when the sound of heavy flapping wings again interrupted him. Again, the winged creature soared in the distant sky. After a few seconds, knowing it had gotten Master Naji's attention, the creature soared away.

At top speed, the creature flew off and landed atop the highest crest of a nearby mountain range. This winged creature, having made his presence known to Master Naji for years, was the Kraylen, Licronus. He and Master Naji shared a relationship more than two decades ago. It was about to be renewed.

Licronus tucked his wings as he landed. He stood for a moment looking out over the vast range of mountain peaks. Then, he knelt. Looking down, Licronus spoke out in the same ancient dead language that Gabris used to trap Death.

"Great Lucifer. Our plan soon becomes reality. We have the Angel of Death. The chain that binds you to Hell is being broken and you will soon be free to have your vengeance. Our vengeance. Give me the power, Great Lucifer, to summon your army so that we may defeat the God of Hosts."

Licronus stood and raised his hands to the sky. The whites of his eyes turned jet black as he spread his wings, opened his mouth wide and released a wind that spread all over the entire world.

Master Naji had resumed his morning meditation and Tai-Chi when suddenly a horrible feeling jarred him from his spiritual state. Something in the air. A feeling of terror came over Master Naji. He turned and stared at the horizon where he last saw the winged creature. A powerful wind suddenly began to blow. There was something about the odor of this wind. Something evil. Something Master Naji recognized. As he stared straight into the wind, hair whipping from its force, Master Naji knew what this was. He stood and faced it head-on.

"Summon your evil forces, my enemy!" Master Naji called out, barely audible over the sound of the wind. "We have been preparing for this moment for thousands of years!"

The monks on the Cuju field were running for cover as the powerful wind disrupted their game. Agean, still near the field, looked to the sky as his hair whipped in the wind. He sensed something. The Mark on his neck began to tingle in a very strange way. Agean placed his hand on his Mark. His memory danced as it searched to remember where he had felt this feeling before. Far back. Back to his childhood. He knew that the tingling, and what he felt deep within him was not a good thing. The wind. His senses. His glowing and tingling Mark told him that something was dreadfully wrong.

As Brand did most evenings since the age of 13, he sat proudly staring at the Credara like a sentinel on guard, watching for the slightest change. Meanwhile, Gradore was in his stable, tending and brushing Shayna.

Suddenly he heard Brand yelling from the house. "Father! Come quick!"

Gradore immediately stopped brushing, turned and kicked over a bucket of horse grooming items. He ignored the mess and hurried off towards the house. He burst into the front door and looked around. Seeing nothing, he rushed farther into the house and spotted Brand, sitting in front of the mantel in his study. Brand had an apologetic look on his face as Gradore, breathing heavily, rushed into the room.

Gradore, huffing and puffing, asked him, "What is it, Son? Is everything all right?"

Brand replied, "Sorry, Father. I thought something had changed."

Gradore looked up at the mantel. The Credara was unchanged. Still out of breath, Gradore tried to squeeze out a smile. "No problem, Son. No problem." Gradore grabbed his chest in exhaustion as he turned and exited the room. Gradore would soon discover that for some strange reason, now, after four years, Brand would begin taking his duty to God and family more seriously than ever before. In fat, it would become an obsession.

After completing the work of the day, Gradore sat at

the dinner table enjoying a delicious meal. Zeta entered the room from his study, stopped, hands on hips, and confronted him.

"You are going to have to talk to your son, Gradore," she demanded.

Mouth full of food, Gradore replied, "He will be fine, my love. He's just… he's just trying to do a good job is all."

"A good job? Well he certainly did not do a good job at his chores around here today," Zeta said. "Gradore, he's been in there for hours."

Gradore said, "I know, Zeta. Believe me, I…"

Suddenly, Brand's yelling interrupted Gradore. "Father!"

Gradore looked at Zeta, dropped his fork and rushed out of the dining room. Zeta rolled her eyes and walked over to the wash bucket nearby. She took a wet plate out of the water and began drying it with a rag. A few moments later, Gradore re-entered the room with a bland look. Zeta smirked. Gradore sighed and then sat back down at the table to finish his meal. Zeta began to snicker, much to Gradore's embarrassment.

The next afternoon, Gradore was in the horse stable sweating through the difficult task of shoeing Shayna when suddenly Brand called out.

"Father! Quickly! Come quickly!" Brand yelled.

Gradore sighed, paused and looked to the sky. A few seconds later, Brand called out again.

"Never mind! Sorry!" he yelled.

Gradore silently mimicked his son and continued his work.

That night, the cool air felt good filtering through the house at the end of a hot day. Gradore lay in bed under the covers reading a parchment by lamp light as Zeta lay asleep next to him.

Suddenly Brand called out from the study, startling Gradore and awakening Zeta. "Father!"

Gradore yelled, "Brand, please! Go to bed, Son!"

"But Father! Come quickly!" Brand yelled.

Gradore laid the parchment down and pulled the covers completely over his head.

Zeta leaned over and poked him through the covers. "You started it." Gradore blew a heavy sigh under the covers then reluctantly got out of bed and put his robe on. His eyes met Zeta's sarcastic gaze.

"Don't look at me like that. I plan to put an end to this here and now," Gradore said. He then headed for the bedroom door, but not before stubbing his toe on the corner of a chest near the bed.

"Ow!" Gradore yelled as he stumbled, grabbed his toe and hopped around in pain grumbling angrily to himself.

He immediately stopped hopping when he caught the smile on Zeta's face. He sighed and then limped painfully out of the bedroom door.

Gradore crept into his study knowing to expect a false alarm.

He said to his son, "Now Brand, we need to talk, Son."

Suddenly Gradore's eyes widened as he caught a startling sight. Brand was sitting, arms folded, legs crossed, with a proud look on his face.

"Look, Father," Brand said.

The Credara was brightly lit and the waters inside were swirling like an ocean whirlpool. Gradore stared for a second, stunned. The sight shocked Zeta as she entered the doorway.

Gradore looked at Zeta, swallowed hard and then turned back to the Credara. "Get my horse."

❧

Master Naji's training room was more brightly lit than normal, with all lamps fully aglow. Master Naji stood in all white with his hands in a prayer position as he meditated. Agean entered quietly and was immediately taken by the brightness of the room, the color of Master Naji's garb, but even more so by his praying stance. He had never before seen him meditate in this position. Master Naji would often choose his position to begin their training for just that, training purposes. One must always be aware, ready for one's enemy from any position, whenever and wherever that enemy may strike. This position, however, was confusing - a position of surrender rather than readiness; as if surrendering himself to God's will. Agean set his Hamen Swords on the table and took his normal position at the kneeling block.

"You are on time today," Master Naji said, never moving from his position.

Agean responded, "You have taught me to be wise, Master."

"Yes. Tell me, Agean. Is it wise for a man of God to teach his student to kill?" asked Master Naji.

Agean replied, "Is it not wise for a man of God to know how to defend against God's enemies?"

Master Naji opened his eyes, lowered his hands and said to him, "We have learned much together, Agean. What I have shared with you over the years was given by God. Know this, my son: He is but one side of an important balance; on the other is evil. But what you as a Hamen Warrior must know, is that while evil looks the same, do not be deceived. There is an evil even greater than the others. You will face this evil, Agean. And when you look within it; in that moment you will find the warrior you were destined to be. For this evil… you must take its head, or you must expose its heart."

Agean gave a confused look. "I will face it, Master?" Master Naji smiled and stared directly into Agean's eyes.

"When I was a Hamen student, the last words my beloved Master shared with me were these: 'You will be wiser to understand that it is not as important to know how to battle, as to know when not to.' Know this. A Hamen Warrior's mind is his sharpest weapon. You will know the meaning of all that I say when the time comes." Master Naji took a step back, standing straight and tall. "I have always looked upon you as a son, Agean. This that I say to you, I say with great honor: After this day, your training will be complete. But remember, my son. All that you must learn begins today."

Agean, honored yet still somewhat confused, bowed in acceptance of Master Naji's wisdom. But what now? Every moment of his life, as far back as he could remember, had been as a student. And what about the unusual praying stance? The white garb? Before Agean could draw in the breath to ask these questions, Master Naji spun into a Hamen fighting stance. Agean reacted instantly. His final training had begun.

With no weapons, Master Naji skillfully attacked Agean in hand to hand combat. Agean reacted masterfully and with focus. Still, something about this training session felt different. Master Naji appeared to be relentless in his effort to defeat Agean. Spinning, flipping and almost floating on air as he utilized his full arsenal of moves to challenge him. Agean met each and every challenge with masterful skill and confidence. Then, with a spectacular move, Master Naji removed a sword from a wall rack and attacked Agean before he had the chance to grab a sword of his own. Agean used everything Master Naji taught him to fend off the attack with his bare hands until he was able to grab a weapon of his own. Much to Agean's surprise, Master Naji not only defended against his blows, he destroyed every weapon Agean used against him. Ancient, irreplaceable weapons from Master Naji's collection all being smashed and broken, one after the other as Agean chose them. Agean did all he could to maintain his focus during Master Naji's relentless onslaught. Then, with an incredible move, Agean was able to grab one of his Hamen Swords from the table, just in time to defend against what would surely have been a death blow from Master Naji.

They both fought with increasing intensity. Acrobatic, precise and masterful, they battled as they had done many times before, except this time would ultimately be different. This time, after several minutes of sparring and with a swift, agile movement by Agean, his blade plunged directly into Master Naji's stomach, halting him in his tracks. Master Naji's eyes began to water as the blood stain on his robe spread. He then fell to his knees, gravely wounded. Mortified, Agean realized what had happened and collapsed to the floor with the Master.

"Master! Oh my God, Master! Help! Someone help!" Agean cried out.

As Agean scrambled to do something — stop the blood, trying to hold him, Master Naji struggled to speak.

"Agean. I knew this day would come. You are now ready, my son," Master Naji said, coughing up blood.

Agean, struggled to understand. "Ready? Master, ready for what?"

"You are The Sitcian. But you must be careful, Agean. They will come after you," Master Naji warned.

Agean was overwhelmed with grief. "Master! Master, I've killed you!"

Master Naji replied, "Agean. Listen to me. The miracle is broken. The Hall of Souls will empty. The Credara is the key."

"Oh God, Master please don't leave me!" Agean pleaded.

Master Naji pulled Agean closer and told him, "My son. Soon you will see this evil. It will show you its face." Tears streamed down Agean's face as Master Naji coughed in pain. Agean continued to hold him.

"Master. I'm so sorry," Agean said, crying. He looked towards the door. "Help me!"

At that very moment, Solis and two monks burst in and saw what was happening. They immediately ran over to help. Agean, in tears, blood covering his hands and arms, did not want to let Master Naji go.

Solis told him, "Agean. Agean! You must let him go!"

"No," said Agean, crying and trying to hold on.

"Agean!" Solis said, finally getting Agean's full attention. Solis looked into Agean's eyes, seeing firsthand the pain he felt. Without words, he convinced Agean that it was okay. Agean reluctantly let go. He and Solis stood.

"You must let us help him," Solis said.

Agean watched as Solis and the other monks attempted to help Master Naji. They tore some of his clothing and pressed it to his wound. Master Naji grimaced in pain.

Master Naji grabbed Solis's arm. "Solis. Go to Iorbus. You must assemble the Court. It is time."

Solis's jaw dropped as he stared at Master Naji, stunned. He then cut a look of shock to Agean, who stood bloody and shaking. Solis knew what this meant. He had also hoped to live his life without ever having to see this time come. Solis then nodded to one of the monks, who immediately rushed out of the room and down the hall. Solis and the other monk continued to assist Master Naji.

Distraught and covered in the Master's blood, Agean sadly picked up his Hamen Sword from the floor. He stared at the blade, seeing his reflection amid the blood from his beloved Master. He then sadly staggered over to the table and picked up his other Hamen Sword. Agean then rushed out of the room.

A fog. Dense. Gloomy. It was all that Agean could see. His beloved Master Naji would surely not survive this horrible tragedy.

Agean sat on the floor against his bed in a daze staring at his hands; hands that were still covered in the Master's blood. How did this happen? What do I do now? Pray? Agean angrily grabbed his hair with his blood stained hands, trying to understand how such a thing could happen.

After a few moments, Agean got up and wandered over to the washing bowl. He trained his eyes on the mirror which hung directly above it. The emotions welled up within him and he began pounding furiously on the wall in disbelief. Blow after blow against the wall as the mirror bounced on the thin chord that held it up, until finally, a blow landed directly onto the mirror itself. It shattered into pieces, leaving one large shard still hanging on the wall. Control this! Try and make sense of this!

Then, a memory. Flowing like silk into Agean's mind, countering his sadness for just a moment. The sound of a crying child. Loud piercing crying. Agean somehow remembered the feeling of terror which accompanied his tears that day. The day he came to this place. The day he first met the calming touch and words of his beloved Master as he picked him up to comfort him. He understood Agean. Understood what he was trying to tell them. He trusted Agean's instincts from the first time he saw him. Master Naji knew... the man was evil - terribly, terribly evil. He must be stopped!

Agean closed his eyes tight as the memory was now pounding against the walls of his skull. He rinsed his face and hands in the bowl, attempting to wash it from his mind. He narrowly avoided slicing his hand open on the large pieces of mirror that had fallen in. Agean stared into the large shard still hanging from the wall; stared at his wet dripping face. He then quickly swapped his blood-stained training garb for regular clothing and tossed the blood stained items to the floor in disbelief.

Now fully changed, he again caught his reflection in the shard of mirror on the wall and stared. He heard Master Naji's words. "You are the Sitcian. They will come after you." Agean decided to grab his Swords of Hamen. He put them on and covered them with a long coat. He quickly grabbed a sack of coins from his desk and then crossed to his cell door. He put his ear to the door for a moment to listen.

Several monks walked quickly through the hall outside of Agean's door. It was an unusual amount of activity for this time of day. Agean had no doubt that the word had spread about Master Naji and what he had done. One of the monks gave what appeared to be important instructions to another and they both scampered off in different directions. Once it sounded as if the hallway was clear, Agean slowly opened his door. He peeked out to see if anyone was around, then exited his cell into the hall.

Quickly, Agean began making his way towards the Great Foyer and the front of the monastery, when suddenly Solis appeared from around a corner, stopping Agean in his tracks.

"Where are you going?" Solis asked.

Agean looked into Solis's eyes for a moment then began to go around him. "I'm going out to get some air."

Solis placed his hand on Agean's chest, stopping him again.

"With those?" asked Solis, referring to Agean's swords. "You're lying. I'm coming with you."

Agean quickly responded, "No! I will be fine alone."

"Agean! I can only imagine how you must feel. You should not be alone," Solis said.

Agean quickly replied, "The one person I cared about, if he is not already, will soon be dead by my own hand. Alone is all I have left."

Solis stared at Agean for a moment, then slowly dropped his hand, allowing him to pass. Agean continued walking quickly towards the Great Foyer, disappearing down the hall. After a few moments of thought, Solis began making his way down the hall after him.

Solis marched through the Great Foyer, determined to stop Agean. Suddenly, Solis slowed. He gazed at the huge statues all around him, studying their faces, their swords… reflecting on their valor… thinking. Solis then quickly walked through to the window to the left of the massive front door. He peered out, watching as Agean galloped through the main gate of the monastery grounds, then on to the forest beyond. Solis's troubled look spoke clearly of his thoughts.

"Be careful of strangers, my boy," Solis said as he turned away from the window.

For generation after generation, the space on the mantel in Gradore's study had been occupied by the Credara. It was now empty.

Zeta and Brand stood watching from the front porch as Gradore rushed from the farm atop Shayna in full gallop. Flittorin screeched and led the way as Gradore headed towards the forest. As Gradore faded into the darkness, Brand turned and looked directly into his mother's eyes. She knew what he was thinking. Brand was a man now.

As dusk transformed the evening sky, an eerie glow was cast upon the town of Dearby and The Dancing Swine. Inside The Swine, the atmosphere was strangely quiet. Quite the opposite of what it was on Agean's last visit. The faces all looked the same, but the energy level was much less. Patrons were drinking. Jacob and Sally were serving.

The front door opened and Agean entered. Although Agean knew there was nothing he could gain from the constant merriment of his favorite escape, he hoped that Jacob might help him somehow make sense of everything. Many a night Agean spent talking to Jacob. He always had a way of easing Agean's troubles. Almost as if he was there for that very purpose. This would not be the case tonight.

The first thing Agean noticed was the strangely modest crowd; nothing like the usual throngs who crammed into this popular pub after finishing the day's work. Then, something else. Agean immediately sensed something was wrong as the Mark on his neck began to glow and tingle, just as it had done earlier in the strange wind. He paused a moment to touch it. Then, something within Agean began to speak to him. Silently, like some sort of new animal instinct that had come alive. His senses were on fire. Agean slowly approached the bar. The patrons and Sally all seemed to be keeping an eye on him.

"Hello, Jacob," Agean said as he stared into his old friend's eyes.

"Hello, Sir. What'll it be?" Jacob asked. What will it be? Sir? Agean's senses were getting keener by the moment. Something was wrong here. Then, Agean saw something. A quick flash from Jacob. A startling change. In that momentary flash Jacob went from his normal form, to that of a dark creature and back again. In that quick instant, he felt an evil emanating from his old friend, the likes of which he had never sensed before. Whatever manner of evil it was, it felt deep and pure. The sight jarred Agean, but he maintained his control.

Jacob asked, "Is everything all right, Sir?"

"Yes, yes. Just a slight headache is all," Agean told him as he placed his hand on his forehead. "I'll have my usual, Jacob. Like always."

Jacob paused, looking Agean directly in the eye. He then grabbed a bottle from the shelf. Agean looked at Jacob, confused by his behavior as he poured the wrong drink. The Mark on Agean's neck began tingling wildly.

Agean sharpened his focus. Then suddenly, the evil in the room began to reveal itself.

The tingling and glowing of his Mark became more intense as it became increasingly clear what Agean was seeing. Jacob, Sally, the patrons, everyone, changed into some dark form of evil. All poised to kill him. Somehow he knew this. Instinctively, he knew this. And just as instinctively, Agean went into action. He immediately backed away from the bar and snatched open his coat, revealing his Swords of Hamen.

"Jacob!… or whatever you are… I'll not be needing that drink," Agean declared.

The fully revealed creatures began drawing their weapons. Jacob emitted a horrid sneer at Agean. Then, without a moment's thought, a Kraylen from behind Agean lunged forth with a sword. Agean's senses, having expanded his awareness to every corner of the Kraylen-filled pub, enabled him to immediately spin to defend himself from the death blow. Then, with a swift and agile move, Agean slashed through the Kraylen with his blade. No moment of caution. Not a second of pause or regret. Somehow, his actions felt instinctive, righteous and pure as the Kraylen burst into a cloud of smoke and black ash before his eyes. His first kill.

The Kraylen horde attacked full force as Agean used

the Hamen Art and his Hamen Swords to vaporize them. His long coat flaring out as he executed move after move, spinning to defend against every Kraylen blow. His confidence enhanced as his senses grew sharper: the way they moved; how they breathed; their odor - all taken in to be utilized against this enemy.

This enemy can fly. Agean utilized his acrobatic skill to flip and spin, utilizing tables, counters, every beam and wall in the space to attack and defend against the flying menace, at times disabling them by slicing through their wings, then finishing them off on the ground. Black blood from injured Kraylen flew in all directions and drained eerily into the floorboards. His swords sang, snapping the Kraylen's inferior weapons in half as he destroyed with the masterful skill of a Sitcian Warrior. Kraylen burned to ash and crumbled as Agean spun, slashed and ripped them apart with his blades. The incredible battle laid waste to tables and chairs as Agean moved through the ale house killing Kraylen after Kraylen, allowing none to escape, until finally the scene ended with Agean alive, and without as much as a scratch. More than twenty Kraylen destroyed; reduced to piles of black ash. Agean sheathed his swords and then paused for a moment to think. Agean quickly turned and headed for the front door.

The sun was gone and a full moon had taken its place.

Agean carefully opened the front door of The Swine and checked the area. There was no one on the street; no one but an eerie shadowy figure peering at him from behind a tree at the very edge of the dark forest - a Kraylen, observing the scene. Much to the Kraylen's disappointment, Agean departed the pub unscathed, mounted his horse and galloped full stride into the forest.

The Kraylen growled in anger, "Half breeds." He then exited in a different direction, no doubt to report his findings.

By the dim light of night, Gradore rode like the wind, dodging trees and leaping over fallen timber. Flittorin soared just above the trees as he raced through the forest. Gradore's senses were sharp and focused as he rode. This was good, because not only did he know that the fate of mankind was riding on the precious item he carried, he also knew for some time now that he was not alone. Someone had been following him, getting closer and closer over time, to the point where he knew he must confront them. Gradore brought his horse to a skidding halt, drew his sword and turned about. Gradore was correct. Only instead of an enemy, it was his son, Brand. Brand rode up quickly and also skidded to a halt. Gradore, sword still at the ready, stared at his son for a moment.

"Took you long enough," Gradore told him.

Brand replied, "Well I think you're just upset because my horse was ready to overtake your precious Shayna there."

Gradore put his sword away and gazed at Brand. "I'm proud of you, Son."

"You once said it was my time, Father," Brand told him.

Gradore smiled proudly. "I think we should get going." Brand began to turn his horse to continue on. "Son," Gradore said. Brand turned to his father. Gradore then reached into a travel sack on the side of his horse and removed the Credara. "Here." Gradore tossed the Credara to Brand, who carefully caught it. Flittorin screeched. "It is for you to take to the Holy Order." Brand looked at his father with pride and then beheld the precious urn. After years of curiosity, he now held the Credara for the very first time. Brand carefully placed it into his travel sack. Gradore smiled and then turned Shayna about. Together, they resumed full gallop through the forest towards the Holy Order of God Monastery.

Hours later, the full moon sitting amongst a heavy cloud cover lit the sky as Gradore and Brand rode like the wind. The main gate of the monastery opened as soon as they reached it. Once they reached the steps of the monastery, Gradore and Brand quickly dismounted. Brand detached his travel sack from his horse and they both made their way up the stairs to the front door. Flittorin screeched as Gradore used the large knocker on the front door to signal his arrival. Flittorin glided in and landed on Gradore's shoulder.

The sound of heavy metal against the large wooden monastery door echoed throughout the Great Foyer. It hung in the air with a weight as heavy as the large brass knocker that had caused it. Seconds later, a monk headed quickly for the monolithic entrance and grabbed its handle. It took surprisingly little effort to open the huge door, its mechanisms and hinges having been meticulously crafted by Europe's finest. As the monk swung the door in, Brand and Gradore with Flittorin entered quickly into the Great Foyer. Gradore had visited the monastery several times over the years, but not once since the birth of his son, Brand.

"You are Gradore?" asked the monk.

Gradore replied, "I am."

The monk said to him, "The Court awaits you in the Court Chamber."

Flittorin took to the air as all three rushed through the Great Foyer and down the hallway to the Court Chamber.

The Court Chamber was a grand room with ornate

pillars, beautiful stained glass windows and walls and ceilings adorned with masterfully painted frescoes honoring God. Seven large throne-like chairs were placed in a semicircle around an immensely large round wood table. Here sat the members of the Court of Seven. A walkway was cut into the table leading from the edge opposite the Court chairs, to a stone pedestal in the middle. There were a total of four additional large chairs, two each on the opposite sides of the walkway entrance.

The Court of Seven: seven wise Elders from the Holy Order of God tasked with maintaining the holy mission of the Order. They were Iorbus, Grandis, Partum, Bethen, Staron, Euriden and Naji. These men were very old and knew the history, the goals and most importantly, the truth of their Order. They were sworn to its secrecy and would honor its mission to their death.

The six members present were dressed in special garb, indicative of their positions on the Court. They, minus Master Naji, were seated and speaking with Solis, who sat to the right of the table walkway.

Gradore and Brand entered as Flittorin screeched and soared into the Court Chamber, landing atop a chair to the left of the walkway. This got the attention of Iorbus, the Court's leader, who looked up to find that Gradore had arrived.

"Welcome, Gradore. It has been a very long time, my friend," Iorbus said.

Gradore and Brand bowed respectfully to the Court.

Gradore responded, "Iorbus. Great Court. Solis." Gradore and Brand then rose.

"Great Court, I present to you my son, Brand. He has recently assumed the family legacy," Gradore said proudly.

"Welcome, Young Man," Iorbus said. "It is an honor to meet the next generation of such an honorable family."

Brand responded, "Thank you, Sir. It is a great honor for me as well."

Iorbus said, "Please... sit. We have grave matters to discuss and time is of the essence." Gradore took the seat with Flittorin. Brand sat next to him.

"How did you know I would come?" Gradore asked.

Grandis answered, "As you can see, Gradore, we are only six."

Gradore looked carefully at the Court.

"Master Naji," Gradore said.

"Mortally wounded by our young Sitcian," explained Solis.

After a brief pause of thought, Gradore said, "Hamorem?"

Bethen said, "Indeed, Gradore. However, although his condition is grave, he does not make the transition to heaven. He lives, and he suffers."

Gradore asked, "Then Death has not come for him? Is this not good, Great Court? That Master Naji might live?"

"It is our opinion that Master Naji should no longer be among the living, Gradore," Staron replied.

Gradore paused for a moment to think. Then suddenly he realized a horrible possibility. "The eclipse. It was Kanaran! The Great Angel! They have him?"

Iorbus responded, "We pray not. However, it would explain Master Naji's condition, as well as the reason for your visit. Such a deed would impact the Hall of Souls and therefore the Credara. It could also mean doom for mankind." Gradore took the travel sack from Brand and immediately opened it to reveal the Credara. The members of the Court stared in awe at this gift from God. Gradore walked the Credara through the walkway in the table and set it on the pedestal which was made for its presence. Once placed there, it lit and revealed its receded swirling waters inside. Iorbus and the Court members gave a confirming look.

Staron stated, "We haven't much time."

"Does Agean know? We must tell him before he encounters the Kraylen," Gradore said.

Agean, now standing in the doorway of the Court Chamber said, "I believe I already have." Agean knelt before the Court.

"Agean. Please," said Euriden as he beckoned Agean to come forth.

Agean rose then walked to the table's edge, looking curiously at the Credara as he approached. The Arc-Pen Symbol on the Credara glowed as the Mark on Agean's neck glowed and tingled. Then the Credara lit brightly, as if it had been waiting for him with great anticipation. Agean touched his Mark. Brand was in total awe at the sight of the Sitcian Mark. It was just as his father had told him.

"The fact that you stand before us means the Master has trained you well," Iorbus said. "Agean, I would like you to meet Gradore and his son, Brand. They are our friends and sworn servants of God."

"Gradore. Brand," Agean said, bowing out of respect. Gradore and Brand returned the gesture.

"Agean. It is good to see you again," Gradore said. "When first we met, you were a child."

"It is an honor," said Agean.

Grandis said, "Agean, please sit. I am sure you are anxious to know what is happening." Agean sat.

Iorbus took a deep breath, then explained, "As you well know, Agean, from its inception, this Order has studied and monitored every form of religion known to mankind. The missionaries we send into the world help to ensure that God is not forgotten. But this Order has an even greater purpose. Since the Great War in Heaven, there has been an evil living among us. They are called Kraylen: Lucifer's army, who, along with him, was cast forever out of Heaven; he into Hell, they onto earth. While Lucifer has been locked away, God saw that the Kraylen would not so easily accept their punishment. Instead of awaiting His mercy to return them to the Heavens, God found them plotting, waiting patiently for the right moment to exact their revenge. This was why all of this was put into place. We now believe, Agean, that their right moment has come."

Gradore directed Agean's attention to the Credara on the pedestal. "Before you, Agean, is one of the holiest items God has ever bestowed upon man. It is the heavenly urn. The Credara. It not only lights the path to the Hall of Souls, but it is much… much more. And right now, it tells us that the Kraylen are trying to release Lucifer."

Agean, unable to believe what he was hearing, "Lucifer? From Hell?"

"Yes, Agean," said Gradore. "And for Lucifer's Lair, the Credara is the key." Suddenly a wave of thoughts pushed through Agean's mind. Visions of his beloved Master Naji, bleeding and near death on the floor saying those very same words began to swirl in his head. Agean fought it off and snapped back into the moment at hand.

Agean asked, "Honored Court. What is it that God would have us do?"

"Stop them," said Staron. "And not us, Agean. You."

Agean stood in total shock. "I am to do it? Great Court, I mean no disrespect. Though I search my memory, I can not even recall how I came to be here. I have failed at a life of service to God, though not a life of my choosing. And if I may say, Great Court, my faith has suffered over the years."

Iorbus replied, "Faith is the greatest challenge to mankind, Agean. We have all been there."

"But am I now to believe that God calls upon me for such a task?" The Court members and Gradore looked at each other.

"It is true, Agean," said Solis. "The Kraylen have begun to act and must be stopped. You, Agean, bear the Mark."

Iorbus immediately stood and walked towards Agean. "The Hamen Mark of Sitcian, Agean. The holy symbol that rests upon your neck." Looking confused, Agean touched the mark on his neck. "Placed upon you at birth by God himself and formed from two symbols. The inner, the Arc-Pen Symbol, represents all things that are directly of God. The Credara and your Hamen Swords bear this symbol. Joined with it is the Mark of Hamen. It is the mark of the Hamen Warrior, one of God's weapons against evil, trained in the Hamen Fighting Art. The very art Master Naji has been teaching you since childhood."

Solis said to Agean, "You see, Agean. You are the Sitcian." Agean paused for a moment, stunned by what he was being told. The Sitcian. Master Naji mentioned this.

"Master Naji. How is he?" Agean asked.

"The wound you inflicted should have ended his life, yet Master Naji lives and suffers still," Iorbus stated. "It is because of this, Agean, that we fear the Kraylen may have captured the Angel of Death."

Agean turned to Iorbus, shocked yet again. "I beg your indulgence, Great Court, but Master Naji, fighting demons, Lucifer, and now you say the Angel of Death may be captured? How is this possible?"

"The eclipse we experienced recently, Agean, was Kanaran. It happens once every fifteen hundred years," Solis explained. "Ancient scrolls tell us it is the only time during which the Angel is vulnerable. They may have discovered a way to reveal him, then take him captive."

Agean said, "But if they do have him, then-"

"No one can die," interrupted Bethen, "no matter the age, disease or dismemberment. Mankind will suffer endlessly until Death is freed. We should all pray that we are mistaken."

Solis spoke. "Agean, this must be kept secret. Reveal

this to no one until you are sure. If word of this gets out, it will cause panic throughout the world. And if we are right, you must get to the Angel as quickly as possible."

Confused, Agean asked, "But why would someone do such a thing? What purpose would it serve?"

"Such an act would force the Hall of Souls to empty," explained Iorbus. Agean paused with a perplexed look, trying to drink it all in. He began to pace back and forth as it all became too much to bear.

"I need to see Master Naji," Agean said. Agean quickly turned to exit the room with Solis in pursuit.

Solis called out, "Agean! Agean, there is more you must know!" Solis stopped and watched as Agean exited the Court Chamber.

Iorbus said to him, "Solis. It is time to tell the boy the truth. His truth."

Solis paused for a moment, staring at the Court members. He then walked over to the Credara, removed it from the pedestal, bowed to the Court, then exited.

chapter seven
A Warrior Learns His Truth

The hall outside of Master Naji's cell was quiet except for the sound of chant filtering throughout the monastery. Quite overwhelmed, Agean walked quickly down the hallway towards Master Naji's door. Two tall candelabras filled with lit candles had been placed on each side of his doorway. This was usually done for monks who had fallen gravely ill; for prayer. Agean paused for a moment then slowly approached the door and opened it.

Master Naji's cell, and those of the other Elders, was grander than those of ordinary monks. This place was indeed a spiritual space for the Master. His cell was both neat and impeccably clean. On the walls and shelves were his most prized possessions. Their colors stood out in contrast against the dark color of the walls and floor. They almost seemed to dance with the light of the candles. The moonlight shining through the balcony door window illuminated Master Naji, who lay peacefully on his bed.

Agean slowly entered. There were many lit candles of varying dimensions, colors, and shapes around the Master's bed. A monk sat quietly reading scripture in Latin to him. The monk noticed Agean and stopped his reading to watch Agean approach with a sad look. Moments later, Solis quietly entered holding the Credara and gestured to the monk, who then closed his book, stood, crossed, and left the room. Agean placed a hand gently on Master Naji's arm.

"Master. How could I have done this? What would you have me do?" Agean asked sadly.

Solis said, "You have many questions, Agean." Agean turned to look at Solis. He then turned back to Master Naji as the flickering candlelight reflected in the tears welling in his eyes.

"He was always there with answers," Agean said.

Solis moved closer to Agean. "Yes. Always knowing things that none of us could ever know. His place in God's heart is truly special." Agean moved his hand to Master Naji's shoulder, and lowered his head in sadness. "Agean, you have always wondered about your coming here, about the visions that haunt you. It is time you knew the truth."

At that moment, the Credara began to light in multiple colors.

Agean glanced over at it. "The truth?"

"Master Naji somehow knew that you would be the one to be challenged, Agean. He dedicated his life to preparing you for this moment," Solis explained. "He accepted it as an honor. We all have." Solis allowed Agean a moment to absorb what he was saying. "You say you've encountered the Kraylen?"

"Yes. At The Dancing Swine. It is a pub in Dearby."

"I am very familiar with it, Agean," Solis said.

"They appeared human at first, disguised as my friends. But somehow my senses allowed me to see through them," Agean told Solis. "That's when I realized that none of my friends were among them."

"They, Agean, are the darkest form of evil ever to walk the earth. The pure enemy of God. Master Naji sensed that they had come out of hiding," Solis said. "I fear, my boy, that you will not see your friends again."

Agean stared at Solis with sadness in his eyes. "Can we not just destroy them, Headmaster?"

"Only those who bear the Mark of Hamen can see through their disguise. Only the weapons of Hamen, weapons forged from Hamen Living Metal, can destroy them. This is why we brought you here, Agean. To protect you, teach you," explained Solis. Agean touched his Mark. "Come with me, Agean. I want to show you something."

Solis turned and walked to the door. After a moment with Master Naji, Agean turned and followed.

The high lanterns in the Great Foyer shone a somewhat eerie light upon the faces of the stark white statues lining its walls. As Solis and Agean approached, their footsteps echoed as if they were entering a cavern deep within the earth.

Solis called Agean's attention to the statues adorning the lengthy foyer. "Tell me, Agean. What do you know of these men?"

"I have been told that they were great warriors of God."

Solis said, "Look at their swords, Agean." Agean moved in for a closer look. Something he had always avoided in the past. "The Arc-Pen Symbol — the same symbol that is emblazoned upon your swords. And just as your swords, they are forged from Hamen Living Metal." Agean touched the handles of his swords, acknowledging a newfound connection to the foyer statues for the first time since his arrival. "They are indeed great warriors, Agean. But more importantly, they are you," said Solis.

Agean responded, "Me?"

Solis said proudly, "They too were Sitcians." Agean took a moment to ponder what Solis had just told him.

"Sitcians? But Sitcian Angels exist only in Heaven," Agean said.

"With the exception of these men... and you, Agean. Born on earth to protect mankind against Lucifer's forces. These very special monuments were erected in their honor, as one will be for you," explained Solis.

Solis held up the Credara before the statues. It immediately began emitting a bright light. Suddenly, all of the statues moved, raising their swords in honor of the Credara's presence. Agean was stunned.

Solis continued, "Their spirits remain, so that they may serve as council to the Elders and whoever bears the Sitcian Mark. They are The Sitcian Council. God's purpose for them was the same as for you, Agean, only they were able to live out their lives never having to face the great threat that now confronts us all." Solis moved to the first statue. "This one was the first — Fitaris." Fitaris's statue repositioned to a standing bow position. Agean marveled at what he was witnessing. "The Credara was given to him. It was he who started this Order. But there is one more, Agean. One whose statue is not yet complete. Your truth lies with him."

Agean, perplexed, said, "I do not understand."

Solis moved closer to Agean. "You know, Agean, practically all of my time here has been spent studying. The ancient scrolls, the Bisalis, and this… the Credara. You, Agean, must learn to trust its power. For you bear the Sitcian Mark. And for he who bears the Mark, it can summon an army. It is also the purest form of truth on earth. And if it is truth you seek, it can bring you face to face with it." Solis took Agean's hand and placed it on the Credara. Then magically, in a swirl of light in their minds, they were both taken back in time.

Solis and Agean suddenly found themselves looking upon a scene from many years in the past; simply observers to a moment in time. The power of the Credara transported them to Master Naji's training room. A younger Master Naji was training a young monk who, just as Agean, bore the Sitcian Mark upon his neck.

"His name was Patharus," Solis said. "Truly talented and always level headed, until for some reason he became headstrong and impatient with his training and his time here as a monk."

Patharus executed a masterful move on Master Naji, causing him to stumble backwards. Patharus reacted overly proud, much to the Master's disappointment. Despite this, Master Naji continued with the training session.

"Master Naji worried about Patharus and his curiosity about the world… about his desire to leave the Order and seek out his destiny. The Master knew Patharus's place was with the Order, not only to fulfill his role as Sitcian but also because Master Naji knew in his heart that while Patharus's Hamen skills were excellent, he was not yet ready."

As quickly as they had arrived, they were again transported in their minds to another place. The Dancing Swine, where Patharus sat at a table with Sirin, a greying older man to whom he listened closely.

"The Swine," Agean said.

"Yes. Patharus, like you, enjoyed The Dancing Swine," Solis said. "As you well know, we never encouraged it, but we knew there had to be a place for you and the others to connect with the world. To keep an eye on you, this Order has a friend there in Jacob."

Sirin passionately told Patharus, "If God has given you a gift, do you truly have a choice? You must take it into the world and use it for the good of mankind. Seek ye thy destiny, Patharus." Patharus nodded his head in agreement.

A younger Jacob tended the bar while observing Patharus and Sirin.

"Patharus had a close friend at the monastery who also became concerned with his behavior," Solis said. "His name was Thaddeus."

Cleaning a beer stein with a cloth, Jacob turned to look to the other end of the room. There sat Thaddeus, a young monk from the Order, dressed as a regular patron at the far end of the bar. Thaddeus gave a nod to acknowledge Jacob and then continued watching Patharus and Sirin, sensing something was very wrong.

Suddenly, in a powerful swirl, Agean and Solis returned to the Great Foyer. Solis had removed Agean's hand from the Credara. Agean looked at his hand, clenching it while looking at the colorfully lit vessel.

"Thaddeus told me the next day what he had observed," Solis said. "It was then that I knew that something was amiss. Despite Master Naji's urging, Patharus decided that evening to gather his things and leave the monastery in search of his destiny. I asked Thaddeus to follow him, to make sure he was okay through the forest at night. This I should not have done."

Solis gestured to Agean to extend his arm. Agean did, and once again Solis placed his hand on the Credara, taking them back in time.

With a powerful swirling of space and time, Solis and Agean were again transported. This time, to the forest beyond the monastery grounds at night.

Patharus, on horseback, rode through the forest. Unbeknownst to him, Thaddeus trailed him at a distance. Suddenly, Sirin stepped out from behind a tree and into Patharus's path, interrupting his ride mid-stride. He swerved, barely missing Sirin and then turned about.

Patharus was totally shocked. "Sirin! What the devil are you doing? I could have killed you!"

"Patharus. My sincerest apologies," Sirin responded. "My home is not far from here. I often take walks at night to clear my thoughts. I find it peaceful. But what an unexpected pleasure. Please. Stop and rest."

Patharus, pausing for a moment, said, "I suppose I should get a good night's rest… get an early start in the morning." Patharus trotted over to a nearby tree, dismounted, tied off and began unpacking his horse. "You must be more careful, my friend."

Sirin responded, "Of course you are right, Patharus. It is fortunate for me that you are such a skilled horseman." While Patharus continued unpacking his horse, Sirin moved in closer to help.

"So, where are you off to, my friend?" Sirin asked. Patharus removed his Hamen Swords, leaned them against the tree, and then resumed unpacking. From a distance, Thaddeus dismounted and continued watching.

Patharus replied, "I thought I'd travel to the North as far as my supplies will allow; then from there, destiny, Sirin. I have you to thank. A good friend's advice is much better than that of cranky old priests — which is exactly what I'll be if I do not get some sleep." Patharus began undoing the straps to his horse's saddle. Sirin picked up one of Patharus's swords and slowly drew it from its sheath. This immediately got Thaddeus's attention as he continued watching from a distance.

Sirin said, "Patharus." Patharus turned, seeing that Sirin had one of his swords, running his fingers along the blade. "Tell me. Do you trust me?"

Patharus leaned casually against his horse. "Of course, Sirin. You are my friend. Why I have more reason to-"

Immediately Sirin spun like a master swordsman and ran Patharus through the stomach with the Hamen

Sword, cutting off his words. Patharus's horse reared up and neighed loudly. The Arc-Pen Symbol on the Hamen Sword and Patharus's Sitcian Mark glowed brightly.

Thaddeus saw this and took off running towards the scene, screaming, "Nooo! Patharus!"

Sirin embedded the sword so deeply that he now stood an inch from Patharus's face. So close that Patharus could feel the heat of his breath.

Sirin asked, "Am I your friend now, Sitcian?"

Patharus, gurgling blood, replied, "Why... Sirin?"

Suddenly, in a deep, evil Kraylen voice, Sirin said, "Your Master was right about you, Patharus. You were not yet ready. Otherwise, you would've known what I am. One of the true angels of Heaven. The name... is Licronus!" Sirin immediately transformed into the Kraylen creature, Licronus. Patharus stared in pain and horror. All he could do was cough and choke on his own blood as it streamed from his mouth and nose. Suddenly, Licronus withdrew the sword, spun and decapitated Patharus with split-second precision.

Thaddeus, still running, trying to make his way to the bloody scene, screamed again. "Nooo!"

Then Licronus, without looking, took a dagger from his waist and threw it like a marksman. The dagger found its mark directly into the forehead of Thaddeus, who immediately stopped and then dropped directly where he stood.

"My heart is still heavy," Solis said. "I should have been the one to die that night."

Licronus walked over and picked up the second Sword of Hamen. He returned to Patharus, knelt next to him, and used his clothing to wipe clean the bloody sword's blade. He stared directly at Patharus's face for a moment, then arose and stood still. He took a deep breath and then transformed himself into the perfect image of Patharus.

With a powerful swirl, Agean and Solis were again returned to the Great Foyer. Agean had a disturbed look on his face.

"Their bodies were never found," Solis said. "When Licronus returned to us the next day, disguised as Patharus and begging forgiveness for leaving, we had no idea the evil we had allowed within these walls. I asked about Thaddeus. He swore he had not seen him. We had no choice but to believe that Thaddeus had either fallen to tragic circumstances, or had himself left the Order. For five years Licronus went unsuspected, living among us, learning our secrets, learning the sacred Art. It was not until you were finally discovered in Gullin, that things began to unfold here for Licronus."

Solis raised the Credara to Agean, who willingly placed his hand upon it, taking them back in time.

Agean and Solis were again transported to the forest beyond the monastery grounds mid-day.

In full gallop, Licronus, disguised as Patharus, made his way through the forest. Suddenly, Licronus's two Kraylen Generals, Poragon and Bralorg, rode up and joined him as they thundered through.

With another swirling of time, Agean and Solis were propelled hours ahead. After having passed through the forest and across the grasslands, a disguised Licronus and his Generals entered the town of Gullin, a rather large town with a sizable marketplace bustling with the day's activities. As they rode farther, they saw the small pottery shop they were looking for.

Agean's mother, a beautiful, dark-haired woman in her early thirties, and his sister, fair, lovely and in her early teens, were outside dusting and tending to items for sale. Agean's father, a strong, dark-haired man in his forties, tended to some items just inside the doorway of the shop. He looked out and spotted the riders approaching. Licronus and his Generals trotted up, dismounted and tied off their horses. As they approached the shop, Agean's father hurried out to greet them.

"Gentlemen... Gentlemen!" Agean's father called out. "In what might I interest you? Perhaps some well-crafted water vessels for your homes... or perhaps-"

"We have come for the boy," Licronus interrupted.

Looking closer, Agean's father now saw the symbolic white and gold sleeve binding Licronus's hair. Agean's father looked over at Agean's mother and sister, who stood watching. Agean's mother immediately ran into the shop.

"I see. You're from the Holy Order. My son is inside," Agean's father told them. He then turned to lead Licronus inside. Licronus silently gestured to his Generals as he entered, setting some unknown plan into motion.

Agean's father and Licronus entered the pottery shop, which was filled wall to wall with plates, cups, and large vessels; some elaborately done, some simple and basic. They walked the thin pathway that wound through to a small side room. Agean's father entered the room, closely followed by Licronus. Sitting in the middle of the room on a thick woven rug was Agean's mother, in tears, holding tight to her son, an almost two-year-old Agean.

The younger Agean was at first preoccupied with some makeshift toys. Agean's father knelt to his wife, touching her lovingly on the shoulder.

"My love, it is time," he told her. She hugged Agean tighter as Agean's father hugged them both. Then she looked into Agean's eyes.

"Never forget us, my brave little boy. You will never be forgotten," she said to him. After a moment of tears, she released Agean to his father and stood. She looked Licronus in the eye. She sensed something strange in this one.

Just as she was about to speak, Agean's father told her, "My darling, please leave us to talk. We will be out soon."

Agean's mother looked into Licronus's eyes again and said to him, "Please, take good care of my son. Give him a better life." She put her hand to her mouth, trying to hold back her crying and then turned and ran from the room.

Agean's father stared at the doorway as his wife left. He knew the pain and anguish she felt. He looked lovingly at his son, knowing that this could possibly be the last time he would ever see him.

"This is my son, Agean," Agean's father said. Agean looked up at Licronus. The Sitcian Mark of Hamen was clearly visible upon his neck. As soon as he saw the disguised Licronus, Agean began to cry.

"He's a fine boy," said Agean's father, agonizing and hugging his son. "It's just this mark on his neck. People are afraid it is the mark of the devil. But he's a wonderful boy. And normally very quiet, but for some reason…" Agean continued to cry loudly and point at Licronus. "Agean, quiet down now. This nice man has come to visit with you." Agean's crying became more intense. "I'm sure you are wondering how it is possible for me to give up my only son. My family has lived here all of our lives, and now this mark has made us outcasts. No one will shop with us. I can no longer afford to feed them." Agean continued crying and pointing as his father tried to comfort him. "But you are a man of God, so I know he will be well cared for. I can move my family somewhere distant." Agean's father held up his young son and looked directly into his eyes. "You'll have a better life than I could ever give you, my son."

Agean, still crying, wailed loudly, "Nooo!"

"Shh. Agean," his father said as he turned to Licronus. "With the bag of gold the Order promised, we can start over."

Licronus leaned down and took Agean from his father's arms to inspect him closer. Agean was not fooled by Licronus's disguise and continued crying. Licronus stared into his eyes.

"Hmph. Sitcian. You will soon bow to a greater god. He bears the Mark! Take him!" Licronus ordered.

Bralorg quickly entered the room and took young Agean from Licronus. Agean struggled.

Bralorg asked, "Should we not kill him now?" Licronus immediately spun towards him in anger, glaring at him for a moment.

"I must first have the book! Take him!" demanded Licronus. He and Bralorg, with Agean in his arms, began to leave the room.

Agean's father, shocked by what he had just heard, yelled, "Wait! What are you talking about? Who are you?"

Before exiting, Licronus turned and slapped Agean's father to the floor. He paused a moment to snarl at him. He and Bralorg then exited the back room with young Agean.

Across the street from the pottery shop, people were starting to gather and observe, the fear of Poragon's intimidating size and deadly blades preventing any attempts at heroics. Bralorg, with a crying Agean, walked quickly out of the pottery shop, followed by Licronus. Then Agean's father ran out, holding his jaw.

Agean's father yelled, "Wait! What are you doing?"

What Agean's father saw next stopped him dead in his tracks. His face turned pale as he set his eyes upon a horrific sight. Licronus's Generals had gagged his wife and daughter and tied them to a nearby post. Hay had been piled at their feet. Poragon stood with two lit torches as they both cried and struggled to get free. Poragon tossed one of the torches to Bralorg, who still held the struggling Agean. Agean's father dropped to his knees to beg for their lives.

"Oh my God, no!" he cried as he grabbed hold of Licronus's ankle. Licronus raised his hand and immediately changed it to its Kraylen form. He then reached down and clutched Agean's father's throat and began crushing it, cutting off his words. He lifted him off the ground while his other hand drew a blade from his waist. Poragon and Bralorg tossed their torches onto the hay and set Agean's mother and sister ablaze. Agean screamed, crying as he witnessed the horror of his mother and sister being burned alive. Their screams of pain rang out as the fire made its way up their bodies, quickly engulfing them. Observers screamed in terror at what was happening, helpless to do anything. Then, Licronus took his blade and plunged it through Agean's father's chest, so deeply that the tip exited his back. He choked and convulsed as the screams of Agean's mother and sister subsided with their deaths. Agean, still crying in Bralorg's arms, reached out helplessly to the burning remains of his mother and sister.

Solis said, "Only much later did we learn of the horror inflicted upon your family."

Again, in a powerful swirl they were returned to the Great Foyer. Agean stood shaking with a blank stare and tears welling in his eyes.

"When you arrived, I immediately dropped everything to welcome you. Although you were young, your Hamen senses were very strong. Your crying and glowing Mark alerted Master Naji that there was something evil about the man we all thought was Patharus. Licronus knew you had somehow seen through his disguise. Realizing he would soon be caught, he knew he had to act quickly. You see, Agean, you have already saved us once," Solis told him.

Solis immediately confronted the stunned Agean and grabbed his hand. Agean resisted.

Solis said, "I'm sorry, Agean. This you must know." Solis forced Agean's hand back onto the Credara — again, taking them back in time.

Solis's abbacy was quiet. Empty. Licronus, maintaining his disguise as Patharus, slowly entered the room and shut the door behind him. He scanned his surroundings for a second and then walked over to the bookshelves in search of something. Not finding it, Licronus scanned the room again. He noticed a wall tapestry which was shifted, revealing an open wall cabinet. Licronus quickly walked over and searched the cabinet. Again failing to find what he wanted, he angrily turned, pushing books from the shelves in frustration. Then he saw it. It shocked Licronus as he approached Solis's desk. But there it lay, hidden in plain sight. Solis must have been studying it, interrupted by the arrival of the boy. He must have thought, the world will continue to be safe; the new Sitcian has been found. Yes, that must be it. Why else would he have left such a precious text just sitting on his desk?

The Bisalis. Licronus slowly approached the book and

opened the cover. Licronus's eyes lit up at what he saw next. On the inside cover and first page were drawings of the Great Passage, the Hall of Souls, the Credara, and the Arc-Pen Symbol atop a mountain crest — Lucifer's Lair.

The evil look in Licronus's eyes intensified at seeing this. But where? He began to turn the page when suddenly the door swung open. Solis entered and was stunned to see what Patharus was doing. Licronus immediately slammed the book cover.

"Patharus! Why have you done this? Give me that!" demanded Solis.

Solis lunged for the book and they both struggled. An angry Licronus revealed his Kraylen form to Solis. Solis's face cringed with terror as Licronus slapped him to the floor, cutting him with his ring and causing a gash across Solis's left eye.

"My dear God, what have I done?" Solis said as he struggled to his feet.

As Licronus went for the book again, Solis quickly grabbed the sword from a suit of armor standing in a near-by corner. He swung it with all the strength he had and sliced off Licronus's left hand. Licronus screamed in agony as his hand fell to the floor, black blood dripping onto the floorboards. The blood, almost as if escaping, was quickly absorbed into the floorboards as the hand changed to its human form. Solis again lunged for the Bisalis, causing it to fly off the desk and under a bookshelf. Solis landed on the floor beside the bookshelf. Holding his arm, trying to squeeze the stump to keep more blood from escaping, Licronus roared angrily at Solis and then quickly exited without the book. Solis wiped the blood from his nose as he gathered himself. He quickly searched under the bookshelf, found the Bisalis and held it tight. He sat there breathing heavily with a look of terror in his eyes.

"I then knew the truth," said Solis. "The Kraylen demon had lived among us for years, learning our secrets. I shudder to think what secrets he may now know of Lucifer's Lair."

Once again, after a powerful swirl, Solis and Agean were back in the Great Foyer. What Solis had just told Agean completely overwhelmed him.

"Licronus knows the Hamen Art, and may now have captured the Angel of Death. You, Agean, were born to stop him. Now… you know your truth."

Mortified, Agean said, "My family. Butchered. Why did no one tell me of this before?"

Solis replied, "It was my choice, Agean. For your training, I wanted you to be free of the anger you now feel; to better prepare you for that which is now upon us."

Agean responded, "Upon us? It is upon me! I have suffered for as long as I can remember. These terrible visions… day and night. All of this time you knew the truth?"

Confused. Dazed. Shaking his head, Agean turned and began walking away. Suddenly, he was halted as a swirl of echoing voices emanated from the statues around him, speaking to him in his mind and through his ears. Penetrating voices with an intensity Agean had never before felt.

As he had experienced so often before, they were reaching out to him. Only this time, they grabbed hold of him with pounding, heavy voices, both randomly and in unison, saying to him, "Agean." "You are the Sitcian." "God has chosen you." Agean turned in amazement. Then, one by one:

"Without you, Agean, mankind will be doomed," said one statue.

"It has already started," said another.

"You must, Agean," said another statue.

"It is your task. Your destiny awaits you," said another.

Agean angrily responded, "My destiny? Was it my destiny to be forced to watch as my family was brutally murdered? Taken from me by a horrid creature of His making?"

Suddenly, the Fitaris statue turned directly to Agean and spoke, "Agean. I was called upon first to make the sacrifice. We have all had to… to be who we are… to be who you are - never knowing if and when the time would come. The holy waters of the Credara tell us that the time is upon us. You must gather His army and lead it against the Kraylen."

Agean looked at the statue of Fitaris in amazement, then lowered his eyes and said, "I am sorry, Council, but this is not my fight."

Agean turned, angrily snatched the sleeve from his ponytail, revealing his coal black oily hair, and began walking away.

"Agean!" Solis called out. Agean continued walking. "Agean, you cannot walk away from this!"

Agean spun in furious anger and stormed back to Solis.

"I had the right to avenge the murder of my family! I had the right to know! I did not ask for this!" Agean yelled.

Solis yelled back, "You did not have to ask! He gave you this!"

Agean responded angrily, "If He wanted me to save man, why did He not save me? He let them take my family! And now Master Naji… He left me nothing!"

Solis yelled back, "He gave you purpose! He gave you a destiny!"

Agean, controlling his anger, became calmer. He said to Solis, "He should have given it to someone else."

What Solis had just heard horrified him. Agean then turned and walked down the hall as Solis watched with a look of terror on his face.

The statue of Fitaris spoke. "Solis, the journey for this one will be difficult. He must find his way."

Fitaris's voice echoed out as all statues returned to their original positions and the light on the Credara dimmed.

chapter eight
A Warrior Chooses His Path

A stale quietness had settled over Master Naji's training room. A few lit candles provided a very somber atmosphere as the door slowly opened. Agean entered the training room, still reeling from what he had just learned. Everything he had wondered... from as far back as he could remember - all of his questions answered in one enormous tidal wave. The visions that had haunted him, which still haunted him, had now been made more horrible with this new knowledge.

He leaned against a post near the entrance of the training room, immersed in his thoughts. Then his eyes caught a terrible sight. A red stain on the floor mat. Master Naji's blood. The stain was huge. Master Naji would surely never survive such a loss of blood. Agean moved closer to the stain, staring at it with a blank look. Horribly distraught, he grabbed his hair trying to somehow rip this entire day from his life. Make it go away.

His hands moved from his hair to his face as he gazed across the room, trying to gather his thoughts. He took his traditional position at the wood kneeling block, hoping that somehow this dream, this nightmare, would end. That somehow, it all never happened.

After a few moments, his attention focused on the small cabinet across the room. The strange cabinet containing the square glass container that Master Naji insisted he look into after every training session; and the question the Master would ask each time without fail. *What is it you see here?*

Agean slowly rose and walked over to the cabinet. He stared at it for a moment. Its plain look never triggered much thought in Agean in the years past. Then, he reached out and took hold of the small brass knobs. He had never opened the cabinet himself, only Master Naji. Agean drew a deep breath and pulled the doors open. A look of complete shock took over Agean's face. What was revealed was no longer the human hand he had seen each and every time, but a dark ugly Kraylen hand bearing a unique ring.

Suddenly, Agean's mind violently flashed back to the memory of his father's murder. The hand crushing his father's throat. Then, more memories rushed forcefully into his head: the memory of Solis severing Licronus's hand, the same hand that violently ended his father's life; the hand with the ring; the hand in the cabinet. For some reason, Agean's senses now allowed him to see what he could not see before; just as his senses had allowed him to see the Kraylen at The Swine — before they could kill him — after they had killed his friends. The anger welled up in him and was completely visible on his face as he realized a horrifying truth: This was the hand of the creature that murdered his family. This was the hand of Licronus.

❧

In the Court Chamber, Gradore and the Court members continued speaking on the grave matters at hand. Brand listened with great interest as undoubtedly the most important men in the world at that very moment discussed the fate of mankind. Suddenly, Solis appeared in the doorway with the Credara. The conversation came to an end when Iorbus saw Solis's bewildered look.

"Solis," Iorbus said. "Something tells me that the truth was not easily received by our young Sitcian."

"I told him everything, Great Elders," Solis replied as he entered the Chamber. "Agean has gone through much for which I must bear full responsibility. My choices regarding him knowing his past have proven unwise."

Iorbus responded, "Then may God show mercy on all of us."

"Elders. The greatest horror ever to befall mankind is upon us," Grandis said. "The Credara tells us that the time is very near indeed. Perhaps we need an alternate plan."

"This is God's plan. There is no alternative," Solis declared.

Euriden asked, "Then what are we to do, Solis?"

After a momentary pause, Iorbus stood. "Gradore. Accommodations for you and your son have been arranged in our guest quarters. I ask that you both please excuse us as we must confer on this privately."

Gradore stood. "You are very gracious, Great Council. Come, Son." Brand stood, and he and Gradore bowed to the Court. Gradore looked over to Flittorin and smiled. "Goodbye, Brave One." Flittorin screeched. He and Brand then turned to exit the Court Chamber and found themselves face to face with Agean, carrying a travel sack.

"Agean," Gradore said, surprised. Agean glowed with a renewed confidence, ready to embark on his mission. He dropped his travel sack, causing a loud thud as it hit the floor. He bowed respectfully to Gradore and Brand and then approached the table. The sight of Agean shocked Solis. He gazed at him with a look of great concern as Gradore and Brand exited the Chamber.

"Great Court. Solis," Agean said, bowing with respect. Solis's brow bristled in reaction to Agean calling him by his first name. It was either a sign of disrespect from a student monk, or a sign that Agean's student days had come to an end. The events of the day made Solis believe that perhaps both were true. "I am ready to accept this task." Silence fell over the Court Chamber.

Iorbus said to Agean, "I see. And now that you know everything, Agean, does your heart burn for revenge?"

"Great Elder, it rages inside me like nothing has ever before," Agean replied.

"Then you must set it aside or else we are doomed," Solis demanded. "Do not forget what is at stake, Agean. For if it is vengeance you seek, it will make you vulnerable. Master Naji knew this, as does Licronus. He will be watching, waiting for the right moment to use it against you."

Agean began to turn from Solis without even a word. Solis reached out and grabbed Agean's shoulder. "Do you understand what we are telling you, Agean? Since being cast into Hell, the full force of evil has been kept at bay because Lucifer holds the key to its ultimate power. A power far greater than even him. If Lucifer is allowed to place one foot… even one finger onto God's earth, the power of the Kraylen will increase. Perhaps to such a level that even you may not be able to stop them."

With disdain, Agean shook Solis's hand from his shoulder, stared at him for a moment and then responded, "I will do as God has asked, Great Court. Destroy Licronus and his Kraylen." Solis continued his concerned look.

All the members of the Court stood. Staron said, "Agean, God bestows upon you the holy Credara. It is one of three given to man. It is a vessel of great Sitcian power, and the key to unlock and lock Lucifer's Lair. Licronus knows that without it, your vast Sitcian power will be limited. If he seeks the power we believe he wants, then he means to have all three, Agean, so you must take great care to not allow it to fall into Kraylen hands." Agean gazed at the Credara as he pondered Staron's words. "He has bestowed upon you the Swords of Hamen. No greater weapons for battle exist for a Hamen Warrior. And He bestows upon you the great hawk, Flittorin, to lead your path to the Hall of Souls."

"The Hall of Souls," Agean said, confused. "Master Naji mentioned this."

"Yes, Agean," said Solis. "It is the 'Pool of Life'; the holy place where the very souls of man pass after death and before life. Waiting to be born… awaiting Heaven… or, for some, damnation." Agean cut Solis a look, believing that perhaps that last option was meant to get his attention.

Iorbus added, "It is that which binds Lucifer to Hell. Only when the Hall of Souls is empty can the entrance to the Lair be unlocked, and Lucifer set free. You must heed the holy waters of the Credara, Agean. For when the holy urn is empty, so too be the Hall of Souls."

Solis told Agean, "Licronus must have a Credara to unlock the Lair. For the protection and safety of the other two, we know not where they are located. What we do know is that Licronus has planned this for thousands of years, Agean. If what the holy urn tells us is true, he may have already stolen one of the others. If you do not stop him, he will unlock the Lair and release Lucifer upon the world. Know that he will stop at nothing to destroy you and steal the remaining Credaras. For this reason it must never leave your sight." Agean took a moment to think.

"Great Court. Would God have me do this alone?" asked Agean. Iorbus stood, removed a small, thin, leather bound book from his garb and walked over to Agean.

Iorbus said to him, "You will never be alone, Agean. That He has promised. It is written for the Sitcian: He gives His mightiest army." Iorbus revealed the Bisalis and handed it to Agean. "It is time for you to have this, Agean. It is the Bisalis. A Sitcian's destiny, and everything you will need to know, to understand, is written here. There are four others of God's Army who bear the Marks of Hamen. They are the chosen. As part of our mission, this Order has ensured that their Hamen training and commitment to God's task has been secured throughout the centuries. To protect them, only one of us in this room knows who and where they are. Therefore, you must trust Flittorin to lead you to them." Agean gave a look of disbelief to Flittorin. "They must all be found, Agean, for their destiny is yours."

Agean received the book, taking a moment to marvel at the Arc-Pen Symbol deeply tooled into its cover. His Sitcian Mark tingled and glowed. Flittorin screeched as Agean tucked the text into a pouch on his waist.

Iorbus continued, "Master Agean, the fate of God's earth is in your capable hands. May He keep, fortify and protect you on your journey and in battle."

"You have my promise, Great Court. I will complete this task," declared Agean. Solis then approached Agean. Agean turned to Solis, confronted by his very suspicious look. Solis then handed him the Credara, which lit upon Agean's touch. Agean considered Solis's look and felt angry. Then, with a renewed strength in his being, Agean turned to exit the Court Chamber. Solis paused for a moment to watch him and then followed him to the chamber doorway.

Agean, with the Credara in one hand, picked up his travel sack with the other and left the Court Chamber, making his way down the hallway. Solis quickly exited the Court Chamber and entered the hallway behind him.

Solis yelled, "Agean!" Agean stopped and turned to Solis, still angry. "What made you change your mind?"

Agean took a few steps towards Solis. "If this thing I am asked to do will lead me to the demon that destroyed my family and will end the Master's suffering, then I will do it."

Solis responded, "Do you not see that this thing you must do is greater than that? Greater than your family? Greater than Master Naji? Greater than you? Then again, you have never been good at looking beyond your own needs."

"Say what you will, Solis! But as it appears, I am all you've got. The rest will have to take care of itself."

Suddenly, the Credara began to glow dimly in Agean's hand. He glared at it for a moment, then tucked it carefully into his waist pouch and returned his attention to Solis, who continued to show concern in his gaze. Then, Agean turned and resumed walking down the hallway, leaving Solis staring. Iorbus approached from behind Solis and watched as Agean disappeared down the hall.

Iorbus asked, "Do we believe he can do it, Solis?"

After a moment of introspection, Solis replied, "We should pray that he can, Iorbus. But first, there is something I must tell you. Something I did which may further complicate things." Iorbus turned to Solis with a look of concern as Solis prepared himself to share his secret.

PART FOUR
The Gathering of
Armies

chapter nine
The Task Lies
Beyond the Gates

"Flittorin, lead the way!"

For Agean's journey, he was provided his pick of any one of the prized horses from the Order's stables. For this, Agean chose the Order's finest Arabian stallion. Darius.

Agean was present when Darius came into the world. Master Naji allowed Agean to assist with the birth, allowing him to form a special bond with the horse. Although the times were many when Agean's feelings towards Master Naji were like that of a son to his father, this was one which stood out most in his memory. Agean gave Darius his name, which in the Persian translation meant "rich and kingly." Agean had a history with this steed, riding him through archery and battle training sessions, as well as on many of his escapes to The Swine. On this clear night, Agean rode Darius full gallop through the forest beyond the monastery, with Flittorin soaring overhead, screeching and leading his path.

Several days had passed. Flittorin soared high in the

hot afternoon sky as Agean trotted at a modest clip along a winding path. The lush greenery stretched as far as he could see along a beautiful fjord that cut through a low range of mountains. The tree lines that followed the peaks in the distance distorted the bottom half of a huge sun. The humid breeze whipping off of the water cooled the anger and bitterness that had held tight to Agean since the beginning of his journey. There was but one solution for this anger and bitterness. For now he would keep his vow to God and the Court and follow the plan. Follow the hawk. "Lead the way, Flittorin", he thought. Lead me to the place. For it is there that I will confront this demon, Licronus, and avenge my family.

Evening. Several more days of travel had passed. The sun was now fully set. Agean's horse was tied off to a small shrub as he slept beneath a thick coarse blanket underneath the moonlit sky. In this moment, Agean slept peacefully. Suddenly a drop of rain exploded on Agean's cheek. Then two more. Then all at once, the rain turned into a torrential downpour. The pounding rain soon awakened Agean. He jumped up, grabbed his things and gathered beneath a nearby rock overhang for cover. He looked over and saw his horse and saddle getting soaked and found that Flittorin had taken to a nearby tree branch for cover. Looking out at the pouring rain, he settled in for an uncomfortable night. He took a hunk of hard bread from his travel pack and tore off a bite.

A few days later, and another hot, sunny afternoon, Agean's supplies were beginning to run low, but most of all, he grew weary of the same food from his travel pack. He knew that if he wanted something more appealing, he would have to hunt. His years of training with Master Naji had prepared him to masterfully utilize a menagerie of weapons in ways far superior to anyone he might encounter along his path. However, hunting was an altogether different subject, especially with no bow.

Agean made his way slowly through a brushy area with a long stick he had fashioned into a spear by whittling the tip to a point. Slowly he crept towards the sound of wild chickens. He approached a tall bush and peeked over the top in an effort to sneak up on them. He could do this. He was a warrior.

He took hold of his makeshift spear, trying to get the perfect balance while eyeing the chickens. The chickens were unaware of his presence. Agean selected his target. The fowl of choice was plump, and therefore much slower than the others. Then, just as he was about to pounce, Flittorin screeched loudly from his perch in a nearby tree. Frightened chickens scattered in all directions at the sound of the bird-of-prey, their rapid clucking sounding almost like laughter to the Hamen Warrior. Agean ran at them, trying to catch one by hand. Then, he surrendered. Frustrated and hungry, he lay on his back and spotted Flittorin on a branch staring at him.

Agean said, "I know, chickens are birds. Probably cousins, right?" Flittorin stared at him. "I didn't think you'd mind." Flittorin continued to stare. "Well what would you suggest I eat, then?" Flittorin screeched and then launched from his perch.

That evening, a day of travel and hunting had taken its toll as the night moon lit the dry, rocky landscape. Weary from the day's activities, Agean chose to settle in for the night. After his epic failure with the chickens, Flittorin had put to task his superior hunting skills to provide Agean his evening feast: a large lizard, the remains of which were mounted on a makeshift spit over a small campfire. With a leg in one hand, Agean frowned as he tore a bite and chewed the bitter flesh while reading a page in the Bisalis. Perched on a nearby branch, Flittorin screeched.

Agean looked over to Flittorin, still chewing, "Satisfied?" He frowned, spit out the meat and then tossed the lizard leg into the fire, no longer able to tolerate the taste. Agean decided that this would be a good night for study.

The next morning as the sun peeked through the mountains in the distance, Agean was already awake and practicing the Art with his Hamen Swords, his silhouette rippling like water against the sun's rays; moving like silk flowing in the wind. Preparation was one of the most important keys to being a Hamen Master, Master Naji had often reminded him.

Days later, after many hours trotting along a rocky path, Agean stopped. He stared up at Flittorin, who screeched and circled above. He then took the Credara from his waist pouch and checked the water level. The swirling waters had receded, but not yet to a dangerous level. There was still time. But patience had never been one of Agean's virtues.

Agean called out, "We must hurry, Flittorin!" The bird screeched as he soared above. Where is he taking me? Agean wondered.

While the life of a monk had exposed Agean to ancient scrolls and scriptural writings, it had provided little opportunity for travel. He had no idea where he was in this new world. Instead of feeling renewed and refreshed, it was an odd feeling he carried with him; a bitter mix of searing hatred and freedom. Seeing the world for the first time felt like escape, yet inescapable was the feeling of being trapped in his anger.

Agean looked out at the horizon and discovered something unexpected. Someone was following him. The best he could tell, it was an elderly man on a horse in the distance, just sitting there watching him. He had no doubt this was some sort of scout for the enemy. Yes… a Kraylen trick. He returned the Credara to his waist pouch, placed a hand on his Hamen Sword and then pressed on.

For the past several days, Flittorin had been leading Agean through a hot dry desert area. By now Agean was feeling quite worn and found himself in serious need of supplies and water. Then suddenly Flittorin began screeching much more than usual. Agean raised his head and shaded his eyes with one hand to block the sun. There before him, was a wonderful sight. In the distance was a town. The first sign of civilization he had seen in more than a week.

Agean smiled and then looked to the sky. "Thank you, Flittorin!" He then snapped his reins and began galloping towards the town.

ℰℑ

All was relatively quiet and peaceful in the small town of Krinn. Conversations were being had as people strolled along, customers patronized a few of the town stores, and a young boy chased down a loose goat while his mother tried to stop him. Suddenly, the front door of the town pub, and the wooden shutters of one of its windows exploded open with two men flying out into the street. Quilin, a thin, quirky, fair-haired young man in his twenties, and Naran, a dark-haired young man of the same age, were best friends and experts at getting into trouble. They both landed and rolled in the dirt, ending up next to each other staring straight up into the sky.

Quilin and Naran said in unison, "Run!" They both got up quickly and took off running in opposite directions. Having been in this situation before, they knew the best strategy was to split up. No sooner had they made their escape than several huge burly men exited the pub, weapons drawn, in hot pursuit. Two followed Naran, while three headed off after Quilin as he disappeared around the corner of a building.

On the opposite side of town, Agean slowly rode into Krinn. Flittorin circled above as Agean stopped and paused to observe his surroundings. An old bearded man carrying a sack over his shoulder strolled by.

Agean said to the man, "Beg pardon. Could you be so kind as to tell me the name of this place?" The man stopped and approached Agean. He paused to thoroughly inspect Agean and to observe Flittorin soaring just above them.

"Why you're in Krinn, Young Fellow. Not much for looks and certainly not the kind of place for a family man, but we get more than our fair share of passers through. Will you be wantin' to trade?" the man asked.

"No… Not today. I will be needing supplies though, if you could help."

The man pointed to a shop just up the road. "You can get plenty of that just up the road there. And get your horse some water, or he won't be lastin' ya long."

Agean responded, "Thank you kindly." The man nodded and continued on his way. Agean paused a little longer to watch a woman and her young daughter drawing water from a well. He rode on and stopped at the supply shop. He dismounted, tied off his horse at a water trough and entered the shop. Flittorin screeched from above.

The supply shop was fully stocked with all the necessities for a traveler: plenty of food, spirits, traps, mountain gear and some weapons. Augustus, a somewhat unkempt middle aged man, was at the counter arranging some items.

Agean entered, looked around, and began picking up a few supplies.

"Can I assist you, Traveler?" Augustus asked. Agean continued picking up supplies. Breads and dried meats mostly.

"I think I can manage, thank you," Agean replied. After a few minutes, Agean set his items on the counter to pay. Just then, Quilin burst in through the front door. Augustus spoke to Quilin without even looking up, making it painfully obvious that this was nothing unusual.

"In trouble again, Quilin?" Augustus asked.

Quilin replied, "Augustus, excuse me!"

Quilin made his way towards the back of the shop when two of his chasers confronted him coming from the back. They wore satisfied grins and carried large, sharp axes.

Quilin said to Augustus, "Umm. Quite all right, Augustus; I'll not be needing anything today!" Quilin turned to exit through the front door, but a third chaser wielding a sword entered, cutting him off.

"Uh-ohhhh," Augustus said, as he and Agean watched with great interest. Agean was rather enjoying the entertainment, as it reminded him of some of the antics of his past.

As the chasers slowly closed in on him, Quilin said, "Okay. Okay, why don't we all just take a moment to breathe and think about our little misunderstanding?"

"You'll have no use for breathin' once we're done with you, Thief. And where's that thieving cohort of yours? I think we'll be wanting to talk with him too," said one of the chasers. At that very moment, Agean took a coin sack noisily from a pouch on his waist, getting the attention of the chasers. He dropped a solid gold coin on the counter to pay for his goods.

The chaser turned towards Agean, brandishing his axe.

"Well now. Looks like we'll be havin' a little chat with you as well, Traveler."

One chaser handed his axe to the other and drew his sword. Agean took a deep breath then dropped several more gold coins onto the counter.

Agean said to Augustus, "Payment in advance."

Augustus picked up one of the coins, bit it and then shrugged. "Fine. Not sure you'll be wantin' to waste your gold on him though." Augustus then picked up the remaining coins, exited to a nearby back room and shut the door.

Agean then quickly turned, slinging open his coat to reveal his swords. Quilin took a stance as well, brandishing his whip. Surprised, Agean took a quick glance at Quilin's weapon.

"Quilin, is it?" Agean asked.

Quilin replied, "That's me, Sir."

"Manage that weapon well, do ya?" Agean asked while keeping an eye on the chasers.

"Trust me, Traveler, I know what I'm doing."

One of the chasers said, "Enough of this!"

Suddenly all three chasers lunged at Agean and Quilin, and the battle was on. Much to Agean's surprise, Quilin fought with masterful skill, Quilin's whip snatching away the chasers' weapons, grabbing, spinning, and sending them crashing into shelves and over bins. Ducking blows from axes and avoiding slashes from swords, Agean skillfully used his Hamen weapons to defend himself against the chasers' blades. The fight did substantial damage to the shop, but Agean and Quilin killed no one. By this time, Augustus had begun peeking out of the back room and watching with great interest, almost being entertained as Agean and Quilin skillfully made fools of the chasers and a mess of his shop. After seeing a full shelf of fragile goods completely obliterated, he bit down again on one of Agean's coins to convince himself that the damages were covered. Once the opportunity presented itself, Agean and Quilin made a quick escape out the front door.

Exploding out of the supply shop, Agean and Quilin quickly untied Agean's horse, mounted up and took off just as two of the chasers exited the shop after them. Flittorin immediately took to the air to follow.

On their way out of the town, Quilin took a sack of gold coins from his pocket and tossed it into a horse watering trough as they passed. As he and Agean headed off in the distance, a young man named Kyler appeared from a hiding spot near the trough, removed the sack from the water, and disappeared around a corner.

chapter ten
From a Single Warrior, An Army Rises

The sun was high and the air was hot. Agean and Quilin slowly trotted along a barren landscape. Agean stared straight ahead in an attempt to curb his anger as Quilin, riding back to back with Agean, put the finishing touches on a bush twig he had formed into an odd circular shape. Flittorin screeched from above. Quilin, covering his eyes to block the sun, looked up to locate him in the sky. He then threw the twig into the air at Flittorin. Its odd shape seemed to give it amazing flight capability as it spun and glided towards Flittorin. When it got close, Flittorin screeched and darted out of its way. Missed him. In his disappointment, Quilin huffed and leaned back against Agean. Agean rolled his eyes, not believing the situation he'd gotten himself into.

Quilin declared, "Hello, this is getting boring!" Agean provided no response whatsoever. "Can you at least tell me your name?"

"Agean," Agean said.

"Nice. So, Agean, what are you then? A trader... an assassin?" Quilin asked.

Agean replied, "I'm a priest."

Quilin leaned forward and said in disbelief, "A priest? Oh, I've never known a priest that could swing a blade like you, my friend." Agean ignored Quilin as they continued along. "So, where are we going anyway?"

"To the nearest cliff to drop you off."

"Oh... why now, that's not very priestly," said Quilin, leaning back against Agean again. Agean stopped his horse.

"Have not been feeling very priestly, Quilin," Agean told him. "You just cost me my supplies and four gold coins." Agean started his horse trotting again.

Quilin leaned forward. "Which has me wondering, Priest. Why did you get involved in the first place? After all, the fight was mine. Aren't priests supposed to be all about peace and love and that sort of thing?" Agean stopped his horse.

"I've only three things to say to that, Quilin. One, you'd have been killed. Two, you'd have been killed quite badly. Three, do not make me regret having kept you from being killed." Agean started his horse again.

Quilin again looked up to watch Flittorin soaring above, screeching. "What's with that hawk? I think I've seen him around here before – strange thing around its neck," Quilin said. "I hate birds."

"Quilin, I have no supplies left. Perhaps you have a suggestion," Agean said.

Quilin energetically swung his legs around to the side of the horse. "I was hoping you'd ask, Father... Priest. What the hell do I call you?"

"Agean!"

"Fine. Agean. Ya see that clump of hills in the distance with the trees between?" Quilin asked, pointing. Agean leaned in the direction Quilin was pointing.

"I see nothing, Quilin."

"The trees. In the hills. It's right there," said Quilin. Agean leaned forward more, squinting, trying to focus, when suddenly Quilin pushed him off of his horse. Agean tumbled to the dirt as Quilin swung around and took the saddle and reins.

"Sorry, my friend. This is where we part ways. I'll set your horse out with food and water after sundown!" Quilin said as he galloped off in an entirely different direction towards an expanse of trees. "Sorry!"

Agean spat out dirt and grumbled as he tried to collect himself. Finally, he stood, dusted himself off and looked to the sky. Flittorin continued circling above.

"You, if anyone, should have known this would happen!" Agean yelled to Flittorin. Flittorin screeched. Agean shook his head as he surveyed the long walk to the trees ahead. He took a deep breath. "Well, let's go then." He then began walking towards the expanse of trees, still dusting himself as he went.

After two hours with no shade, the sun had finally set. What turned out to be a cool evening had helped to quell Agean's anger and frustration as he followed Flittorin's lead through the trees.

Agean continued his trek through the thick brush when suddenly, out of nowhere, a small farmhouse appeared, tucked into the background. Agean was amazed.

Though he could see no one in the darkness, the pale moon provided ample light to see a dirt path leading up to the farmhouse. Though not a soul was in sight, Agean's keen senses kicked in, telling him he was not alone. He was being watched. Flittorin screeched, confirming that his senses were dead on. Sensing no Kraylen in the area, Agean removed both of his swords, still in their sheaths, and moved forward a few more steps towards the path. Suddenly, from behind trees and out of the deep brush, a dozen young men armed with swords, axes and knives, surrounded Agean. He took a defensive stance, still leaving his swords in their sheaths.

A deep firm voice rang out from behind him, "What is it you want here?"

"I seek a man called Quilin!" Agean replied while watching everyone around him.

"Why do you seek this man?" the voice asked.

Agean responded, "He has stolen my horse!" Agean continued to rotate, allowing his senses to guide him.

"You dishonor this man by calling him a thief. For this you must pay," the voice said. Suddenly the young men took a step towards Agean, who raised his sheathed swords to protect himself from their weapons.

Quickly, the voice yelled out, "Wait! Wait! Back off, Brave Warriors!" Quilin suddenly appeared from behind a tree. He cleared his throat and coughed lightly. "Sorry about the voice. I'm still working on it." As the men lowered their weapons, Agean eased his stance, looked around and then shot Quilin a stern look. "Oh, come on!" Quilin said. "Don't give me that look. I had to take your horse. This is how we stay safely hidden from those with less than good intentions." Agean continued his stern look. "By the way, how did you find us?" Agean nodded his head, directing Quilin's attention to Flittorin, who was perched on a nearby branch. "Ughh, I hate birds!"

Suddenly, Kyler stepped forward. "Quilin, who do we have here?"

"Ah. How rude of me. This, my dear brothers, is Agean, a priest," Quilin announced. Collective groans came from the group.

Agean responded, "Not to worry. I've not come to judge. Just to kill a certain horse thief."

Quilin responded, "Oh, everyone wants to kill me. You'll feel differently after a good hot meal." Laughter comes from the group.

"Well, all of us here are certainly worthy of judgment," Kyler said as he turned to Quilin, "especially this one." More laughs from the group as Kyler shook Agean's hand. "Tell me, Agean. Why did you not draw your swords?"

"I seek to harm no man. Even those who would seek to do me harm," Agean replied. Kyler turned and looked at Quilin.

"What can I say? He's a priest," Quilin said. Kyler turned back to Agean.

"Welcome to our home, Agean," Kyler said. "Come. You're just in time for supper."

Agean's eyes lit up in response to Kyler's words. He returned his swords back to his waist and gladly followed as they walked the path towards the farmhouse.

An hour or so later, the moon shone bright in the sky as Agean, Quilin and the others gathered around a roaring fire outside the back of the farmhouse. What remained of a huge wild hog continued slowly roasting over a fire pit. Everyone was happily gorging on roasted meat, tearing bread and drinking. There was occasional laughter while some were regaled by stories of the past, and others brought to dance by a fiddle being played in the background. Flittorin sat atop a post, giving off the occasional screech while Kyler's dog barked at him. Kyler's dog was definitely more interested in playing than making a meal of Flittorin. Kyler called the dog over and shared a bit of his food with him.

Agean happily cleaned his plate, wetting his fingertips to pick up every crumb. When there was nothing left, he looked up at Quilin. Quilin smiled and gestured that it was fine to get more. Agean reached in for more meat and continued to gorge himself.

"So, Agean, how was it that you've traveled our way? Have you come to save us from our sins?" asked Kyler.

Agean replied, "No, not at all. I travel on a mission…" Agean paused, considering his next words, "…from God." A few of the men laughed.

"Well, you don't sound very sure, my friend," Quilin said, taking a voracious bite of meat.

"A mission from God?" Naran asked. "Why, Quilin here is on a Godly mission himself."

"What do you mean?" Agean asked.

Quilin scooted in and explained, "It is what we do. You see, we're thieves, but we do it to help the poor and starving. The dry conditions won't let much grow around here, so people need help. You know… to feed their families. And when they do have something to trade, they get taken to task by those criminals." Agean gave a confused look. "The traders back in Krinn. So that's where we step in. Besides, money is such a burden on those fat thugs. Makes them gamble and drink and all sorts of other nasty things. We're really doing them a service, we are. So, perhaps Naran's right."

"Oh my brother, a noble gesture indeed, but we all know that could not be further from truth," said Kyler, laughing. He then turned to Agean. "You see, Quilin here is of the devil. He's got the mark to prove it."

Quilin responded jokingly, "Oh that hurts my heart, Brother." Everyone laughed except Agean, who suddenly became more serious.

"A mark? May I see it?" Agean asked.

Quilin, taking another bite of meat, asked, "What for? It's just a stupid birthmark gone way wrong. I've been teased about it since I was a lad."

Kyler interrupted, "Out of love, Brother, only out of love." Everyone laughed again.

"May I?" Agean asked.

Quilin, after pausing for a second, said to him, "Fine. But I must warn you. It's not very exciting." Quilin pulled back his hair and collar and revealed the Mark of Hamen on his neck. It was exactly as Agean's, only without the

Arc-Pen Symbol. They all noticed as Agean reeled at the sight.

Quilin asked, "Is everything all right?" Agean then opened the neck area of his coat and revealed his Mark. Everyone was shocked.

"It's almost exactly the same," said Naran. Quilin quickly took a closer look and then backed off. He suddenly became noticeably uncomfortable.

"Quilin, what's this about?" asked Naran, looking at Agean suspiciously.

Quilin responded, "It's all right. He's a good man." Quilin then turned to Agean. "Meet me in the stables. I'll get you the supplies you need."

Quilin paused for a moment, gazing at Agean and then walked off towards the horse stables. Agean set his plate down and stood. He cut a look to Naran, who was still suspicious of what was going on and then began making his way towards the stables. As Kyler watched, his dog sensed something in the distance behind them and began growling. Kyler, familiar with this growl, slowly turned to see what was there.

The stables were small, fairly modest, and home to a quality team of horses. Built of strong wood matching the house, there was plenty of hay in the lofts and on the ground. Bridles and saddles hung from the crossbeams and rails.

As Agean approached, he passed several horses that were in the corral, including Darius.

Agean paused and looked at him. "We really need to talk about your loyalty, my friend." Darius neighed as Agean began to slowly make his way inside to look for Quilin. As he moved farther in, he saw light coming from an open storeroom. He slowly walked over to the room, looked in and saw Quilin.

Agean entered the storeroom and found Quilin leaning against a shelf, fidgeting with his whip. Agean noticed that the room was full of supplies of all sorts.

"You were right," Agean said. "You have all the supplies I need." Quilin continued fidgeting.

"Ever since I was born, I've felt something," Quilin said. "This mark. As a child I was teased about it. Someone brilliant suggested it might be the mark of the devil. Then I had to keep it hidden because no one would give me work if they saw it. And once they did see it, I was quickly tossed out. That's when I honed my thieving skills. Then one day an unbelievable thing happened. A man came to me who bore the same mark. He led me to this farm and said, 'It is yours. All I ask is that you allow me to teach you to serve God - to become his warrior.' I was shocked. No one had ever given me anything before. So I agreed. Then he gave me this." Quilin snapped his whip. "He spent each day of many months teaching me to master it."

Suddenly, beginning at the handle, the whip began coating itself with small armor plates until it reached the tip. Before Agean's eyes, Quilin had transformed his ordinary whip into a shining metallic Hamen weapon with a razor sharp bladed tip — The Hamen Whip. Upon its handle, the Arc-Pen Symbol. With a snap, Quilin lashed it, causing the tip to disconnect and hover, spinning in slow motion between him and Agean. "He told me my Mark was a gift from God. And before he left, he said to me, 'You are now prepared, should the Sitcian come.' I suppose that's you. I asked if I would ever see him again. He told me if I did... God help us all."

Quilin lashed the Whip again and the tip reconnected. The whip then returned to its normal form. Agean stepped closer to Quilin, removing the Credara from his waist pouch.

"Quilin. I understand your feelings. My story is not a pleasant one either," Agean said to him. "Because of this mark, my entire family was slaughtered at the hands of the Kraylen. Did your Master tell you about them?"

"I have never met one face to face, but I was told not to expect pleasantries," Quilin responded.

"We did not meet by chance. I was led to you so that we can destroy them. And the key to everything... is this." Agean handed Quilin the Credara. It lit up, showing its swirling waters. "It is given by God. The waters inside tell us that we haven't much time."

"Yes. I was told of this," Quilin said. Suddenly Quilin's and Agean's Marks, and the symbol on the Credara, began to tingle and glow wildly. They both reacted, putting their hands to their necks.

Quilin said, "This Mark. I guess the tingling comes with the honor of having it."

Agean replied, "No. This is different." Suddenly they heard Flittorin's screech. "Come on!" Agean quickly returned the Credara to his waist pouch as they both rushed out of the storeroom.

Agean and Quilin dashed out of the stables to find several Kraylen near the horse corral. What Quilin saw visibly shocked him. They were much more menacing looking than he had expected. These horrid, evil looking creatures were the things he had sworn, and was trained… to kill.

"Agean," whispered Quilin. The Kraylen had cornered a few of Quilin's friends against a fence. Agean drew his swords and Quilin transformed his Hamen Whip. They both took Hamen fighting stances in preparation for battle. But as Agean observed the scene, something within him took over. Seeing the Kraylen, Agean's memory flashed – back to his family – back to the visions of their gruesome murder. The fury began coursing through him. Agean clenched his Swords of Hamen tight as his anger reached the boiling point and beads of sweat began to form on his brow. His need to save his new friends gave way to his need to destroy this enemy.

Seeing his level of anger rising, Quilin asked, "Agean, are you all right?"

"Stand aside. Let me handle this," Agean told him. Agean then called out to the Kraylen. "If it is I you seek, I am here!"

Agean could see nothing but fire as he began walking and brandishing his swords. The Kraylen turned and revealed a bruised and beaten Kyler. The other young men and women quickly hustled out of the way.

Seeing Kyler, Quilin yelled, "Agean! Wait!"

Agean, blind with fury, continued towards the Kraylen, who then threw Kyler to the ground. Then, one of the Kraylen stood over him and raised his sword.

"You would be wise to stop, Priest!" the Kraylen said.

Quilin yelled out again, "Agean!"

Agean continued, completely deaf to Quilin's voice. Then, just as the Kraylen began driving his blade down for the kill, he exploded into black ash and smoke, the tip of its sword missing Kyler by mere inches. The bladed tip of Quilin's Hamen Whip had struck the Kraylen like a missile. The tip then returned back to Quilin's whip. Kyler painfully crawled off to the side as Agean and Quilin immediately rushed into an intense battle with the remaining Kraylen. Though highly skilled, the Kraylen fighting tactics were no match for the masterful fighting skills of the two Hamen Warriors. Unlike the fight at the supply shop, both Agean and Quilin utilized their Hamen skills to take on the Kraylen in deadly fashion. Agean's Hamen Swords spun and slashed through the Kraylen intruders, turning them instantaneously into clouds of dust. The deadly bladed tip of Quilin's Hamen weapon tore through Kraylen as if it had a mind of its own, while his whip ripped the enemy apart with little effort. Kyler's eyes lit up at what he was witnessing. In all the years of knowing him, he had never before seen this level of fighting from Quilin, and never knew he wielded such an amazing weapon with such incredible skill. Agean and Quilin continued vanquishing Kraylen until none were left standing. Quilin and Agean then immediately turned to Kyler.

"Kyler, are you all right?" Quilin asked.

"I'll be fine, Quilin. What's going on? What were they, and why were they here?" Kyler asked.

Quilin responded, "Come. We'll talk about that later. We need to get your wounds dressed." Quilin and Agean helped Kyler to his feet. A few others rushed out to meet them as they and Quilin helped Kyler to the house. Quilin stopped halfway and looked back, shooting Agean an angry look. He then continued on to the farmhouse to help his brother. Agean stared as they walked away still sweating and breathing heavily from his anger.

More than an hour had passed as Agean stood on the back porch of the farmhouse staring into the distance. The moon. The forest just beyond. His thoughts drifted to his beloved Master Naji and the suffering he still endured. Every Kraylen life he took brought the Master closer to the end of his suffering, and him closer to vanquishing the one who destroyed his family.

Suddenly, Agean's thoughts were interrupted as Quilin exited from the farmhouse back door and onto the porch with a large sack of belongings and supplies.

"Shall we go?" asked Quilin as he walked past Agean on his way to the stables.

Agean followed. "Quilin."

"Kyler will be fine," Quilin said without turning around.

Agean repeated, "Quilin!"

Quilin stopped and turned angrily to Agean. "You could have gotten him killed!"

Agean paused for a moment then responded, "I'm sorry, Quilin. But every last one of them must be destroyed."

Quilin tossed the sack on the ground and threw his hands up.

After a few paces back and forth, he moved closer to Agean. "I've never had a mother… or a father or anyone." Quilin paced back and forth again in frustration. "What you see here is my family. Practically all of us orphaned from day one. Most just like me, tossed away like trash. But we've looked after each other. Now finally, I have what I've always wanted." Agean's eyes glistened as he pondered Quilin's words. "I made a promise, Agean. Should the Sitcian come, I would give my life to the task that God has set before us. I owe a debt to God and to my Hamen Master. But I never promised to die for your personal war." Quilin moved in even closer and looked Agean in the eye. "For all of our sake, I really hope you are all that you are supposed to be, my friend." Quilin stared into Agean's eyes for a moment and then turned and picked up his sack. He dusted it off, then looked back at Agean. "It was a terrible thing they did to your family, Agean. I feel for you. I really do." Agean gave a blank look as Quilin turned and continued to the stables. After a brief moment of thought, Agean followed.

chapter eleven
Enter the Wise Master

Three days of travel had passed. The cool night air felt good on bodies scorched by the hot sun. A low campfire had been burning for more than an hour, the evening meal was finished, and Agean had even managed to spend some time with the Bisalis. Initially, boredom was the main reason for his interest in the text over the course of his lengthy journey, but Agean had now established a somewhat spiritual connection with the book. Reading it was almost like looking within, exploring his inner self and the very foundation of who he was. The words that lay within took on more and more meaning with each turn of the page. It began to feed his spirit. Agean knew that for now, time was on his side. He also knew that as he got closer to his destination and the confrontation he sought so passionately, his focus would shift to battle and the annihilation of the enemy. For this, he would need his Hamen skills to be their very best.

The light of day had returned as Agean practiced the Art with his swords and Quilin sat on a rock, eating an apple. Bored, Quilin passed a little time tossing pebbles into the fire. He spotted Flittorin sitting on the branch of a dead tree and flung a pebble at him, scaring him into the air screeching. As Agean continued his practice, Quilin got an idea. He got up and walked about twenty paces away from Agean. While Agean still swung his blades, Quilin transformed his Hamen Whip and released its tip directly towards Agean. Agean did not see the spiraling bladed tip racing towards him, but just as in Master Naji's training sessions, his Hamen senses picked it up. Agean immediately spun himself and his blades to block the tip from its path. Quilin, who had now taken a Hamen stance, focused his senses to control the tip, creating his own incredible battle training session for Agean. Quilin's arms, hands and feet moved as his senses swung the bladed tip at Agean from every possible direction. Agean displayed masterful swordsmanship as the ringing of his sword against the deadly spinning tip filled the air with the music of battle. Although Agean showed incredible ability in fighting off the tip, he came up with an idea, mid-battle, that could bring an end this sparring session with him as the victor. At the first opportunity, Agean swatted the tip away, did an amazing back flip, and utilized his Hamen Sword to slice off a thick branch from a nearby dead tree. As the tip returned, Agean caught the branch and swung it at the tip with pinpoint accuracy. The razor sharp tip embedded itself into the tree branch. Agean then swung the branch, tip embedded, with great force at the trunk of the dead tree. With a loud crack, the tip was now deeply embedded into the tree. Agean, exhausted from his efforts, leaned against the tree while catching his breath. Quilin eased his focus, quite impressed with Agean's tactics.

"Hmm. Nice job," Quilin said.

Agean, still breathing heavily, responded, "Thank you. You as well. I must say, you have truly mastered your Hamen skills, Quilin. I hope you'll hold no harsh feelings against me for planting your weapon into this tree."

Quilin responded, "What tree?" Quilin focused his eyes on the tree and pointed the butt of his whip directly at it. Instantly, sounds of sawing and tearing of wood penetrated the air. Then, suddenly, the tree Agean was leaning against began to crack and tilt as it fell away from him and slammed to the ground. Agean stumbled as the tree toppled. The tip from Quilin's Hamen Whip hovered above the pile of sawdust and the remaining tree stump. Agean was both impressed and shocked by what this Hamen weapon was capable of. He looked at Quilin, only to find a very smug and proud look as the tip slowly returned to his whip. Quilin transformed the whip back to its normal form.

"It appears you are not the only one who has a way with timber," Quilin smirked.

"Nice trick."

"Oh, I have others," Quilin replied, grinning.

Agean smiled. "Of that I am sure, Quilin." Quilin returned his whip to his waist as they both prepared to press on with their journey.

Agean and Quilin galloped along through rough, rocky terrain. Flittorin had taken his usual place, soaring high above and leading their path as they rode.

Agean peered out at the landscape, taking in the majestic beauty of the distant snow-capped mountains and rock formations. Then, almost unbelievably, he spotted the Follower far off in the distance, sitting on his horse and watching them. Agean slowed his horse to a trot. He squinted, trying to see more clearly. Quilin noticed Agean and slowed as well.

"Are you all right, Agean?"

"Yes. Everything is fine, Quilin."

"Is it?" Quilin asked. "Do we even know where or how much farther we are going?"

"It is Flittorin who leads our path, Quilin. Where he goes, we go," Agean replied.

"Wonderful. We follow a bird to our destiny. Or shall I say our doom." At that very moment, a huge splotch of bird poop splashed onto Quilin's shoulder. "Oh, that is just wonderful," Quilin added.

Flittorin screeched as Quilin, with a look of disgust, took out a rag and began wiping his shoulder. Agean continued staring off into the distance at the Follower who was still looking directly at them.

"Quilin, why do you think he follows us?" Agean asked. Quilin looked out into the distance, seeing nothing. Flittorin, soaring above, screeched.

"Who? I see no one out there," Quilin said. "Besides, who would follow us? We who follow a bird?" Quilin ducked and looked up to locate Flittorin. Agean continued looking as they slowly rode along. Quilin noticed Agean obsessing.

"Well Agean, if you see someone skulking in the shadows, I think one of us should have a look," Quilin said as he took off riding up an embankment.

Agean yelled, "Quilin!" Quilin ignored Agean and continued on. Agean again turned to see the Follower, who, much to Agean's surprise, slowly faded from sight. Right before Agean's eyes, he vanished. Meanwhile, Quilin darted around some brush, dismounted, and climbed up a nearby rocky hill. When Quilin reached a landing near the top of the hill, he paused to catch his breath.

Quilin yelled, breathing heavily, "Agean! I told you there was no one here!"

"Not exactly," said a voice from the other end of the landing that seemed to come out of nowhere. Quilin quickly looked around to find, not the Follower, but a tall confident looking warrior in his thirties, standing at a distance, wielding a beautifully carved wooden staff.

The warrior masterfully spun his staff, lifted a stone from the ground with the tip, then spin-slapped it at Quilin. Quilin immediately reacted and drew his Hamen Whip. He then lashed it, sending the bladed tip directly at the warrior. Immediately, the warrior spun his staff, batting the tip away while Quilin cracked his whip, exploding the stone to dust. The warrior then moved quickly towards Quilin, spinning his staff as he approached. The tip returned to Quilin's whip just in time for Quilin to begin his battle with the warrior. They both battled brilliantly, whip against staff. Quilin marveled at how well this warrior defended himself against his Hamen skills. Quilin, however, was determined to prove himself the superior fighter as they both used their weaponry and even the rocky landscape around them to try to gain the upper hand. It was not long before Quilin realized there was something very familiar about this warrior's technique, almost as if he had fought this battle before. Then suddenly a magnificent metallic Staff of Hamen pierced the ground between them, bringing their battle to an end. Quilin immediately recognized the staff and looked up to find Gajir, the Hamen Master who had trained him. A wise looking elderly man, Gajir was also a true warrior. As Leader of Gannus, Gajir was more than the protector of his people, he was their King. He had been standing out of sight on a small landing above them, watching. Quilin stared in disbelief.

"Brilliant!" Gajir said. "You have remembered everything I taught you."

Quilin, still stunned, replied, "Master Gajir. God help me." Gajir began making his way down to Quilin.

"No, Quilin," Gajir said. "As were my last words to you... God help us all." Gajir removed his Hamen Staff from the ground and transformed it to its wooden form. He then placed a hand on Quilin's shoulder. "It's been a long time, my boy." Quilin knelt at Gajir's feet.

"Great Master," Quilin said.

Gajir responded, "Stand, my son. You have made me proud."

Quilin stood. "I have tried to be true to your teachings, Master."

"You have kept your promise and held true to your destiny, my boy." Quilin stood, still in awe as Agean made his way to the landing and approached them.

Agean called out, "Quilin!"

"It's all right, Agean!" Quilin replied.

Quilin turned to Gajir and said, "Master Gajir, this is-"

"The Sitcian," said Gajir, as he approached Agean. "I have felt your coming. My son, Tordin. I am Gajir. Welcome to Gannus."

Gajir directed everyone's attention to the grand mountain realm in the distance, just beyond where they stood. Agean noticed Gajir's Mark of Hamen as he and Quilin moved in to see. Gannus was a marvelous place of dwellings carved into solid rock, with three waterfalls flowing throughout. An intricate cascade of winding paths, entrances and homes. Agean and Quilin both marveled at its beauty.

"I trust a good meal would suit you both," Gajir said.

Agean responded, "It would indeed, Master Gajir." Flittorin screeched and landed on a nearby rock.

"How about a nice juicy bird to enhance tonight's menu, Master?" Quilin asked, watching Flittorin.

Gajir leaned in for a closer look at the large white stain on Quilin's shoulder. "Hmm. I wondered what that was." Gajir then turned to acknowledge his old friend. "Flittorin! Wonderful to see you again." Flittorin screeched as Gajir turned to Quilin. "I see you still possess your sense of humor, Quilin. It is nice to know it-"

Quilin interrupted, "I know, I know. It is a gift."

Gajir responded, "I was going to say it is nice to know it has not yet resulted in your death." Agean and Tordin laughed while Gajir and Quilin both smiled. "Come!"

Agean and Quilin followed Gajir and Tordin down the hill towards Gannus.

❧

The accommodations of Gajir's home were beautiful yet modest. The entire structure was carved into the stone of the mountain. Agean, Quilin, Gajir and Tordin sat eating at the dining table, it too rising from the very stone of Gannus Mountain. Tordin's beautiful young wife, Kisara, who was with child, assisted with removing the plates.

"Are you finished, Master Agean?" Kisara asked.

Agean replied, "Yes, thank you." Agean gazed at Kisara's stomach as his Mark tingled and glowed. "Many blessings on your new child."

"Thank you, Master Agean," said Kisara.

As Kisara passed by Gajir, he took her hand. "Kisara, and soon my grandchild, are my son's greatest achievements, and a true blessing upon this family." Just then, Agean noticed Gajir's other hand running his fingers across a small notch in the stone table. Gajir's eyes turned retrospective as memories emerged from within. "We lost the love of my life, Tordin's mother, God rest her soul, when he was but a child. Many years had passed before an angel stepped in and became everything two heartbroken men needed. Kisara is now the heart and soul of this family." Agean watched as Gajir moved his hand away from the notch.

Kisara smiled, walked over and hugged a proud Tordin. "I'm afraid Father's pride goes much further than we deserve."

"I cannot imagine being more proud of my children. Including you, Quilin. You are like a son to me," Gajir said. Quilin smiled, blushing a little. "Master Naji felt the same of you, Agean."

"You know of Master Naji?" Agean asked.

"Oh yes. He was the Master who taught me the Hamen Art," Gajir explained. "The Credara. It is with you?"

"It is, Master Gajir," Agean replied.

Gajir asked, "And the waters?" Agean removed the Credara from his waist pouch and set it on the table. The Credara lit, showing that its internal waters had continued to recede, now to a dangerous level.

"We must leave immediately," Gajir continued.

Tordin responded shocked, "We, Father?" Gajir stood to face his family.

"My children, what occurs at this very moment is unlike anything ever confronted by mankind; an evil that must be stopped. God has chosen those who will stand against it. Therefore it is I who must go," Gajir explained.

"Father, no!" Kisara said.

"But father. My training," Tordin said to him. "You say that I am ready,"

Gajir explained, "What I have taught you, Tordin, you will need for your own child, and to protect and lead your people. It is I who bear the Mark of Hamen — I who am called to this task. The realm is now in your hands while I am away, my son. We must travel east towards the Seas of Gilan — to a place I have seldom spoken of. Quintana."

Tordin was shocked at what he was hearing. "Quintana? Father…"

"Yes my son, it is real," Gajir said.

Flittorin, perched in a window, screeched.

chapter twelve
Evil Gathers

In this forest there were no leaves that blew. No branches that swayed in the wind. No crumbling bark or encroaching moss. Girjan Forest. Petrified and long abandoned, these trees, frozen in time, no longer had life. They were said to exist only as a reminder of the evils of man - relics of sins past. Hunters would hunt no form of beast in this place. Those who knew of it stayed away, for it was said that death lingered here.

Dust, dead leaves, dried up moss and old cobwebs had combined over the centuries to create huge dark sheets and strands that hung from the trees like capes, moving with every gust of wind and giving each tree a wizard-like appearance. The full moon had an eerie haze about it that made the stone trees stand out like evil creatures lurking.

Alone, lit by the moonlight in a huge clearing of Girjan Forest, Licronus knelt, staring at the dirt. He scooped up a handful and stood, clenching the dirt in his fist. As he raised his eyes to stare at the moon, the sound of horses and wagons approaching from all directions filled the air. All at once, hundreds of Kraylen arrived out of the forest: some on foot; some on horseback; some by air. A dozen or so covered wagons rolled in and stopped along the perimeter. Kraylen jumped out and uncovered them, revealing massive amounts of swords and other weapons. The Kraylen grabbed weapons and then converged on the center of the clearing where Licronus stood. Now armed, the Kraylen encircled Licronus and then stopped. Then, the Kraylen dragged forward from out of the crowd a man who had succumbed to a horrible beating. His body was dirty, bloody and limp; but he was alive and conscious. The man's eyes met Licronus's gaze. Licronus unclenched his fist and allowed the dirt to blow and fall between his fingers.

He raised his arms and said to the crowd of Kraylen, "Patiently we have waited after being cast out from our kingdom! But tonight we bring a new war! Lucifer will rise again, and we will take back what is rightfully ours!" The Kraylen roared with cheers. "Go! Arm your brothers and bring them to the battle!" All at once the Kraylen raised their weapons and yelled. Licronus turned to the beaten man as the yelling ceased. "But first, a gift for their so called Sitcian."

The beaten man begged and struggled as the Kraylen continued cheering. They drew him by binding both wrists and ankles with rope and spread him out face up, tying each rope to the saddle of a separate horse. Then finally, despite his terrifying plea for mercy, the horses drew the ropes tight, painfully suspending the man above the ground. After inspecting the torturous handiwork, Licronus sneered, drew his sword and looked into the man's tearing eyes.

"You should be proud, filthy human. For today I have decided that your worthless life will have meaning." Licronus raised his sword and smacked one of the horses on the rump. The man screamed out as the horse reared up, causing the other three to do the same. The horrid sound of agony and tearing flesh as the man was quartered quickly replaced his screams. A look of satisfaction grew on Licronus's face as the Kraylen resumed yelling. Then, in a mass exodus, the Kraylen took to their horses and to the air like disturbed bats in a cave.

chapter thirteen
A Warrior Is Tested

As days passed, Agean, Quilin and Gajir rode as they could, and walked as the path required; traveling by day, and at times night, through streams and across grassy highlands. They traversed deep gorges and treacherous mountain passes. Agean and Gajir both monitored the waters of the Credara as they went. Gajir knew the place; Flittorin knew the way.

Along the journey, Agean and Quilin engaged in deep conversation with Master Gajir, taking in his seemingly endless wisdom. Often before bedding down for the night, Gajir and Agean studied the Bisalis together. Gajir knew that a Sitcian must know. A Sitcian must understand.

Gajir assisted both Agean and Quilin in practicing the Art. Being ever challenging to the Sitcian, Quilin at one point used his whip to snatch the sword from Agean's hands during one of his spars with Master Gajir. But Agean's skills were razor sharp, and both Quilin and Master Gajir knew it. With his sword suddenly gone, Agean was forced to catch Master Gajir's needle-like staff between his palms to prevent being impaled through the eye. Gajir was impressed. Quilin applauded.

Several days into their journey, Agean, Quilin and Gajir spent most of one sweltering day making their way through dense wooded forest. Though the denseness slowed their horses, the shade proved to be a blessing in disguise. They could not see Flittorin, but his screech let them know they had not strayed from the path.

Then suddenly, Agean, Quilin and Gajir came upon a sight that took them completely by surprise. Before them lay the Girjan Forest in all of its eerie splendor. As they approached, Agean and Quilin were stunned by the sight of the thousands of empty stone trees. The winds created a low howling sound, much like that of mortal agony, as if a thousand condemned souls moaned to be set free. An odd feeling of death seemed to fill the air.

Flittorin circled overhead as they slowed their horses.

Quilin asked, "What is this place?"

"For some reason, our friend Flittorin has led us to Girjan Forest. I never thought I would see it again," Gajir replied.

Agean asked, "Shall we enter, Gajir? Has God abandoned this place?"

"God abandons no place, Agean. As well, Flittorin leads us through," Gajir replied. Agean took a moment to think.

"Where he goes, we go," Agean told them.

Quilin responded, "Oh great. Where have I heard that one before?" Agean, Quilin and Gajir proceeded into the petrified forest, keeping a sharp eye out as they passed the skeletal remains of fallen beasts lost from their path, as well as those of a few humans who had befallen the same fate.

After an hour they came upon a huge clearing. Agean saw something very strange. He brought everyone to a halt as he monitored his senses. Several wagons sat along the perimeter of the clearing.

"Tread carefully," Gajir said. They each trotted over to a different area of the clearing, looked around and then dismounted to inspect the scene. Quilin walked over and stared into a half-empty wagon of swords, axes and other weapons.

"There has been a gathering here!" Quilin said. Gajir spotted a black feather on the ground, stuck to a twig and blowing with the light breeze. He speared it with his Hamen Staff and then raised it to eye level. The symbol on his staff glowed, as did the one on his neck. Quickly, in a puff of smoke, the feather turned to ash.

Gajir called out, "They were here!"

"Looks like hundreds of them," Quilin added.

"They are massing for battle!" Gajir said. "They know the path and are ahead of us! We must continue on!"

Meanwhile, a horrific sight stunned Agean and stopped him in his tracks while he inspected an area in a different part of the clearing. A bloody human arm ripped from its torso, bound at the wrist by rope. Agean stared for a moment. Then suddenly, what he saw next shook him to his core. The fingers on the hand began moving, gripping the mud beneath it. He squeezed his eyes tight and shook his head to clear his mind, then he looked again. Nothing. Was it his imagination? Agean stared horrified for a moment. "The Angel of Death," Agean said to himself. Suddenly, the gruesome sight of a pack of wolves at the edge of the clearing, devouring the torso, diverted his attention.

Agean turned away. "We need to move quickly!" Agean quickly headed back to the horses. They all then hastily mounted up and rode off.

The Kingdom of Kateren. A beautiful city of stone situated within one of the fertile valleys of the Bameron Mountain Range. Stone carvings honoring kings and heroes of the past littered a canvas of beautiful stone buildings and homes. On the outskirts of Kateren were lush green rolling hills bordered by vast forests and the great Aegean Sea.

What had been for many years a tranquil place of peace,

was now gearing up for war, as every available soldier and horse quickly assembled near its great stone gates. The determined warriors and their horses were covered in battle armor, the crest of their kingdom set upon their shields and chest plates. Massive battle catapults constructed of heavy wood, pulled by dray horses, were moved towards the outer gates in preparation for war. Kateren's King Gassan rode steadily through the massing army, inspecting and taking his rightful place as leader over his legion of men. He was in his mid-fifties, strong looking with plenty of greying brown facial hair about his wrinkled face. Once he reached the city gates, he nodded to his General, who directed a clarion trumpeter to signal "forward." Then King Gassan, bannerets carrying huge banners displaying the crest of the realm, and thousands of soldiers, wagons, and several catapults moved through the huge gates. Crowds of subjects yelled chants of support, threw flowers and applauded the bravest of the realm as they filed out of the city and on to face their enemy.

The journey had been steady and tiring; an entire day of nearly continuous riding. Agean, Quilin and Gajir thundered along a path winding through the vast Girjan Forest as Flittorin led the way. Then, finally reaching the edge of the forest, Quilin spotted something far off in the distance and pointed. They slowed and stopped when they came to a cliff that overlooked what appeared to be a small town.

"What do you think? Looks harmless enough," said Quilin.

Agean took a moment to inspect what he saw. "It would take us a great distance from our path. Perhaps we should keep going."

"The horses, Agean. We've ridden them very hard for quite a while now. They are in need of food and water," Gajir said.

Agean looked up at Flittorin who soared in the direction of the town. He then nodded in agreement and they galloped off, following Flittorin's lead.

The town was merely a lengthy dirt road lined on both sides with mostly tents and stands where traders offered their wares. Most of the offerings consisted of exotic spices and foods from all over the world. The town was dusty, yet bustling with activity. A nearby shipping port was the only reason this town existed. When the steady supply of goods dried up, a town such as this would be all but abandoned. But for now, bounteous goods were available and offered up for sale.

Agean, Quilin and Gajir trotted cautiously through

as Flittorin circled above. Since their arrival, their Marks had been alerting them that there were Kraylen about. But how is it that the enemy seemed to be all around them? In every town, even at his beloved Dancing Swine, Agean wondered. Was it that evil was simply everywhere? Was it incredible luck? Luck, and at times the absence of it, was something Agean had much experience with. Were they being watched? Perhaps the Follower who trailed them would provide suitable explanation, once they were finally face to face.

Suddenly, Agean slowed to a stop as a familiar sound got his attention. Scanning the area for its source, a sight caught his eye. In a tent with sausage hanging and drying in the doorway, two Norse traders sat at a table shuffling a deck of cards. The sound and the sight of the cards moving in slow motion as they were shuffled brought back memories for Agean. He recalled the pleasures of game and drink at The Swine. Those were happier times. Simpler. More carefree. Before he mortally wounded his beloved Master; before discovering the horrible truth of his family's gruesome demise. Agean stopped and stared with interest.

Quilin said, "Agean, we must keep moving."

"Go on ahead. I won't be long," Agean responded.

Gajir said to him, "Be careful, my boy. My senses tell me that the enemy is near."

"I will be careful, Gajir," Agean said.

Gajir looked up to the sky and called, "Flittorin!" Flittorin screeched and landed on a nearby rail. "You can never be too careful."

Gajir and Quilin then continued on as Agean dismounted and tied off his horse to a nearby rail.

The sky was thick with clouds and a brisk wind blowing from the east in the Kingdom of Grendane. Located near the northeastern coast of the Black Sea in the Khanate Territory, Grendane sat on a vast and abundant farmland. It was home to thousands of land-working families dedicated to the people of the realm, and to the sovereignty of their kingdom. King Soranem, sitting tall and straight upon his steed, was positioned face to face with a massive legion of warriors heavily armed with weapons, shields, helmets and chest plates. Their horses, armored about the head and chest, stood almost motionless, committed to the will of their riders. Rows of catapults and other heavy battle equipment meant to inflict massive amounts of death sat and waited to be hauled into action. In his early fifties but looking younger, King Soranem's long dark hair complemented the several tribal piercings in his face and ears. Beside him was a banneret and clarion trumpeter.

Aligned five rows deep and as far left and right as the eye could see, thousands of loyal warriors in full battle armor awaited the order. Behind them were the King's loyal subjects: women, children and men too old for battle.

"There is a curse upon our lands!" yelled Soranem. "Steady your minds and your weapons, Warriors of Grendane! The King of Kateren will either lift his wretched curse, or the blood of his people will spill upon their lands. God bless Grendane!" All at once, loud cheering from the loyal subjects filled the air as the swords of every warrior were raised to the sky. Suddenly, a clarion call signaled the exodus of the massive army as they turned and moved along a wide road leading out of Grendane. King Soranem, flanked by his bannerets, clarion trumpeter, and two top Generals, galloped to meet the front of the line as they began a lengthy journey across a dry rocky landscape to do battle with their enemy.

⌘

Flittorin perched on a post at the entrance of the Norse traders' tent while Agean approached. Several gold coins rested on the table in front of the men, along with glasses and a bottle of spirits. The traders continued shuffling.

One trader appeared to have gotten on in his years, with mostly grey hair, a beard and wrinkles telling his age.

He smoked a pipe that almost seemed to grow from his hair-covered lips. He drew in and released a strong aromatic smoke that engulfed his head. He had done this so often that the smoke had left behind a yellowish tint on his skin. The other trader was a younger man, perhaps his son or an apprentice. His dusty appearance showed clearly who did what, with most of the heavy lifting relegated to his strong arms and back.

Agean entered the tent and tossed a gold piece onto the table. The coin bounced and then rolled right in front of an empty chair at the table, positioned with its back against a drawn curtain. The older man turned to Agean to look him over. He pulled the pipe from his lips and blew a cloud of smoke. He then spotted Flittorin at the entrance. Agean noticed the sweat running down both their faces, his Hamen senses still telling him that the enemy was near – very near.

The old man spoke to Agean in an old German language, one thankfully Agean was familiar with. "How much for the bird?" Agean paused for a moment, looking at the deck of cards in the old man's hand. The old man reacted to Agean's interest.

"Well," said the old man. "It appears we have a customer of a different sort. Perhaps the gentleman might be interested in a hand of Pochspiel? Not very popular in these parts, but it was the game of my father and his father before. I'm sure I could teach it to you."

Agean scanned the room then responded in the trader's language, "I am familiar with the game. It is not one of my favorites. However, my interest is in your landjager. I will have four of your oldest."

The old man responded, "Landjager? It is in your eyes, young fellow. A much better use of your coin is what you seek." The old man proceeded to take a small glass sitting overturned on the table and turn it upright. He then popped open the bottle of spirits and filled the glass halfway. Perhaps a gentleman's game of your own choosing. Please, sit." The younger trader adjusted the empty chair, inviting Agean to sit. Agean paused for a moment then lifted the glass from the table. The old man grinned and chuckled while blowing another cloud of smoke into the air.

Agean's Hamen senses tingled wildly as he glared at the two men. The looks on their faces turned to that of dread as he then set the glass of spirits down on top of his gold coin.

"Thank you for the invitation. I will take them from the front," Agean said. Agean turned and walked back to the front. He took a dagger and cut down four sausages. He turned to take another look at the card game.

"A single hand would not keep you from your journey, my friend," the old man said. Despite a momentary pause, Agean won against temptation, turned and exited.

The trader yelled, "Hey! What about the bird?" Agean disappeared from the entrance as Flittorin took to the air. The trader slammed the deck of cards on the table, sweating more now than before.

Agean made his way back to his horse and tucked the sausage into his travel pouch. He then mounted up and slowly rode off as Flittorin circled above. Though the sound of a horse riding off was nothing at all unusual to the two traders, this day it would be the worst and the last sound they would ever hear.

Sitting still in their tent, frozen in their chairs, beads of sweat running down their faces, the two Norsemen swallowed and gazed at each other in horror. Suddenly, a Kraylen burst in from behind the drawn curtain gripping a young woman and holding a menacing-looking blade to her throat. He violently threw her on top of the table, which smashed into pieces, sending everyone crashing to the floor.

"Your daughter's life is meaningless to you!" said the Kraylen in the traders' language.

The old man responded, "We tried! I swear it! We wanted him to sit but he would not! He was not interested!"

The Kraylen growled in anger, drew another blade, then lunged forth. The screams. The blood flying. The sounds of ripping flesh. Violently, the Kraylen made quick work of the three. Although what the demon left behind was barely recognizable, its victims would receive no mercy in death – only endless and painful suffering.

As Agean continued trotting slowly down the road, the angry Kraylen exited the trading shop with his blades drawn and dripping blood. He walked out to the middle of the road and stopped, breathing heavily and watching Agean with an angry glare.

The tingling of Agean's Mark intensified as he sensed that the enemy was behind him. He slowed his horse to a stop and then paused to focus. After a few seconds, Agean reared his horse around and drew his swords. Ready for the kill, Agean's senses and focus were razor sharp. Nothing. Whatever it was, it was gone. No Kraylen in sight. Only two small pools of blood in the middle of the road. Agean scanned the area as the tingling of his Mark began to settle. He then returned his blades to his waist, turned his horse around and resumed making his way down the street.

For the next two days, the sun became a brutal foe. Agean, Gajir and Quilin trotted along the path of a hillside peppered with dry brush. Nearby hilltops, seeming to march along with them like soldiers, provided lifesaving shade as they slowly made their way through the winding passages in order to preserve energy for themselves and the horses. Flittorin screeched and soared above, seemingly unaffected by the sun's burning rays.

For the past few hours, the journey had been somewhat secluded, with various hillsides and mountain ranges blocking the view of the lands in the distance. Finally, an opening in the cascading hills allowed for a change of scenery. However, it was not what anyone expected.

What Agean and the others saw brought their ride to a standstill. They all stared out into the distance at two heavily armed legions of warriors, each with thousands of men facing each other and prepared for war. Shields, lances, bows, arrows, maces, swords and just about every other manner of weapon were held firm and aimed directly at each other. On both sides, various giant catapult systems had been pulled into place by dray horses and positioned within striking distance. Banners were proudly displayed high, in front, and alongside the Kings of each realm.

King Gassan of Kateren and King Soranem of Grendane each wore the crest of their kingdom and wielded sword and shield.

Whatever the reason, both King and warrior were ready to die for it.

The two Kings, each with a single banneret alongside him, began galloping towards each other.

Quilin said, "I don't think we want to be around for this."

"Can you smell it, Quilin? It is in the air. A repulsive odor which has followed mankind throughout its existence. It is the stench of war," Gajir said.

Quilin asked, "What can we do?"

Gajir replied, "I fear in moments like these, there is nothing much to be done." Agean thought of the Angel of Death and the horrible consequences of what was about to occur.

"But we must try, Gajir," Agean said as he galloped off in the direction of the pending confrontation.

Gajir yelled, "Agean!" Gajir turned to Quilin. "Stay here, Quilin." Gajir then raced off in pursuit of Agean.

Meanwhile, the Kings and bannerets continued towards each other. When they were within speaking distance, they stopped.

In a strong voice, King Soranem spoke, "King Gassan. The people of Grendane and I, their King, hold you responsible for the unholy curse placed upon our lands."

"The curse is yours, Soranem! And my people will see justice done until you release us from whatever wizardry you have cast upon us," said King Gassan.

King Soranem responded angrily, "My people are suffering and have since the day your ministers paid visit! My men bleed from recent battles and suffer from grave injury but do not die! This will not go unanswered, Gassan."

"We sent our ministers to share with you the bounties of our land, Soranem. We cast no spell upon your people. And yet you repay us with a wretched plague! No disease, not even dismemberment, has taken lives in weeks throughout my kingdom. There is a great panic spreading across our lands. I cannot fathom what we have done to deserve such, but you and your men will surely die if you do not instruct your wizards to end this pestilence!" King Gassan responded, drawing his sword. King Soranem drew his sword as their horses shifted about, sensing the danger of the situation.

Suddenly, the sight of Agean and Gajir riding towards them at top speed captured their attention. Seeing this, warriors on both sides became restless but held their positions.

Gajir yelled out as he and Agean rode up. "Your Highnesses! Please, Your Highnesses!" The Kings turned towards Gajir and Agean, and readied their weapons. "Please! I beg of you! A word!"

King Gassan asked, "A word? Who are you?"

"I am Gajir, King of Gannus," Gajir replied.

"King Gajir of Gannus. Why have you come here? As

a King, you should know that defending one's realm is an act of honor to be challenged by no one," said King Soranem. Gajir turned and looked at Agean, then turned back to King Soranem.

"We mean no disrespect, Your Highnesses. We have come here to ask that you not go forward with this battle," Gajir said. "I make such a request respectfully as a King to Kings."

King Gassan said, "As a King to Kings? I have heard of you, Gajir of Gannus. You are said to be a very wise leader of your people."

Gajir responded, "The honor of being King requires wisdom, Your Majesty."

"Then would it be wise for a King to insult another and dishonor himself with such a request? Do you forget that we are brave men who must remain so in the eyes of our own?" asked King Soranem. Gajir paused for a moment and looked directly into the eyes of King Soranem, then King Gassan. Gajir then gazed in the distance at the two armies.

After emitting a heavy sigh, Gajir said, "I mean no insult Your Majesties, and beg your-"

Agean interrupted, "Then it is I who make the request."

King Soranem asked, "And who are you?"

"A priest, Your Majesties," Gajir said.

King Gassan asked, "A priest?" King Gassan's suspicion grew once he spotted Agean's swords. "Do you think us foolish, Gajir of Gannus? That we would believe a priest would carry such weapons?"

"I am from the Holy Order of God. My swords will remain at my sides," Agean said.

"The Holy Order of God?" King Gassan asked as he looked at King Soranem. "I have been told of the warrior priests of the Holy Order. I have also been told it is a thing of legend. How do we know this to be true?" Agean began reaching down into his travel sack. Gajir's eyes widened. He could not believe what Agean was about to do. The Credara was never to be seen by ordinary man. How could this Sitcian not know this? Gajir's heart pounded as Agean began to pull an item from the sack. Then, much to Gajir's great relief, Agean drew his white and gold hair sleeve from the sack: a symbol distinguishing a priest of the holiest of orders from all others. The Kings bowed their heads in acknowledgment of Agean's status. For the first time, Agean felt a sense of value and power from his life in the priesthood.

"We are honored to be in your presence, Priest. However, this matter is not one of the church, it is a matter among men... among Kings," said King Soranem.

"I ask not in the name of the church, Your Highnesses. I ask in the name of God himself," Agean said. "Do not spill blood here this day. Allow yourselves till this day in the coming month. So that your anger may be cooled. So that the suffering of many might be spared."

King Soranem said, "The suffering of many is the very reason we are here, Priest. However, I have respect for your request, and for God and Church."

"As do I, Priest," said King Gassan.

"Leave us," King Soranem continued. "We will consider what you have asked of us." Agean and Gajir bowed respectfully to the Kings, looked at each other, then turned their horses and began galloping full stride back to Quilin. The Kings watched as they rode off.

Agean and Gajir made it back to Quilin. "What happened?" Quilin asked.

"We must go and we must hurry!" Agean said.

Quilin asks, "Why?"

Gajir looked directly into Agean's eyes, "It is not your Hamen senses this time, is it?" Agean's face showed his concurrence with Gajir's words. "Man's pride and ego. At times, a weapon mightier than God."

Agean, Gajir and Quilin looked out into the distance to find the Kings and their bannerets returning to their men. Almost instantaneously, horns blared from both sides signaling the beginning of battle. Suddenly, thoughts of horror raced through Agean's mind. Thoughts so terrible that it became unbearable to consider. What if the Angel of Death had truly been captured? What horrible consequences were about to unfold before his eyes? While the distance between them and the battle concealed the reality, Agean's gut wrenched at the possibility of what might be. He used everything within him to keep from losing his stomach at the mere thought of it.

As the two armies violently collided and weapons clashed, horns signaled the go-ahead to the catapults and boulders began smashing mercilessly through a sea of living bodies. Swords, lances and maces tore and ripped through flesh. If Agean's greatest fears were true, flesh that would not die. Agean could not see it, but he could feel the horror in his heart. He prayed he was wrong.

Agean turned away with a disheartened look. Then he, Gajir and Quilin rode off, choosing not to watch the devastation of battle, but instead to get back to the greater task ahead.

PART FIVE

Anger and
Purpose Collide

chapter fourteen
The Road Less Traveled

The past few days of travel had been hot and at times dangerous as Agean, Quilin and Gajir reached a treacherous portion of their journey along the edge of a steep bluff. The perilously narrow path along the side of the bluff was bordered by a straight drop to a deep body of water below. They walked their horses carefully as rocks tumbled off the side of the bluff with each step. Forever curious, Quilin paused and leaned forward to peek over the edge of the bluff. He then quickly leaned back, taking a deep breath.

Quilin asked, "Are we quite sure this isn't a Kraylen trick to finally be rid of us?"

"This path is meant to be dangerous. Only those meant to survive it, will," Gajir replied.

What happened next was what they all feared the most: part of the narrow path gave way from under Quilin's feet. He slid off the edge of the bluff, falling and yelling all the way. Agean and Gajir immediately knelt down and peered over the edge to find out Quilin's fate. To their surprise and relief, they discovered that he had somehow grabbed hold of a tree branch that was sticking out of the hillside, and was hanging precariously above the lengthy drop.

Quilin yelled, "Hey! Help me!"

"Quilin! Are you all right?" Agean yelled.

Quilin continued screaming, "Agean, get me down from here!" Suddenly, Flittorin, who was circling above, screeched and then soared towards Quilin. He landed on Quilin's branch and began pecking at his fingers.

Quilin responded, "Hey! Stop it! Damned bird! Ow!" Flittorin kept pecking, despite Quilin's yelling. "Agean! Make him stop! Ow!"

Flittorin made a final peck on Quilin's fingers and he let go, yelling and dropping like a stone. Flittorin took to the air just in time to escape the enormous paw of a huge lioness, swiping out and destroying the entire branch Quilin was hanging from. It even took a few of Flittorin's feathers with it. Agean and Gajir, startled, reared back. The frightening roar of the lioness reverberated throughout the hillside as Quilin plunged into the water below. A lion's den. At the same spot on the bluff as the tree.

Quilin flailed about in the water looking up at the huge cat. The lioness roared again, sending shock waves through everyone. The lioness then turned away and retreated to a cave entrance on the hillside where several cubs awaited her return. Quilin yelled as he swam to the nearby water's edge, still frantically acknowledging the event.

"Did you see that? I could've been killed!" Quilin yelled. Agean and Gajir looked at each other with relief.

Gajir yelled to Quilin, "Just stay there, Quilin!"

Quilin climbed and crawled up a rock and onto shore, out of breath and completely overwhelmed by what just happened. Breathing heavily, Quilin looked up to see Flittorin landing on a rock nearby.

Several minutes later, Agean and Gajir finally made it down the bluff, horses in tow. They quickly made their way over to Quilin and discovered something they never thought they'd see. A soaked Quilin was seated on a rock in front of Flittorin, feeding him food from his waist pouch and mumbling kind words to him. Agean and Gajir were amazed.

"We see you've made a new friend," Gajir said.

"Aw, isn't he great? Look at him. This magnificent creature just saved my life," Quilin said.

As Quilin continued adoring and feeding Flittorin, Agean looked up and spotted a bridge off in the distance, high upon another hilltop.

"Look! There!" Agean said, pointing.

Gajir looked up to discover that Agean had spotted the landmark he had hoped to reach before sundown.

"The Bridge of Eternity!" Gajir said. "We need to move quickly!"

Agean and Gajir took the reins of their horses and began walking along a path towards the bridge. Still soaked,

Quilin walked over to his horse and removed one of the leather straps from his saddle. He wrapped the strap around his arm several times and then coaxed Flittorin onto it. He then happily grabbed the reins of his horse and began to follow the others, carrying and mumbling adoring words to Flittorin all the way.

After several hours, amidst the backdrop of deep darkness, a bright crescent moon and stars lit up the sky. Sitting on the peak of a small ridge of shoreline hills was the Bridge of Eternity, a frail looking wood-and-rope bridge that looked as if it could have been there since the beginning of time. Resting on the edge of the hillside, it extended out about one hundred feet into a vast dark nothingness. Agean, Quilin and Gajir arrived in the moonlit darkness of night. Flittorin flew over and perched on a bridge post. Agean and Quilin stared in amazement as they approached this heavenly marvel.

Gajir said to them, "My boys, before you is the pathway to Quintana." They continued staring in amazement. "As you see, before the sun rises this bridge leads to nowhere. No one dare cross at night. Some have tried. All have failed and have paid the highest price." Gajir turned away and began to unpack his horse. "We must rest here for the night. Trust that we will need all of our strength in the morning."

Quilin asked, "Should not one of us stay awake, Master, just in case?"

"My boy, you will soon learn that your newfound friend is quite special. A hawk can see and hear far better than any man. And, this hawk is a Hamen Warrior. He will watch over us, protect us, even die for us if need be," Gajir told him. Suddenly, a bright metallic sound rang out as Flittorin's talons turned Hamen; gleaming, metallic and needle sharp. "Now, get some rest, Quilin." Quilin looked at Flittorin and smiled as Gajir began unpacking. He then turned to Agean, who nodded, reassured by Gajir's words. They both began unpacking their horses and preparing to bed down for the night. Flittorin stood guard from the bridge post.

The night was cool and calm as everyone slept peacefully — everyone but Agean, who sweat, tossed and turned from yet another nightmare. As always, it jarred him from his sleep. Agean bolted upright, breathing deeply for a few moments, then wiped the sweat from his face. Trying not to disturb anyone, he got up, walked over to the bridge and stared off into the distance. Solis's truth telling had not only revealed the tragic realities of his family's gruesome murder, they had also unlocked memories Agean had thought were lost forever; memories of his life before the Order. His thoughts turned to pleasant remembrances which were slowly resurfacing about his family: the loving embrace of his mother, and her calming beauty. The sound of her voice danced through his mind. Then, memories of his loving young sister began to fill his head. He remembered her golden hair and the touch of her skin as she kissed his cheeks, playing with him and teaching him as if he were her own. And his father, tossing him into the air and chasing him around the pottery shop — proud to have him as a son despite his having broken quite a few costly items. Their happy faces became ever clearer to him, smiling and laughing, until suddenly fire entered his reminiscence. Intense flames caused his family to cry and reach out to him, screaming out for his help. Suddenly, the flesh on their faces began to melt, quickly liquefying and pouring off like the wax of a candle, leaving behind only their skeletal remains screaming out in agony. Then, as quickly as it came, Agean was startled out of it. The horrid vision was gone, chased from him by the touch of Gajir's hand. Awakened by Agean, Gajir had gotten up to find out what it was that disturbed him.

"Could not sleep, my boy?" Gajir asked. Agean was surprised to see that someone was awake.

"My apologies, Gajir," Agean said. "It was not my intent to wake you."

"Something burdens you, Agean. What is it?"

Agean lowered his eyes and said, "Things which are mine to bear, Gajir."

Gajir knowingly nodded his head. "I see. I know about your family, Agean."

Agean was surprised and paused a moment. "Master Naji has entrusted you with much. You must mean a lot to him."

"Oh, yes. He and I were at times like oil and water. But our hearts were the same," Gajir told him. "He gave his life so that you could realize the gift of yours."

Agean said surprised, "His life? How did you know?"

"He has only spoken to me about this once. It is called Hamorem," Gajir explained. "To be moved from this life to Heaven by the blade of a Sitcian. Master Naji felt that it might come soon, and that it might be by your blade." Agean gave a stunned look.

"How could this be?" Agean asked. "He was like a father to me."

"Master Naji knew in is heart that he would be the one to train the Sitcian who would be called to save us all," Gajir said. "To do this, he would have to train you to the ultimate point; well beyond his own skill. To the point where you would be able to kill even him. The point of Hamorem." Agean turned away with sadness, again staring into the darkness beyond the bridge.

"Don't feel bad, my boy. Naji was right. You are that Sitcian. And you gave him what he cherished most. There is no greater honor for a Hamen Master."

"Sitcian. I assure you I am not worthy of such an honor. For some reason, God has chosen me to lead us into battle, yet the greatest battle wages within me. A battle Solis was so willing to start."

Gajir said, "Ah. Solis. I know him well."

"He kept the truth about my family from me, only to reveal it now, when the fate of mankind is at stake," Agean said.

"Perhaps he realized that the path to your destiny could only be paved with the truth," Gajir said. "After all, goodness and truth are the source of a Sitcian's power."

Agean looked out at the stars and said, "And now I dishonor Master Naji with this rage I cannot shake."

"Let me share something with you, Agean. When we were having dinner at my home in Gannus I told you of Tordin's mother. That she had died."

Agean said, "Yes, Gajir. I remember."

"It wasn't as simple as that, my boy," Gajir said. "It was the worst day of my life. A day when I was faced with the most difficult choice I have ever had to make." Gajir's eyes became glassy as his emotions flowed with the telling of his story. "My wife was the most beautiful woman

I had ever set eyes upon. My one and only true love. She gave me a beautiful son in Tordin. Looking back, those were the happiest times of my life until that day." Agean's heart bled with compassion as Gajir's story unfolded, taking Gajir back to a moment in his life he had tried so desperately to shake: his first encounter with the Kraylen.

"I was speaking with a few of the Gannus Council members just outside of our home when I heard her scream. I immediately ran to her aid. And there, in my home, were three of them. Three Kraylen threatening my wife and my son."

Gajir shuddered as his words brought back the vivid memory of two creatures standing over his newborn son's cradle with blades drawn — the third pinning his wife down on the dining table, one of its dark calloused hands around her throat, the other holding a long dagger called a cinqueda above her heart.

"She was pleading, thinking nothing of herself, begging them not to harm our son," Gajir continued. "Almost without thinking, I raised my Hamen Staff and saved my son's life. Then, I turned to my wife, but it was too late. The Kraylen had driven the dagger so deeply through her heart that its tip cut a notch in the stone table beneath her." Agean's memory took him back to the dinner at Master Gajir's home, where he had noticed Gajir's fingers running across the notch in the stone table. "The creature took her life and then I, in return, took his. I know in my heart that saving Tordin was the choice she would have wanted me to make, but I was angry. More angry than I had ever been. Angry at the Kraylen... angry at God... even angry at Tordin for a very long time. So you see, Agean, I know how you must feel — but you have a choice, just as I had. I chose to raise my son to be a good man, and to be a king. Although he is not chosen, I trained him in the Art so that he could protect his family and his people. I chose not to allow those demons to strip away what was in my heart." What Gajir had just shared stunned Agean.

Gajir took a deep breath. "Yes. It is difficult to set such feelings aside, my boy. But to honor Master Naji is to remember his words, and to trust that he has prepared you for your destiny," Gajir told him, "...as we trust you to lead us, Agean. Your destiny is ours. You will know which path to take when the time comes. Look out there, my boy." Gajir directed Agean's attention back to the darkness in the distance. "You see the darkness before you. When the time is right, the sun will rise on your heart..." Just then the sun began rising over the horizon, lifting the darkness from the distance and revealing a heavy, thick white cloud floor. The bridge no longer ended at darkness, but now extended directly into the clouds. "...and reveal the very path you must follow."

What Agean saw astonished him. Quilin, awakened by the light, stood and joined the others to share the moment.

"Is this what we've been waiting for?" asked Quilin.

Gajir replied, "It is indeed."

Quilin asked, "Is it safe?"

"There are times when one must step out on faith, Quilin. The darkness has lifted. Leave the horses. We must hurry!" said Gajir.

Agean, Gajir and Quilin gathered their things quickly. Flittorin remained perched at the first post of the bridge. Once they were ready, Gajir paused, looking for Agean to go first. No one moved. Master Gajir then stepped onto the bridge.

"Master Gajir!" Agean said, stopping Gajir. "I believe it is I who should go first." Gajir gave Agean a smile and then stepped off the bridge.

"I could not agree more, Master Agean," Gajir said. Agean returned the smile, took a deep breath and then stepped onto the bridge.

"Agean!" Gajir said. Agean turned to Gajir. "As God has led your path, so shall you lead us into Quintana and beyond. Such is your destiny, as it is ours to follow you." Agean gave Gajir a reassuring look then turned back to the bridge. He took a few steps onto the bridge, followed by Quilin, then by Gajir.

Agean and the others moved forward to the point at which the bridge entered the clouds. Suddenly, his Hamen senses kicked in, somehow letting him know that he needed the Credara. Agean took the Credara from his waist pouch and held it directly in front of him. As they slowly moved forward, Flittorin took off and then soared directly down, disappearing into the clouds. All that could be heard was his screech, echoing from all directions.

With Quilin and Gajir now directly behind him, Agean took a leap of faith and stepped into the clouds. Quickly, the clouds began whirlpooling at his feet, swirling with lightning and wind. After a few seconds, the clouds were suddenly sucked down into its center, revealing Flittorin soaring just above a great whirlpooling body of water. The bridge now extended directly into the water's center, seemingly anchored to something below. Agean held the Credara high as Flittorin soared and circled above. The three carefully walked along the bridge until they were at the whirlpool's center. Dark storm clouds amassed above as the wind churned with lightning flashes and cracking thunder. They held on tight to the ropes of the bridge to keep from being swept off by the strong winds.

Quilin yelled, "What do we do now?"

"I'm not sure!" Agean answered. Then Flittorin screeched as he began to fly closer. Agean continued to hold the Credara high.

"Look!" Quilin yelled. All eyes turned to Flittorin as he swooped down and took the Credara from Agean's hands. He flew it high above the center of the whirlpool then dropped it in. The winds became stronger and lightning struck the very center of the whirlpool. Suddenly, a wall of jagged rock emerged from the waters like a mountain range, creating a circular enclosure in the sea, a lagoon several miles across.

Then, the waters began to recede. It was as if a huge drain had been opened. The water whirled down and vanished, leaving completely dry sandy ground with the Credara half-buried in it.

"Gentlemen, behold... Quintana!" announced Gajir.

A wondrous sight to behold, the fabled Quintana was a virtual hole in the sea with high walls of sea rock surrounding it, holding back its waters. It consisted of five huge monolithic rock pillars. Two smaller stood guard to three larger ones. The outer two of the three larger pillars had cascading waterfalls spilling from their top. The largest pillar sat at the center of the three and had a massive entrance in its center. Agean and Quilin found themselves speechless as they took in the beauty of this truly magnificent place. Flittorin soared, weaving in and around the pillars, screeching as if he were home.

"Yes. Speechless is what I was the first time I saw it, "Gajir said. "Come."

Agean, Quilin and Gajir made their way across the remainder of the bridge which ended in the sandy floor. The seafloor was strangely barren. No trace of sea life or plant life. They immediately walked over to the Credara and plucked it from the sand. Agean returned it to his waist pouch. They then proceeded towards the huge center pillar entrance.

As they got closer, the huge entrance began to open. The air filled with the sound of rock scraping against rock. Then, a man dressed in beautifully ornate garb stepped out to greet them.

"Gentlemen, I am Turon. Please, come this way. He awaits your arrival," Turon said.

Agean and Quilin looked at each other curiously. Quilin, now permanently wearing the leather strapping, whistled for Flittorin, who soared down and perched on his arm as they entered.

chapter fifteen
Heaven on Earth

Quintana. Upon entering, Agean and Quilin found themselves overwhelmed by what they saw. They realized they had entered another world, with its own sky, its own warming sunlight, and its own clean fresh air. Quintana was magnificent and beautiful. There were the most exquisite exotic flowers, glistening waterfalls, and sparkling paths. There was every ethnicity and age of man, woman and child. Every animal roaming free. Agean, Quilin and Gajir stood in awe.

Turon said to them, "Please, Gentlemen. Wait here." Turon then departed.

"I truly believe that I could visit this place a thousand times and still marvel at its magnificence," said Gajir.

After several moments, Turon returned with two others. One was a middle aged man with light hair and a kind face, dressed in obvious leadership garb laced with gold and precious stones.

"Gentlemen," he said, "I am Janirin. Welcome to Quintana."

Gajir added, "Otherwise known as... Heaven on

Earth." Janirin smiled and laughed. He crossed to Gajir and shook his hand.

"Master Gajir. Despite the circumstances, it is a pleasure to have you with us again, Old Friend."

"So you were aware of our coming?" Gajir asked.

Janirin replied, "Indeed. I have been made fully aware of the situation. I knew the Sitcian would soon arrive, and that you, of course, would be with him." Janirin turned to Agean. Seeing his Swords of Hamen, Janirin knew that he was the Sitcian. Janirin crossed over to Agean and placed his hands on his arms. He took a moment to admire his Mark. "It is a great honor to meet you, Young Man. You are the hope that God has promised. What is your name?"

"I am Agean," he replied.

Janirin said, "I will pray for your success each day of your journey, Agean." Janirin then turned to Quilin. "And you, Young Man?"

"I am Quilin," he replied, "and this is Flittorin."

"Yes. Flittorin, welcome back. He has visited with us many times," Janirin said. "Gentlemen. Come with me."

They all followed Janirin and the others to a beautiful golden open horse-drawn carriage with a driver.

Janirin said to them, "I hope this will be comfortable for you." Agean and Quilin looked impressed. Janirin, along with Agean, Gajir and Quilin, boarded and began a trip along beautiful paths, passing exquisite orchards, fields, animals and playing children. The sky was filled with pristine white clouds.

Along the way, Agean noticed something odd: an endless field of golden grain swaying in the wind. The field was bordered by a golden path. Along the path were men and women in standing prayer positions, seemingly awaiting something. Agean was immediately taken back to that fateful day. His beloved Master Naji chose this very same position as his last.

"Janirin, wait!" Agean said. Janirin gestured to the driver to bring the carriage to a stop. Agean and the rest stared at the scene. "What is happening here?"

Janirin responded, "This, my friends, is the Gateway to Quintana. Out of God's golden fields they come. We wait and welcome them here. Sadly, with each day their numbers are fewer."

"Because of the Hall of Souls?" asked Gajir.

Janirin responded, "Regretfully, yes. And we pray that you, Agean... all of you... will be victorious against the Kraylen." Agean gave Janirin a solemn look. "There is more, Agean. I will show you." Janirin started the carriage going again. They traveled a little farther up the path and stopped behind another horse-drawn carriage. A man, a woman and a child stood in the carriage with bright smiles on their faces, staring off into the distance.

"Ah. We are in luck," Gajir said. In the distance was a wondrous sight. A magnificent sparkling waterfall with the clearest water they had ever seen. In the sky above the waterfall was a cloud formation with a spectacular flow of light bursting through it and beaming directly onto the flowing falls. A huge, magnificent crystal structure formed an altar. A golden path led directly to it. As if floating on air, the falls sat dead center, and were completely surrounded by a wide circular opening with an endless drop. The only way into the falls was across this opening, making it impossible to reach without taking flight. The water from the falls spilled directly into the opening.

On this occasion, a woman dressed in flowing silk garb walked the golden path, reaching the altar. As she stood, she held her arms out wide and high as a bright sparkling light appeared from the cloud formation. Then, all at once, stunning white wings were formed upon her back. She lowered and clasped her hands in front of her. Then suddenly, she was lifted from the altar and began floating across the opening, her wings moving ever so gracefully. Tears of joy and happiness flowed from the eyes of those in the carriage watching her. As she entered the falls, her body pierced the flowing water. It poured over her body and wings like precious oil as it opened up and received her. Then, she was gone; moved on to Heaven, much to the awe and delight of those watching.

"It is called The Great Passage," Janirin said.

"The Great Passage?" Agean asked.

"Yes. It is where one makes one's final transition from Quintana to Heaven when it is time", Janirin explained. "I stood here and watched as my wife received her wings. She lost her life on the earth side and was re-awakened here in Quintana as only the most fortunate of us are. She floated across as an angel… and through the waterfall to Heaven. I hope to join her someday." All shared the tender moment as Gajir placed a hand on Janirin's shoulder.

The carriage started up again and the trip continued until they reached the almost palatial residence of Janirin, a home consistent with the beauty which surrounded it. The carriage stopped and everyone disembarked. Flittorin then left Quilin's arm and soared off into the distance.

"It appears Flittorin has appointments of his own," Gajir said. All made their way up a beautiful stone path to the foyer entrance. There was no door, only a beautiful open archway into the residence. Janirin's home was a dwelling fit for royalty. The high ceilings were beautifully painted, the passages incredibly crafted with archways unlike any ever seen. The pillars were trimmed in gold, encrusted with precious stones and draped in silk. The floors were of the rarest marble and the furnishings were crafted of the finest and most priceless materials in existence. All who called it home worked together to maintain its exquisite beauty. There were neither slaves nor servants.

"Welcome to our home, Gentlemen," Janirin said.

"Our home?" asked Agean.

"Why yes, my boy. Quintana belongs to us all. All of us here work together to maintain its beauty," Janirin said as he directed Agean's attention to the steady flow of people milling about.

"It is beautiful, Janirin," said Agean.

"Thank you, Agean. We all share in the abundance that God provides."

Quilin noticed a doorway off to the side of the foyer and walked over to take a look. The doorway led to a beautiful garden. Quilin took one step into the garden and there before his eyes was Istya, a beautiful, young and slender, dark-haired woman. Upon her neck was the Mark of Hamen, but Quilin was so taken by her beautiful brown eyes and lovely form, he didn't notice it.

As well, Istya did not notice Quilin at first as she was keenly focused, working one of the six Priya she kept attached to her waist. Three on the left, three on the right. Beautifully carved out of flawless Ebony, the Priya was an ancient Hamen weapon formed from two disks attached by a small metal cylinder in their center. Attached to the cylinder was a length of string made from the strongest fibers on earth. Attached to the other end of the string was a perfect sphere of Onyx. Each Priya was masterfully crested on each side with the Arc-Pen Symbol.

With a snap of her wrist, Istya extended and retrieved the Priya with impeccable skill. Quilin recalled hearing stories of such a weapon. It was used by a village's most skilled hunters — skilled in hunting live prey from the trees.

Suddenly, while executing a magnificent move, Istya spun and extended the Priya to its full length. The Priya then transformed from its wooden form to its Hamen form of glistening silver metal. Then, in the blink of an eye, razor sharp blades sprang from its edges while the string transformed into an unbreakable metallic line. This was no ordinary weapon. It sensed the will of the master who wielded it. Each of its razor sharp blades retracted individually, allowing it to be held safely by a Hamen Warrior. It was among the deadliest of the Hamen arsenal. The Hamen Priya.

Istya spun, aimed and sheared off a high, thick branch from one of the nearby trees. "Hmm. Tree cutting. Now where have I seen this before?" Quilin mused. Quilin was impressed with the capabilities of this weapon, but he was even more impressed with the woman wielding it.

"Now that is beauty," Quilin said to himself as he moved farther into the garden.

Istya retrieved the Priya, transforming it back to its normal form. She continued to skillfully work the weapon when suddenly she caught Quilin's movements out of the corner of her eye. She looked up and saw Quilin doing his best to avoid making eye contact. She smiled softly, pausing a moment to admire his good looks, then decided to ignore him. Quilin meandered farther into the garden and then walked over to a plant, pretending to admire it, and to not see her. Istya folded her arms and turned, looking directly at Quilin. When Quilin, trying to be coy, looked up and found Istya watching him, he quickly retreated back to the plant. Istya smiled, shook her head and then continued working the Priya. After a few moments, Quilin decided to approach.

"Oh, hello. I didn't see you there," he said. Istya rolled her eyes and continued what she was doing, ignoring Quilin. Quilin moved closer. "My name is Quilin. Your garden is quite lovely." Istya said nothing. Quilin took one more step closer. Istya, without as much as a glance, extended her Priya at him, stopping him in his tracks as it hovered on its string between them.

Istya's actions took Quilin completely by surprise. "That's not very friendly," he said. Istya then retrieved the Priya and continued working it, ignoring Quilin. Quilin decided to meet Istya's unfriendly challenge by lashing his whip and catching her Priya by the string. Istya immediately drew another Priya from her waist and extended it directly into Quilin's groin, doubling him over in pain. Quilin's eyes crossed as he fell over like a downed tree. He groaned as Agean, Gajir and Janirin entered the garden. Janirin saw Quilin curled up in a fetal position on the ground.

"I see you've met my daughter. And I see in her own way she has already introduced herself," Janirin said. Quilin continued to groan as Janirin walked over to Istya. "My dear, you must find a better way to greet our guests." Janirin turned back to Agean and Gajir. As he was about to speak, he noticed the tree branch lying on the ground and turned back to Istya. "Istya, dear, didn't we just speak about not using the garden trees for practice?"

"Sorry, Father," Istya said, embarrassed.

"Oh, she speaks!" said Quilin sarcastically, still curled into a ball on the ground. Istya cut him a stern look.

"Gentlemen, I would like you to meet that which is most precious to me. My daughter, Istya."

"A pleasure to meet you, Istya," Agean said. "I'm sure for Quilin as well."

"How incredibly rude," Quilin said, still writhing on the ground.

"You started it!" Istya proclaimed. Gajir walked over to Istya.

"Istya, I am Gajir. We met long ago when you were very young. Trust me, we are in no doubt certain that our Quilin was in some way at fault," Gajir told her. Quilin blazed a stern look towards Istya as she smirked with satisfaction.

Janirin, clearing his throat, said, "Well, perhaps we should all go inside. We do have much to discuss."

"Indeed," Gajir said. He then leaned down to Quilin. "Hurry along, Quilin." Quilin rolled his eyes and sighed as Janirin, Agean, and Gajir walked to the doorway to exit the garden. Istya followed.

Quilin, struggling to get to his feet, mocked Istya. "You started it."

Istya heard him and smiled, flattered, as she exited the garden. Quilin took a deep breath and groaned, then limped along after them.

Janirin and the others made their way into the main room at the front of the house.

"Please make yourselves comfortable," Janirin said. "Would anyone like some tea?" Janirin crossed to a table where a tea service awaited, hot and ready to serve.

"Your hospitality has always been most gracious, Janirin," Gajir said. "Please do not think me rude, but I am afraid we have little time." Janirin stopped pouring, appearing uncomfortable.

"Yes, you are right. What is happening in the Hall of Souls must be stopped," Janirin said. Janirin returned the tea pot to its place and nervously turned to the others. "Perhaps we should discuss a plan; a way to keep the Kraylen from reaching their goal." Gajir walked over to Janirin, placed his hands on his shoulders and looked him in the eye.

"My friend, I know she is your only daughter, but delaying her destiny will not keep her from it," Gajir said.

Hearing this, Quilin immediately jumped to attention. "What? Her? But God is to provide us a warrior, not an… an impetuous girl."

Istya quickly turned to Quilin, removed a Priya from her waist, and drew back. Quilin ducked, tried to block and fell clumsily from his chair. Istya chose not to strike him, but instead returned the Priya to her waist.

"Master Gajir is right," Agean said. "We must act quickly. I fear things are more grave than we think."

"I understand. Please, forgive me," Janirin said. He then walked directly over to Agean and took a deep breath. "Master Agean. To God's Army I give my precious daughter. Trust that she is ready and has mastered the Art. Her weapons of Hamen will serve you well in destroying the Kraylen. I know there is no place for selfishness in this, but I ask that you do everything in your power to bring her back to me."

What Istya heard shocked her. "Father!"

"Istya, I am simply asking-"

"I am chosen, Father," Istya said to him, interrupting. "I am a Hamen Warrior."

Quilin coughed loudly and cleared his throat. Istya turned and blazed an angry look at him.

"Sorry. Sorry. Something stuck in my throat," Quilin said.

Agean turned to Janirin, "As God is my witness, I will do all I can to return her safely to you, Janirin. But from what I have already seen, I do not doubt that she can take care of herself." Agean and the others turned their eyes to Quilin.

"What?" Quilin asked.

Janirin said, "That is all a loving father can ask, Agean. Thank you." Istya scowled at Agean and Janirin, then turned, folded her arms in a huff and stared out of a nearby window.

❧

At the entrance to Quintana, Turon waited as Janirin, Agean, Quilin, Gajir and Istya all arrived by carriage. Just as they exited the carriage, Flittorin soared in and landed on Quilin's arm.

"Ahh, there you are," Quilin said.

Janirin crossed over to Agean. "Agean. I have no doubt

you will succeed. I shall patiently await your return. We have retrieved your horses. A vessel is prepared for the next leg of your journey."

"We are grateful for your assistance, Janirin," Agean said, respectfully bowing. Janirin then walked over to Istya, who gave him a stern eye.

Janirin said to her, "Your mother used to give me that same look. I really miss her so." Istya held her look. "Istya. No smile for an old foolish father?" Istya tried to maintain her look but could not and smiled. She lovingly hugged Janirin, who smiled and held their embrace. "This is all happening so fast. It was the same way with your mother."

"I remember, Father," Istya said as she released her embrace and looked into Janirin's eyes.

Janirin said, "I put something in your travel pack." Istya's smile turned serious. "Mention it to no one, and reveal it only if absolutely necessary. It was never intended to leave this place. For this I will seek God's forgiveness. But know that I will not be forgiven if it is lost to the Kraylen." Istya's expression turned to one of deep concern.

"Father…" Istya said.

"Whatever happens, Istya, I am proud of you," said Janirin, interrupting. Istya's smile returned as Janirin raised his hand. "Open the entrance!"

Again, the sound of rock scraping against rock cut the air as the entrance to Quintana opened. As Agean, Quilin,

Gajir and Istya began to exit, Istya paused and turned to give her father a reassuring look.

Istya called out to Janirin, "I promise to return soon, Father!"

"Be safe, my daughter! God's warrior!" Janirin said proudly.

Istya smiled as she ran to catch up with the others. Turon, Agean, Gajir, Quilin and Istya all exited the center pillar.

Much to their surprise, to the left of the entrance sat a sailing vessel large enough to comfortably stow their horses and supplies, and allow comfortable space for sleep. Where did such a vessel come from? Agean pondered this as they all went aboard. A few men finished loading the horses and supplies onto it and then disembarked. Flittorin found his perch at the bow of the ship.

Agean walked over to his horse, which was secured in his hold, to make sure he was comfortable. "Well, Darius, off we go, my friend." Once they were ready to depart, Turon gave one last wave. He then entered the center pillar and the entrance closed. All at once the waterfalls atop the two large pillars began to pour forth with greater intensity. Suddenly the dry sand floor began to fill with water as if a giant spigot had been opened. The waters rushed in with a fury, splashing against the rock pillars and the vessel. The vessel began to rise. A whirlpool formed and the vessel began circling its center. When the water rose high enough, the rock walls slowly descended into the sea. Flittorin then began to screech and spread his wings. All at once the winds kicked up, grabbed hold of the sails and moved the vessel out into the open sea.

chapter sixteen

The Heart of a Hero Emerges

The sunlight of the day danced off the small ripples in the water. There were no waves and no wind, yet the boat cut through the still water as if being pushed along by the hand of God. With Flittorin, a Godly navigator at the helm, such a thing was truly possible.

At sea for three days now, everyone passed the time in various ways: practicing the Art, studying the Bisalis, and taking in wisdom from Master Gajir. At one point, as Istya watched, Quilin demonstrated to Agean how to launch the bladed tip from his Hamen Whip, using the aft mast at the stern of the vessel as his target. With a quick movement and a lashing of the whip, the tip disconnected from the Hamen weapon and entered the thick post like the head of an arrow. Quilin cracked the whip again, and the tip dislodged and returned. Agean decided to give it a try. He took hold of the whip and instantly felt his Hamen senses connecting with it. His Mark and that on the whip started to glow. Agean cracked the whip, sending the deadly tip ripping through the air towards its target — only this time, when the tip met its target, the wood exploded, leaving a gapping void in the post. The top portion of the mast, along with its topsail, snapped its lines, tilted and fell off into the sea. The tip then magically returned to the whip. Quilin and Agean could only stare at the remnants of the mast in total disbelief and embarrassment.

In the midst of the terribly awkward moment, Agean turned to Gajir and asked, "Gajir, was that piece important?"

Gajir raised an eyebrow at the question. "Need I remind you both that we will need the entire vessel in order to make it to our destination?" Agean and Quilin both continued to look embarrassed.

Several more days had passed. A new morning broke through the clouds in the distance. Storms over the past three days had, for the most part, kept everyone behind closed doors. However, on this clear morning, Agean was definitely in the mood to practice the Art. Quilin appeared uninterested as he stood staring into the distance, gnawing on a chunk of bread. Istya lay napping in the warm sun.

Agean turned to Gajir and asked, "Master Gajir, are you up for a challenge this morning?"

Gajir replied, "I must say I admire your commitment,

Agean. Master Naji has done well with you. However, this old man must preserve some of his energy for what lies ahead." Agean shrank with disappointment. "There is, however, one here whom you have yet to challenge." Agean gave a confused look.

"But I have sparred with each of you, Gajir. Several times," Agean said.

Gajir said, "Ahh, but you haven't. Flittorin!" At Gajir's calling, Flittorin left the bow and soared high into the air. This immediately got the attention of both Quilin and Istya, who began to watch. Suddenly, Flittorin's talons turned Hamen and the symbol on his pendant began to glow. Seeing this, Agean drew one of his swords and took a Hamen fighting stance. Flittorin proceeded to attack. Their sparring session was unlike any Agean had experienced. Agean spun and swung his blade at Flittorin with laser-like precision while Flittorin attacked and defended like a Hamen Master with wings. Gajir watched as Quilin and Istya cheered them on. The sound of Agean's sword against Flittorin's talons rang out as they challenged each other. Agean ducked and dodged as Flittorin's needle sharp talons continually zipped past his head. After a good amount of time had passed, Gajir brought the session to a halt.

"Enough!" Gajir yelled. Agean paused mid-move,

breathing heavily and sweating from the workout. Flittorin's talons returned to normal as he landed on the edge of the vessel. Gajir walked over to Agean.

"Be thankful we have him, Agean. Remember, our enemy can fly," Gajir said. Agean realized the importance of Gajir's words. He lowered his sword and walked over to Flittorin. With great respect, and with sword in hand, Agean bowed to him.

"Master Flittorin," Agean complimented. Flittorin screeched and then took to the air.

Quilin crossed over to Agean. "So... How does it feel, Master Agean?"

"How does what feel, Quilin?"

Quilin crept closer and said in a whisper, "Being nearly beaten by a bird." Quilin began chuckling when suddenly a huge splotch of bird poop landed on the railing near Quilin. Quilin looked up to Flittorin.

"Aha! Missed me!" Quilin said, laughing.

"A Hamen Warrior never misses, Quilin," said Gajir, nodding his head and directing Quilin to look again.

"What?" Quilin asked as he strained his neck, checking his shoulders. Then, he saw it, oozing down his back. Agean, Istya and Gajir immediately began laughing as Flittorin screeched from above.

"Aww..." Quilin growled.

"I think he prefers the term "Warrior", Quilin," Agean said.

Quilin looked up and found Flittorin circling. "I was just kidding! I thought we were friends." Flittorin screeched again as Agean and the others continued laughing. Quilin then took a rag from his waist pouch and did his best to reach it. After several unsuccessful attempts, he put on a childlike grin and tried to hand the rag to Istya, who put her hands up, declining the offer. As he turned his pitiful look to Agean and Gajir, they both declined and walked off. Quilin rolled his eyes, knowing he was on his own.

❧

On a hot afternoon, a dry rocky mountain range appeared frighteningly destitute with little evidence of life, except for a lone figure standing atop the highest ridge of a dead volcano. Licronus, the light breeze blowing the loose elements of his garb, looked directly into the sun, as if challenging it to do him harm. Suddenly, Poragon and Bralorg approached from the air, landing beside Licronus and tucking their wings.

"It is done. They await your orders," Poragon said. Licronus continued to stare directly into the sun for a moment more. Then, he lowered his head to gaze deep within the crater of the volcano and set his eyes upon a sight he had waited centuries to see. Down within the volcano's belly was the culmination of years of patience and planning. Gathered on the crater floor, fully armed, and ready for war were tens of thousands of his Kraylen warriors. Licronus had amassed an unimaginable sea of evil that filled the entire inner cavity of the massive volcano.

"Our moment has arrived! Go! Go and take back what is rightfully yours!" Licronus yelled. A tremendous roar swelled from within the volcano as the Kraylen raised their weapons to the sky. Then, all at once, an eruption of Kraylen blasted into the sky, as if the dead volcano had once again come alive. Licronus and his Generals sprouted their jet black wings and joined the evil legion as it took to the air.

⧼⧽

A few more days at sea had passed. The morning meal was complete. Quilin settled in for another long day with a nap as Gajir meditated. Agean was tending his swords with a precious grey crystal that lit up with each stroke as he ran it along the blade. Istya meticulously worked her Priyas, catching Agean's eye with her stunning movements.

Agean said to her, "I know of this weapon. The Priya. It is very ancient."

"Yes. My mother chose it for me. She had been training me since I was a child. I was still a child when she left," Istya told him.

"Your father shared with us how much he loved her," Agean said.

"Yes, as did I. There wasn't even a chance to say goodbye," Istya said sadly. "My father told me that Quintana is a place for those souls who have departed too soon; who still had something to finish when their lives ended. He told me that her purpose was fulfilled in me." Istya looked off into the distance. "I still miss her." Agean felt for Istya, as he felt for the loss of his own family.

"I imagine it is very difficult," Agean said.

"My greatest hope is to make her proud of me," Istya replied introspectively. "Perhaps when I finish God's work, my father and I will be able to see her again." She then perked up and slung a Priya out and back. "But to answer your question, yes. Almost as difficult as this Hamen weapon." Istya slung and retrieved the Priya again. She then stopped and sat by Agean.

"It was difficult. But my father is a good man, a very patient man. He understood God's purpose and eventually, so did I. So, he took over my training and changed his rebellious little daughter into a Hamen Master."

"Master Istya," said Agean bowing his head. Istya nodded in acceptance of the title.

"What about you, Agean?" Istya asked. Agean purposely avoided speaking about his family.

"The swords? Definitely not rebellious," Agean replied. "If anything, I was much too anxious in the beginning. Master Naji taught me patience. He has given his life to teach me the Art." Agean paused to reminisce. "Like your parents, he meant everything to me."

Istya smiled at Agean. "And what of your parents, Agean?" Agean looked directly into Istya's eyes. She could see that there was something burning beyond the surface. A fire. Pain.

"Though I think of them often, I remember little of them," Agean replied. He immediately resumed tending his sword, stroking the blade with the precious crystal with more intensity, more anger, until suddenly he cut his finger. Agean grimaced as he watched the blood trickle from the small cut. Istya reacted quickly and reached into her travel sack which lay nearby. She removed a thin white head scarf, and wrapped Agean's hand.

"There, that should do it," Istya said. Agean looked embarrassed as Istya attempted to change the subject.

"My father always told me that I was part of a sort of puzzle. We all are. You, me, Quilin, Master Gajir. But you, Agean... you are the most important piece of this puzzle. It is the swiftness of your sword that God and mankind are counting on."

"And Master Naji," Agean said, as his embarrassment turned to anger again. He stopped tending his blade and looked forward with a blank stare. "It is too late for my parents, but the Master still needs me. I assure you, Istya, for Licronus my sword will be swift." Realizing he was saying too much, Agean stopped speaking and resumed tending his blade. Istya showed a look of concern as Agean rubbed the crystal against the blade with even more intensity; with more anger.

The next afternoon found Agean near the bow of the vessel studying the Bisalis as Gajir and Istya tended to their horses. Quilin, standing nearby and looking off the port side of the vessel, turned to Agean and observed him - wondering what he was thinking. Quilin's hair blew in the brisk sea breeze as he watched Agean take the Credara from his waist pouch. He had seen this look of concern on Agean's face before as he inspected the receding waters.

Quilin asked, "So. How are we doing?"

"We're running out of time," Agean said as he returned the Credara to his waist pouch. He then went back to reading the Bisalis.

Quilin said to him, "Agean, you have read that entire book at least four times."

"Five actually," Agean replied. "There will be no more time for study from this point on, Quilin. Our focus must now be on destroying Licronus. But I must say, I have read many scrolls and texts during my time with the Order, none of which I care to read again. But this book... I've never seen anything like it."

Quilin noticed as Agean turned from a page filled with writing, to a blank page, and then again to another blank page.

Quilin said, staring at the book, "I can see why. A book with blank pages isn't much of a book."

Agean was confused by what Quilin was saying. He touched the blank pages in total awe.

"Look at these pages, Quilin. I struggle to understand the symbols and language, but surely it was written by God's own hand," Agean said.

Quilin, reaching down to pick up his whip, said, "Well, God must not have much to say because those pages, my friend, are blank. You know, you're starting to give me a scare, seeing things as you do. First followers that aren't there and now this... I definitely see leeches and bloodletting in your future, Agean."

Just as Agean began to argue with Quilin, something caught his eye. With no forewarning, it appeared where first there was nothing.

Agean stared, mouth open in total awe, and yelled, "The Passage of Rizarnia!" Quilin looked up to see a vision that practically knocked him from his feet. The Passage of

Rizarnia was a magnificent stone passageway, rising from the sea like a gigantic guardian, and etched along its towering pillars, top to bottom, with symbols. At the very top was the Arc-Pen Symbol.

The size of the passageway dwarfed their vessel as they passed through. By now, Gajir and Istya had heard Agean yell and were taking in the sheer beauty of the stone passageway. Flittorin screeched as they passed through. Agean quickly flipped to a page in the Bisalis showing a detailed drawing of the beautiful passageway in the sea. He ran his fingers across the page in admiration and then looked up at it again.

Quilin said, "Incredible."

"Seen only by those who travel this path," said Gajir. "These are God's waters. Passing through Rizarnia means we are nearly there. But, as I feared, we are not alone." Seeing Gajir gaze into the distance, everyone turned to look and saw a thick dark cloud approaching from the distance.

"Is that a storm?" Istya asked.

Agean focused and saw that the cloud was not a cloud after all, but instead a huge swarm of Kraylen.

Agean replied, "That is no storm, Istya."

Suddenly, everyone's Marks tingled and glowed, confirming the Kraylen.

"There must be thousands of them," said Quilin.

"What do we do? They will surely not miss us," said Istya.

Agean declared with increasing anger, "We do what we came to do. If it is a fight they want, then fight we shall."

Quilin looked at Agean with amazement. "Fight them? That many?! We'll be slaughtered!"

Istya said, "Agean, you can't be serious?"

Agean, with eyes still focused, began to boil with anger. He placed his hands on his swords and stared at the cloud of Kraylen, beads of sweat forming on his brow.

"He is, Istya," Quilin said. "I have seen that look before."

Istya, gravely concerned, asked Gajir, "What do we do?" Gajir looked at Agean and then turned to Istya and Quilin.

"We have no choice. The Sitcian has decided. We fight them!" Gajir said.

Istya and Quilin looked at each other astonished. They then accepted their fate. Istya drew four Priya from her waist, two in each hand, and transformed them into their Hamen form. Quilin drew and transformed his Hamen Whip. All turned and faced the approaching menace, determined and ready to die in battle if they must. Suddenly, a screech from Flittorin disrupted Agean's anger and focus. Then, he remembered what Solis had told him about trusting the Credara and its power. Agean struggled against his anger. His eyes closed tightly, squeezing to understand. Then, his eyes opened as his searing anger was broken.

Gajir, Istya and Quilin took Hamen fighting positions for battle, when suddenly, with a burst of pure energy, they all, including the entire vessel, became transparent like water.

Stunned with disbelief, they all looked around in total awe at each other and their water-like limbs. They looked out at the transparent vessel and marveled at the incredible change. They turned to Agean and found him transformed as well, holding up the Credara. Its Arc-Pen Symbol was glowing as waves of energy engulfed the vessel. Flittorin, unaffected by the Credara's power, was still perched at the bow with his wings spread.

The Kraylen, as they passed directly overhead, saw only what appeared to be a lone hawk gliding above the water. Agean and the others, as well as the vessel, were completely hidden, blending in with the water below. The disturbing rumbling sound of thousands of Kraylen flying overhead penetrated the air. Once the swarm had passed, Agean lowered the Credara and all returned to normal.

Quilin proclaimed proudly, "Now that's more like it!" Gajir gave Agean a proud look as he stood in awe of what he had done. Then Gajir directed everyone's attention ahead to the shore and the forest in the distance.

Gajir announced, "There! The Badril Forest. Prepare to have their full attention once we arrive." Agean and the others looked towards the forest.

The Badril Forest was a thick, lush, tropical forest of high trees. Little did Agean and the others know, Licronus and his Generals had already arrived.

Licronus stood among the trees near the shore with his two Generals, gazing out at Agean and the others as their vessel approached.

After a moment of seething anger, Licronus turned quickly and walked off into the forest. Poragon and Bral-org followed.

જી

The air which ripped past Tan's face like cactus needles was dry and hot as he and his horse tore through the final few miles of their journey. Their destination: the ancient province of Shao-Tan. Tan's previous encounter with the knife wielding Kraylen made him fully aware of what was at stake and what he now faced. The enemy, having not yet decided to make every effort to slay him, had surely been tracking him since their last meeting. All was at risk as long as he was out in the open. Tan was now vulnerable to attack from the air and all directions. Making it safely to Shao-Tan was all he could think of. It is there that he would find shelter, food, water, his family, and the Shao-Tan Temple where he would do God's work.

Located northwest of the great lands of China, in the religion tolerant Mongolian territory, this small province was non-existent until the ancient Shao-Tan monks decided to make it their home. The structures and main entrance of the grand Shao-Tan Temple were formed mainly from rammed-earth, giving them the appearance of having risen from the ground on their own.

Not long after the completion of the Temple, Chinese refugees escaping persecution and the turmoil of war in China began inhabiting the land surrounding the Temple. In the decades that followed, and as word spread, many families and others seeking the comfort of religious freedom and the Temple's brand of spiritual enlightenment, made Shao-Tan their home. It wasn't long before the area was teaming with families tending huge expanses of intricate rice terraces, small farms with livestock, and other food sources. Generations had taken hold, getting physical nourishment from the land and spiritual nourishment from the Temple. On the perimeter of a vast hot and dry landscape, Shao-Tan was a green and lush oasis of beauty. The adjacent mountain made this possible with its melting snow cap bringing an ample supply of water to the province. Solis told Tan that there would be much to share and much to learn.

As Tan raced along towards the small province, he thought about the great responsibility he was about to take on. All that Solis and the Order had taught him over the years began surging through his mind. Then, he saw it in the distance: The entrance to Shao-Tan. A feeling of relief brought a sense of coolness to his entire body as he knew he was almost there - almost home.

Tan could see the main tower of the Temple, Shao-Tan's centerpiece, in the distance. Then, he noticed something strange. A crowd had formed; a large crowd of Shao-Tan inhabitants at the entrance. While Tan expected his arrival might be anticipated by the monks, the exact time of his arrival could not have possibly been foreseen. Even he had no idea when he would arrive. Tan pushed his stallion to go faster, knowing he chanced losing him at any moment from exhaustion. Closer and closer Tan came to the crowd and his long awaited destination. Now close enough to distinguish the crowd's makeup, Tan could see that men and women, young and old had gathered along with children as young as newborns. Guided by what he knew of the enemy, Tan kept his guard up and his senses focused. Just as Tan was about to slow his horse, it skidded to a halt, nearly tossing Tan from his saddle. His horse neighed loudly and began turning in awkward directions as if confused. Tan tried to settle the horse as he continued to neigh, snort, kick its feet and turn left to right. Although Tan tried his best to calm the animal, he knew full well what was happening. He quickly dismounted, just in time for the horse to drop onto his front knees in the dirt. Tan continued to try and calm his horse, muttering words of apology for riding him beyond his breaking point. The horse then snorted and collapsed onto its side.

"Hold on, my friend," Tan said to the horse. Tan rubbed the horses face as it began to calm, then stood looking down on him for a moment. He turned towards the crowd and began walking. He placed his hands on his waist to make sure his weapons were intact – they were. He knew this could well be a Kraylen trap.

As he approached the crowd, he noticed the faces of the people. There was fear and anguish in many, as if they had been forced there against their will. One of the older men stepped forward and met him face to face.

"I am Tan," said Tan, speaking in his native Mandarin and exchanging bows with the man. "I am a missionary from the Holy Order of God. My family and I are from here. My horse needs help." The man looked out into the distance at the horse.

"No," the man responded smugly in Mandarin. Tan stood baffled at the man's response.

"My family awaits my arrival. The Shao-Tan monks are expecting me at the Temple. I assure you I bring no ill will. I must get water and food for my horse or he will die," Tan said.

"Then die he will. Unless of course you are willing to pay," the man said.

"I am but a poor missionary of God. I have nothing with which to pay you."

"Then we will take that!" The man said, pointing to the scroll case hanging across Tan's chest. He then transformed into the Kraylen, Barejis. Tan was momentarily startled by the transformation. Then, he quickly gathered his senses, retrieved his Bouma from his waist and took a Hamen fighting stance. His peripheral vision sharply focused, his senses dialed in, Tan awaited Barejis's next move.

"It appears I did not make myself clear during our last encounter, Kraylen," Tan said.

"Ahhh... but you did, young monk. However, this time... we are not alone." Barejis laughed. Then suddenly, from Tan's left, a man stepped from the crowd, took his Kraylen form and drew a curved blade. He lunged at Tan. Tan did an incredible back flip to avoid being impaled by the Kraylen's deadly weapon. He then spun and kicked the Kraylen across the face, spinning him around and then landed a crushing kick to center of his back. After stumbling forward, the angry Kraylen huffed, turned, then drew a second blade and began slashing away. Tan used his Bouma to block each death blow with incredible precision, eventually striking the Kraylen across the face, kicking him in the chest, then striking the Kraylen under the chin. The force from the Bouma's blow lifted the Kraylen from his feet, causing his blades to fly from his hands. The Kraylen hit the ground unconscious. Immediately, another man on his right took a winged Kraylen form, drew two blades and launched into the air. Tan instantaneously hurled one of his Bouma, striking the Kraylen on his right wing. The Bouma tore through the wing sending half of it fluttering to the ground. As the Kraylen tried to gain control, Tan sent his second Bouma ripping through its remaining wing, causing the creature to plummet to the ground. It then transformed back to its human form and lay there writhing in pain. Both of Tan's Bouma swirled around and returned to his awaiting grasp. Tan took a Hamen fighting stance in Barejis's direction, only to find that Barejis was no longer there. Tan found himself facing the crowd.

Suddenly, Barejis's voice rang out. "Entertaining, Monk. You have the fighting skills of a true Hamen Warrior." Tan scanned the fearful looking crowd, trying to locate Barejis. "Now, let me tell you what I know. I know you are no Hamen Warrior for you are not chosen. You cannot see through our disguise, can you, Monk?" Tan continued scanning the crowd. All he could see were frightened men, women and children. All he could hear were babies and young children crying along with their worried mothers. Suddenly, Tan's keen hearing sensed the sound of a blade in the air. He drew his Bouma and sent it flying. The Bouma connected with the blade, deflecting it from its deadly path. The Bouma returned to Tan who grabbed it and returned to a ready stance. Then, from out of the crowd, a blade slashed through the sleeve of Tan's garb, making a small cut in his arm. Tan spun, ready to throw his Bouma, but he could find no enemy to strike; nothing but innocent Shao-Tan inhabitants staring at him in fear. Barejis laughed again.

"Only the chosen can see what you cannot, young monk. So... which one of us will your weapons strike next?" The crowd began moving, surrounding Tan. Tan, maintaining his Hamen stance, rotated to observe what was going on around him. Tan scanned for the enemy, until he found himself surrounded. The Kraylen was right. Tan could not tell which were Kraylen, and which were not. Then, suddenly and randomly, creatures in the crowd began taking their Kraylen form, then quickly changing back. A child, to Kraylen, then back. A mother, to Kraylen, then back. An old man, then an old woman, then a child, and so on.

"Even a great warrior cannot fight what he cannot see. Unless of course you plan to do battle with innocent men, women and children," Barejis said.

The crowd became more worried about their fate. Tan could hear children crying and mothers beginning to beg him not to hurt them. After a moment, Tan relaxed his Hamen stance and returned his Bouma to his waist. He knew what he now faced. His vow as a monk would not allow him to bring harm to the innocent.

"Your God has betrayed you, Monk. He has put you in our grasp, and left you powerless against us," Barejis proclaimed. Then, suddenly, dark grey clouds began to gather directly overhead. Lightning blazed across the sky and thunder cracked as Tan continued to survey his situation and decide his own fate. As the storm formed, Tan bowed his head and placed his hands on the scroll case.

Barejis said from the crowd, "You have no choice but to give us what we want."

"What I have belongs to God Almighty. I will harm no innocent man, woman or child. You may take my life. What happens to me is not important. What happens to this, only He will decide." A crack of thunder exploded in the sky as the dark clouds swirled above, blocking most of the sunlight. Tan knelt in the dirt and placed his hands in a prayer position. He looked up into the swirling clouds.

"If it is thy will," Tan said. He then bowed his head, submitting to his fate, willing to die at the hands of the Kraylen in order to fulfill his vow to God. Barejis, in his human form, made his way out of the crowd. Another loud crack of thunder rumbled as he stared at Tan for a moment. Barejis then crossed over to Tan and got down on one knee as lightning danced across the sky. Barejis slowly reached his hand out towards the scroll case strapped to Tan's body. Tan did not move. Just as Barejis's fingers were but inches from the case, a drop of rain landed on the back of his hand. Barejis's attention was quickly diverted from the scroll case to the rain drop as something very peculiar occurred once it landed. Smoke began rising from it. Then… pain - sharp, searing pain. Another drop landed on Barejis's outreached hand and more smoke began rising from his burning flesh. Barejis looked at his hand in horror but then realized that he was being scorched by every drop that landed on his body. He screamed out in pain as drop after drop burned like fire.

Immediately, Barejis stood, spread his jet black wings and launched into the air, heading directly towards a small grain shed just to the left of the gathering. He slammed head-on into the old wooden structure, blowing a hole through it as he penetrated it with hurricane force. Just as he did, the rain began to pour down with greater force. Every disguised Kraylen began smoking and burning – writhing in pain with every raindrop that landed upon them. The creatures all revealed themselves and took their winged Kraylen form as they looked up into the sky, their facial features breaking down and disintegrating as the rain drenched them from head to toe. Evil screams of pain filled the air as some of the Kraylen tried to fly out of the downpour. Their effort proved futile as every Kraylen exploded in masses of smoke and ash. Vanquished.

Soaking wet and still kneeling, Tan raised his head and opened his eyes, not knowing what to expect. Tan was shocked by what he saw. Smoldering mounds of ash lay on the ground. Many from the crowd appeared to have vanished, leaving only a couple of dozen frightened men and mothers holding tight to their crying children. Tan realized that the rain, a pure act of God, had destroyed the Kraylen. Immediately, Tan checked to make sure he was still in possession of the scroll case. Then, a strange sight in the distance caught his eye: an old man sitting atop a horse a little way up the main road into Shao-Tan. The old man simply sat and stared at him. Tan paused a moment to observe, but something deep within drew him to the old man. Those in the crowd stood perplexed. Unable to see the old man, no one knew what it was that held Tan's attention. Then, suddenly Tan's horse neighed and stood, seemingly fully recovered, and slowly made its way over to him. Tan stroked his horse's mane then turned back to observe the old man. As quickly as it began, the rain suddenly ceased and the clouds began to dissipate. The old man then turned his horse and began slowly trotting up the main road towards the Shao-Tan Temple. Tan took the reins of his horse and began to follow on foot. Something within Tan knew that from this moment on, his life would change forever. The crowd of Shao-Tan inhabitants turned and began making their way back into the province.

Once the clouds had dissolved completely, the sun revealed something unexpected in the sky - a winged Kraylen. A Kraylen who was somehow smart enough to soar above the dark grey clouds which had suddenly formed; a Kraylen that avoided the vanquishing. Suddenly, the Kraylen dropped from the sky like a meteor, landing hard in the dirt, partially knelt with two razor sharp silver blades drawn. The Kraylen was Jirsa. As she looked towards the Shao-Tan main road, she observed the filthy humans as they returned to their meaningless lives, and the monk as he made his way to the Temple. All around, piles of smoke and ash from her downed brethren blew in the wind. For

Jirsa there would be no sympathy for those vanquished — no excuses for their failure.

Suddenly, Jirsa heard an odd noise. She scanned the area to find the source. The grain shed near the entrance of the province. Just as she gripped her blades tight in preparation for battle, Barejis kicked open the door of the shed and stepped out into the sun. Still breathing heavily and smoking from the drops of burning rain, his eyes quickly found the glaring stare of Jirsa. Barejis knew now that Licronus would soon know of his failure. Jirsa glared at him with contempt. Barejis was a mere half breed; worthless for anything more than menial tasks and sacrifice in battle. Jirsa sneered at what she saw as she stood tall and returned her blades to their sheaths. She would soon take delight in relaying her findings to Licronus.

chapter seventeen
Embracing Destiny

It had been several hours since Licronus and his Generals witnessed the arrival of Agean and the others. Licronus and his Generals slashed and cut their way through the thick forest brush and made their way to Napaji Village, a beautiful village of tree dwellings and above ground walkways. The Napajians, with their beautiful brown skin, and brown eyes to match, had handed down the art of tree living from generation to generation. Napajians were taught at an early age that safety was in the trees. As such, the villagers continued to create elaborate dwellings and unique spaces that made it less of a necessity to be on the ground for extended periods. Incredible networks of pathways were made of wood from a specific part of the forest and reinforced with vines and strands of cultivated tree bark. It was truly a sight to behold.

Departure from the trees was rare for the majority of Napajians, the exception being those who had proven themselves brave and skilled enough to have earned the special status of hunter. Hunters were the strongest and smartest of the village. They hunted on the ground for meat, returning to the trees with their bounty. All else could be gotten by others using their exceptional gathering skills in nearby trees. The frequent rainfall had allowed them to develop a duct system that captured fresh rainwater from the forest canopy, to be used for drinking, sanitation and other needs.

Licronus was unimpressed with Napaji. He had seen this place before and knew the hawk would lead the Sitcian there. Licronus had made great effort over the centuries to find the ones called God's Army; the ones bearing the Mark. He knew that one of them lived here. A Hamen Master with blades made to kill Kraylen.

Licronus and his Generals continued to spy on the village when suddenly a loud crack of thunder caught Licronus's attention. Under normal circumstances such an occurrence would mean nothing, however this sound appeared to come from all directions, as if rolling in from the Heavens. Over the thousands of years of imprisonment among the humans, Licronus had become well acquainted with such sounds. He knew the difference between an act of nature and God's handiwork.

"He walks among them… working against us at this very moment," Licronus said as another crack of thunder erupted. "The power of our enemy increases with each passing day. Our time draws near." After a moment of pause, Licronus and his generals refocused their attention on the village in the distance.

The ground was still wet from the recent downpour. Tan and his horse trotted along a muddy Shao-Tan road as he approached a small house just below a series of rice terraces. Just as he reached the path leading to the front door, Tan stopped and stared at the small, modest house and the several pack mules tied to a railing along its side. Memories from his childhood flooded his mind and brought a subtle smile to his face. He dismounted and walked his horse up to the railing with the mules and tied him off. After pausing a moment to take it all in, he slowly approached the front door. He noticed that nothing much had changed in the more than twenty years since he lived in this house. The door, with its familiar scratches and markings, appeared just as he remembered it.

Tan lifted the latch to the door and slowly pushed on it. It creaked loudly as it slowly swung open. Tan walked in to the house, thinking to perhaps surprise his family, but finding no one.

"Hello?" Tan said in his native Mandarin. He slowly walked farther into the house, items he recalled from his youth catching his attention as he scanned the large combined living and dining area. "Hello?" No answer. Tan's attention was caught by the room where he and his sister slept when they were young. He walked over and stared through the doorway, smiling at the memories. Then, suddenly, an uncomfortable feeling came over Tan. Why was no one around? The sudden downpour would surely have forced everyone indoors. Then it occurred to him. The Kraylen. Could they have brought harm to his family?

"Hello?" Tan said louder as he moved quickly to his parents sliding bedroom door. Tan quickly slid open the door and placed his hand on his Bouma. And there, huddled in a corner, was his aging father in a wheeled chair, his elderly mother holding up a kitchen knife in defense, and his younger sister standing strong by her parents' side. Tan was taken totally by surprise, as was his family. For a moment, all stood staring at each other, stunned.

"Tan?" said Tan's mother, speaking in her native Mandarin. "Tan?"

Tan relaxed and smiled. "Mother." He rushed over to his family.

"My son! Oh, my son! Tan!" said Tan's mother happily as they all embraced.

"My boy! God has brought you back to us," Tan's father said as he embraced his son.

Tan's sister asked, "When did you get here?"

"I've only just arrived," Tan replied as he stared at his sister, realizing he hadn't seen her in more than twenty years. "Jie. You are all grown up."

"So are you, big brother," Jie responded.

"Your father and I say she grew up too fast," Tan's mother said. After a pause, they laughed. "We are so happy to see you."

Tan responded, "It is good to be home. But what is happening here? Why the knife?"

"Oh, Tan. Something horrible has happened. Devils came today and started taking some of our people. We did not know what to do. Your father can no longer walk since his accident in the fields so we could not run. We did not want them to take us. They may still be here, Tan," replied Tan's mother.

"No need to worry, Mother. They are gone," Tan said.

Jie asked, "But how do you know?"

Tan revealed to his family the newly received Mark of Hamen upon his neck. "The demons you saw are trying to destroy God's kingdom. This Mark means that He has chosen me as one of His warriors. It will tell me when they are near."

Confused, Tan's father said, "I do not understand, Tan. Why would you be chosen for such an honor?"

"It is not for me to ask why, Father. But what I do

know is that we must defeat them… or all of mankind will suffer." Tan turned to his sister. "Jie, is there still a local tanner here?"

"Yes. Just down the road. He makes shoes and saddles," Jie said. Why?

"Perfect. Jie, I will need you to do something very important, but it is also very dangerous. Will you help me?"

Jie replied, "Of course, Tan."

Tan and Jie turned to their mother and father. Although greatly concerned about what Tan has asked of Jie, they nodded their approval. Tan lovingly held both of his parents' hands. "I promise I will explain more to you soon. But for now we must hurry."

"We can go now if you want," Jie stated.

"Yes." Tan replied as he looked into the eyes of his worried parents. "God will keep us safe. I will tell you all you need to know when we return."

Both of Tan's parents again nodded their approval as Tan and Jie hurried out of the bedroom, leaving their parents both happy and terribly confused.

❧

The Great Foyer would lie in pitch black darkness were it not for the faint glimmer of candles strategically placed along its length. The flickering of the candlelight cast an eeriness upon the swords and statues which stood watch like sentries. The faint yet seemingly ever present sound of chant flowed through like a length of endless fine silk. The combined ambiance contributed to his somber mood as Solis peered through the window near the front door, just as he'd done on so many other nights since Agean's departure. The texture of the handmade glass made it more difficult to see during the night than during the day. Nevertheless, he made his way to the window every evening to stare into the darkness, hoping and silently praying for the young Sitcian's success, while at the same time, worrying that Agean's self-centered ways and vengeful desires would bring a horror the likes of which has never been faced by mankind. As well, Solis wondered what had become of Tan. Had he made it to Shao-Tan? Suddenly, from behind him, a voice filled the air; a deep penetrating voice with which Solis had already become well familiar — the statue of Fitaris.

"Your faith abandons you, Solis," Fitaris says, his statue turning its head towards Solis. Solis is neither surprised nor startled by what he had just heard.

"Fitaris. I was wondering when you might decide to join me here," Solis responded, still staring out into the night. "My faith in God is unwavering. It is Agean who concerns me."

At that moment, Fitaris stepped down from his position and landed on the foyer floor with a loud thud and a large puff of dust. He turned and walked over to Solis.

"Your worries go far beyond Agean, Solis."

"And how do you know this?" Solis asked, turning to face the statue.

"Have you forgotten? I am Sitcian. I have the privilege of knowing many things." Fitaris's statue said.

"Then tell me. Why is it that I stare out of this window every night?"

"Because you fear you have made a terrible choice, Solis."

Solis turned back to the window. "I have already come to terms with that, Fitaris. Agean and I have already spoken on it."

"Not with Agean. It is young Tan you worry so much about." Solis turned back to Fitaris, momentarily pondering his words. "You placed the young monk in grave danger."

Solis snapped back, "I realize that. But I had no choice. I had to do something in case…"

"In case what, Solis?" Fitaris asked.

Solis slowly walked back to the window and stared out into the night. "In case… Agean fails."

"I see." Fitaris raised his Hamen Sword to eye level. He

stared at the Arc-Pen Symbol cast into its handle. "Agean is one of us, Solis. He is one of God's."

Solis, still staring out of the window, said, "I know... I know, but I was unsure of how he might react once he learned the truth." Solis turned and walked over to Fitaris. "Now look at what I've done. I've released an anger in Agean unlike any I have ever seen – and I have risked young Tan's life."

"Solis, what you have done has reached God's heart. You alone took it upon yourself to try and protect His kingdom."

"I fear I may have sent Tan to his doom." said Solis. "With all that I taught him, everything I did to prepare him... What if they have somehow discovered what it is he carries?"

"This insidious evil seeks us out," said Fitaris. "It crawls under rocks and into cracks. It dwells underneath and upon the very crust of all that is good."

Solis's look changed to one of dread. "Tell me, Fitaris. Did Tan encounter the Kraylen?"

"He did, Solis."

Solis immediately turned away, a look of horror set upon his face. "You have the privilege of knowing, Fitaris. Please. Tell me his fate."

"This one was brave beyond measure, Solis. You would

have been proud. He willingly surrendered his life to protect the lives of others." Solis walked slowly back to the window with a look of sadness and peered out, expecting to hear the worst.

"It was the hand of God which vanquished the enemy… and saved the young monk's life," Fitaris told him. Solis's eyes opened wide as he quickly turned back to Fitaris.

"Before God he proved himself worthy," said Fitaris. "Your young monk is now chosen. You have trained a fine Hamen Warrior. He now returns to join the Sitcian and God's army against the Kraylen. The precious item you bestowed upon him is in safe hands." Practically in tears, Solis rejoiced at Fitaris's words.

"There is more. Our young Sitcian's journey has proven difficult. His anger and his quest for vengeance have endangered the lives of the others," Fitaris said. Solis's look of happiness slowly faded to one of concern. "All is not lost, Solis. Our young Sitcian still fights to learn his purpose and to find his way. The balance between anger and destiny within him is shifting. That which threatens to destroy him now strengthens him. His bond with the Credara and his alliance with the Hamen Warriors grows ever stronger. Each day he grows closer to becoming the Sitcian he was born to be. But he will soon be tested by the Kraylen. He will soon be forced to make a choice."

Fitaris turned away from Solis and began to make his way back to his place among the statues.

"Wait! Fitaris! What will happen?" Solis asked with great concern.

"I cannot say how this will turn out, Solis. But know that the holy waters of the Credara have reached a critical level… and the time for Lucifer and our young Sitcian to meet draws near."

Fitaris's statue stepped back into place among the others. Then… silence. Solis stared down the length of the Great Foyer – knowing he could do nothing but await the coming fate of mankind.

❧

After a couple of hours of darkness, a few Napajians were still out tending to the last of their daily chores while most had taken to the safety and comfort of their elevated homes for the night.

"Useless vermin!" Licronus growled. "Because of Him, I've been forced to live for centuries among this human filth."

"It is difficult. Especially knowing that we were once like them," Bralorg said. Suddenly, an angry Licronus turned to Bralorg and back slapped him with tremendous force, lifting him off his feet and sending him crashing into the nearby brush.

"I was never like them!" Licronus declared as he placed his hand on his sword. "First, you question my orders and now you dare part your lips to insult me? Once more and I will tear the tongue from your mouth with my bare hands!" Bralorg sat up, wiped the black blood from his mouth and stared at Licronus.

Poragon asked, "Shall we kill them all?"

"Your desire to spill their blood impresses me, but no. There is no death as long as we have the Angel. However, perhaps now is a good time to strike a blow," said Licronus. Licronus then stood and transformed into a Napajian villager. "Follow me. Be silent." He then crept forward towards the village. Poragon walked over to Bralorg, extended his hand and helped him to his feet. The Generals then transformed themselves into villagers and followed Licronus.

❧

The light of a new day had returned to the Badril Forest. Although Flittorin had watched over them in the night, knowing that the enemy was near made sleeping difficult. The waters of the Credara had become dangerously low, requiring an early start.

Morning routines had already kicked in as Istya readied herself by practicing with all six Priya at once, spinning the Hamen weapons with such great speed that they created an almost invisible protective force around her. Then, instantaneously, all Priya stopped, floating in mid-air as she stood in a defensive Hamen stance. Meanwhile, Agean and Gajir practiced a slow synchronized Tai-Chi style spar. Bored again, Quilin decided to take this opportunity to sneak behind them, planning to once again use his Hamen Whip to snatch Agean's sword. Istya spied Quilin sneaking about, readying his whip. She quickly got that he was up to something and brought the practice to a halt by binging him in the head with a Priya.

Quilin yelled, "Ow! Hey!" Istya smirked as Quilin rubbed his head. "Hitting a man in the head with a... a toy is not playing fair."

Istya walked over and confronted Quilin eye to eye. "A toy?"

"Well, it's certainly no weapon. I mean who couldn't work one of those things?" Quilin asked.

A confident Istya responded, "Oh really? Would you like to try?" Istya offered Quilin a Priya.

Agean, stepped in. "Quilin, I wouldn't if I were you." He then turned to Gajir. "I hear a river to the North. Perhaps there's food." Gajir sensed that Agean needed time to his thoughts to prepare himself for the battle soon to come. He gave Agean a knowing look.

"Take your time, my boy," Gajir told him.

"Time is something we have little of, Gajir," Agean said. "I will be back shortly." Agean headed into the forest.

Quilin continued with Istya. "Come on. Let me have that thing."

Istya handed Quilin a Priya. Quilin took the Priya and set it firmly in his hand. Suddenly Quilin's Mark and the symbol on the Priya began to glow. The Priya instantly transformed to its Hamen form. Quilin slowly and carefully slung the Priya. Istya's eyes widened as the swishing sound of the Priya going wildly out of control resonated. Unable to control the ancient weapon, Quilin was now completely tied head to toe to the tree he had been leaning on. The Priya dangled from his finger. Flittorin, perched on one of the branches of the tree, screeched.

Gajir leaned in for a closer look. "Indeed, my boy."

"Uhmm. Help?" said Quilin. Gajir and Istya looked at each other and burst into laughter. Istya smiled and touched Quilin's face flirtatiously. Their eyes met for a touching moment.

"Something about being tied to a tree kinda ruins the moment, Istya," Quilin mumbled.

"Hmm," said Istya. She immediately went to the back of the tree and began counting.

"What are you doing?" Quilin asked.

Istya said, "I must count the loops."

"Count the loops? Why do you have to count the loops?" Quilin asked.

"Five… six… seven… Because, my dear Quilin, if I get it wrong, instead of releasing you, this toy will cut you and the tree in half," Istya answered.

"Oh," Quilin said, swallowing uncomfortably. Istya walked back around to Quilin. She took hold of the dangling Priya.

"Okay… seven. It was seven, wasn't it?" Istya asked.

Quilin's expression turned to one of great concern. Then suddenly, Istya let go of the Priya and turned to Gajir.

"Where did Agean go?" she asked.

Gajir said, "North, for food. There is a river."

"Oh. I can help with that," Istya said as she moved in closer to Gajir. "As a child, my mother told me of a particularly delicious berry in this forest. I'll be quick." She and Gajir shared a smile as she headed north into the forest.

"Istya!" Quilin yelled, as Istya disappeared. Flittorin screeched.

Quilin's eyes turned to Gajir. "Master?" Gajir gave Quilin a raised eyebrow. Quilin rolled his eyes, knowing to expect no help from him.

The sound of rushing water was a delight to Agean's ears. Fast-moving water fed by the melting snow of the surrounding mountains. A cool freshness floated in the air. Agean took a few minutes to take it all in. The smell rejuvenated his senses. It perhaps meant a bath and fish to eat. He was confident he would fare better with fishing than he did with those wild chickens. If only there was time.

Agean walked along the river's edge, then knelt next to the rushing water to gather his thoughts. He paused to take in his surroundings and then took the Credara from his waist pouch. It glowed colorfully.

Istya trudged through the thick brush, hacking away at it with a blade. A small clearing provided some relief and a moment for her to rest, leaning against a tree. As she wiped the sweat from her brow, a strange feeling came over her. A familiar feeling. Her Hamen senses. She thought back to the ship. Yes. The same feeling when the Kraylen approached from the sky. Suddenly, her Mark began to tingle and glow. No question needed answering. No pondering of choice. Istya focused her senses. She set her hands upon her waist. Five. Five Priya. Then, from out of the trees they appeared. Several Kraylen, armed and ready, approached. Istya's mind immediately went to work. Though she'd never had to before, she knew exactly what to do.

Istya grabbed the five Priya from her waist and tossed all five high into the air. At the same time, the Kraylen rushed to attack from all directions. Istya began running top speed towards the flying Priya, then leapt into the air, taking control of each of them. All five immediately transformed into Hamen Priya once she grabbed hold. Istya then spun, extending all five of the razor sharp Priya into the trees, quickly cutting through several large branches. The branches fell, landing on the attacking Kraylen, knocking them to the ground. Istya landed directly in the middle of the fallen Kraylen, then smirked at them as they shook it off. Now. The battle was on.

The Kraylen all gathered themselves and rushed in. Istya slung her Priya with incredible precision, their blades ripping through Kraylen as they attacked. Istya's remarkable Hamen skills allowed her to avoid the heavy blades of the enemy while keeping them totally off balance until, one by one, they were vanquished from existence. After the last of them exploded into ash and smoke, Istya paused a moment to think. She then raced off back through the trees in the direction of Gajir and Quilin.

Istya moved as quickly as she could through the thick

brush in order to get back to Gajir and Quilin. Retracing her path helped as the brush had already been cut away. Her Hamen senses were aglow as she rushed through the forest.

Istya quickly made her way out of the forest and into the clearing where she found Quilin still bound to the tree. Gajir stood in front of him poised in a Hamen fighting stance, his Hamen Staff in hand. Istya gave Gajir a confused look, wondering why he stood guard with no enemy present. Then, her eyes met Gajir's and with them, he directed Istya's attention upward to the tree canopy. Istya slowly gazed upward, finding a few dozen Kraylen positioned among the high branches, ready to pounce. She looked back at Gajir and then her eyes met Quilin's.

"Istya, get me out of this!" Quilin said.

Knowing there was no time to think, Istya took a deep breath then darted forward, running top speed towards Quilin. The Kraylen launched from the trees as Gajir stepped aside. Istya did an incredible forward flip, grabbing mid-air the Priya that bound Quilin to the tree. The Priya instantly became Hamen and released Quilin. All three Hamen Warriors then went to work vanquishing Kraylen. Gajir's skillful spinning of his Hamen Staff enabled him to vanquish Kraylen on the ground and in the air without missing a beat. Flittorin activated his Hamen

Talons, navigated through the trees, and began tearing through Kraylen, mid-flight, as a full-on battle ensued.

Having found the perfect spot along the river's shoreline, Agean delicately set the Credara on a stone at the water's edge. Agean stared at it as the vivid colors danced off the ripples of the water. Then, in his head, he heard snippets of Master Naji's voice. "The Hall of Souls will empty. The Credara is the key." Agean's face frowned and his eyes closed tight as Master Naji's voice changed to those of his mother and sister, screaming in agony. This new nightmare, enhanced by what Solis revealed, burned even hotter in his head. He could see his father's face now. His look of terror as Licronus crushed his throat and rammed a blade into him. He could see his mother and sister's faces as they darkened from the burning flames that consumed them. Just as Agean hit the breaking point, taking all he could bear, the imagery in his mind changed. Suddenly there was darkness; a deep penetrating darkness, followed by a thick grey gloom. Agean's brow furrowed as he tried to understand what was happening. At first, glints of eerie swirling light followed bursts of foggy clarity; clarity which singed Agean's senses with even brighter light. Then, the fog settled low and made way for a vision which Agean had never before seen. A rotating sphere of fiery white light suspended beneath him. As he looked down on it, the long beams of the hot light rose up and pierced his skin. Despite the pain, he hovered above, unable to escape. The more the light burned through him, the more it revealed. Agean struggled to escape the vision's grip — shake loose of its hold. Then, they were there. Three strange dark figures standing in the fog reaching up to the blazing sphere. He could not make out who they were or why they were there. Thin white streams of smoke rose from their bony fingertips and were being sucked directly into the center of the sphere from below, feeding it evil, giving it energy. Just as it seemed as if the light would blow Agean's mind apart, he quickly snatched open his eyes. Breathing heavily, his brow glistening with sweat, Agean then noticed the Follower had again appeared in the distance across the river, sitting upright upon his horse, watching him. Agean's Mark and the symbol on the Credara began to tingle and glow. Suddenly the sound of a war axe flipping through the air cut through the sound of the rushing river. Agean immediately leapt and spun while drawing his sword and smashed the axe in half, the two parts splashing into the river. Agean landed in a kneeling Hamen fighting position, focused and ready for battle.

"Thinking about your family, Agean?" Agean swung

around and spotted three Kraylen standing in the distance. Then he saw it. That moment he had longed for had finally come. It was him. Seeing the missing hand, Agean realized he had finally come face to face with Licronus. His anger began to rise. A focused, piercing anger that invaded the very core of his being.

"Licronus!" Agean yelled. Licronus and his Generals began to move in closer to Agean.

Licronus said to him, "Very good, Agean. But I see your Hamen senses are a little slow. Perhaps it's because you are still tormented by what I did to your father. You know, Agean, I believe I can still taste his blood on my fingers." Licronus held up his one hand and admired his fingers. Agean's anger visibly welled up within him. Flashes of the murder scene, once again, filled his mind. The Follower across the river disappeared.

Licronus continued, "And have you met my friends? I'm sure you recognize them. Think back to that day, Agean. They were kind enough to set fire to your mother and sister."

Agean's anger began to escalate. Beads of sweat began to form upon his brow as he drew his second Hamen Sword.

He yelled, "Licronus! You and your murdering demons will die for what you have done!"

"You are no Sitcian!" Licronus replied. "You are a fool! And every man, woman and child of God will suffer because of it! Besides, you are outnumbered… Priest."

Swords out front, Agean rushed up the shoreline to the Kraylen Generals and began the battle. Agean's anger was apparent in his flailing moves as he attempted to vanquish the Kraylen Generals, slashing and turning from one to the other, barely blocking Kraylen blows and showing little of the masterful skill of a Hamen Warrior. Agean's blade, nevertheless, made contact with the Kraylen. It slashed and pierced their flesh, yet they remained unvanquished, able to continue fighting.

After a few moments of battling, Agean realized what was happening, but it was too late. Poragon made an incredible move, spinning in the air, his sword slashing diagonally across Agean's body. What little control Agean had of his Hamen skills enabled him to rear back as the razor-sharp blade of Poragon's sword passed within an inch of Agean's chest and stomach. While Agean felt the breeze explode against him as the sword tore through the air and his clothing, his Hamen moves were enough to avoid the fatal intent of the Kraylen's blade, which produced a slash in Agean's garb, just at the waist. No consequence. While Agean's move succeeded in saving his life from Poragon's death blow, it was not enough to prevent Bralorg from landing a kick to Agean's head, sending him tumbling backwards onto the ground, bleeding from his mouth. The Kraylen Generals then simultaneously released a weapon consisting of curved steel hooks at the end of a thin wire. The weapons wrapped and captured Agean's wrists, and the Generals pulled them taut in preparation to tear him apart. Stunned and bleeding from his nose and mouth, Agean struggled to get loose. Then, he looked up to find Licronus removing the Credara from the stone where he had placed it.

"You and your so-called 'warriors' have done an admirable job against our half breeds, Priest. In fact, they are probably slaying a dozen or so of them as we speak. But you do not fare so well against the true enemies of God," Licronus said as he moved in close, face to face with Agean, so close Agean could feel the steam coming from Licronus's breath, which reeked of death. "We are the true angels of Heaven." Agean panted heavily, sweating, trying to catch his breath. "For thousands of years I have searched for a way to defeat your God. The wait has been too long." Licronus held up the Credara, admiring it. "Kill him!" he ordered.

The Kraylen Generals began to pull with great force. Swords still in hand, Agean's Mark and the Symbol on them began to glow brightly. Bearing the pain, Agean slowly raised his head and stared directly into Licronus's eyes. Master Naji had always told Agean that there, in the eyes, was where one truly discovers one's enemy. As Agean looked deeper into Licronus, what he found was even more horrible than he had expected. So much so that it burned, forcing Agean to look away. When he looked up again, his eyes found the Follower, sitting atop his horse on a nearby hill, staring at him. As the Kraylen Generals began pulling with greater force, the thin wire began forcing its way into Agean's skin. Struggling against the searing pain, Agean heard his beloved Master's words: "When you look within him, then you will know you are the warrior you are destined to be." Agean then turned his eyes back to Licronus.

"You are wrong, Licronus! I am Sitcian!" Agean yelled.

In a remarkable move, struggling against the strength of the two Kraylen, veins bulging in his neck and forehead, Agean forced himself to his feet. Then, with every ounce of strength within him, he spun both of his swords. Their blades sparked as they cut through the wires. The Kraylen Generals stumbled backwards. He then spun into a Hamen fighting stance. Just as the Generals recovered, Gajir and the others appeared out of the forest. Flittorin screeched as they all ran to Agean's aid.

Quilin yelled, "Agean!" The Kraylen Generals assumed a fighting stance in preparation for battle.

Licronus said quickly, "No! Another time. But soon, Priest."

Licronus and the Kraylen Generals unfurled their wings and flew off into the distance, high above the forest canopy. Agean dropped to his knees as Gajir and the others made their way to him.

"Agean, are you all right?" asked Istya.

Agean, struggling and breathing heavily, said, "Licronus. He has the Credara."

Shocked, Istya responded, "The Credara? Agean, how?"

"Solis tried to tell me. Licronus used my anger against me. I failed," Agean explained. Gajir and Quilin helped him to his feet.

Gajir told him, "Not failure, Agean. A lesson. I assure you, you will get another chance."

"Gajir. I looked into his eyes. His evil was unlike anything I've ever known… it is pure," Agean said. "I sought out his heart and there was none; only a swirling pit of darkness and hatred. But even more, Gajir… I saw myself. I saw my own hatred within him. It gave him strength. That's when I knew… I cannot let him do this evil he seeks to do."

Gajir smiled proudly at what he was hearing. "Alas. A Sitcian now knows. A Sitcian… now understands."

Quilin said, "Well we must go after him!"

"No! Licronus called me a fool and he was right," Agean explained. "Until now I have been led by my anger, and I have put your lives at risk. For this I ask your forgiveness. Now Licronus has the Credara. We are only five. God's Army requires a sixth Hamen Warrior if we are to defeat the Kraylen. If we go after Licronus now, we will not be complete. I will not allow him to distract me again."

Gajir said, "Flittorin leads us to the Napaji Village."

"Then there we must go. We must try and make it there before the Kraylen do," said Agean, grimacing as he dabbed his bloody nose and lip with a cloth.

Quilin, concerned, asked, "But what about the Credara?"

"Licronus has a key but can do nothing with it before it is time," Gajir explained.

Istya said, "And we still have time. Trust me. But we must go now."

"Wait! Licronus mentioned something else. Half breeds," Agean said.

Gajir asked, "Half breeds?"

"The Kraylen we have confronted thus far have been half breeds. I believe he speaks of the Kraylen born of human breeding."

"The true Kraylen are the original demons cast out

from heaven. They will be stronger. Harder to kill," Gajir said.

"Yes, as I have just discovered. But Master Naji shared something with me. He spoke of the evil greater than the others. Perhaps this is what he meant. He said we must take off its head, or expose its heart."

Gajir said with confidence, "Then so it is fellow warriors. We must take their heads or we open their chests."

"But which are the true Kraylen?" Istya asked.

Agean responded, "You will know only in battle, Istya." Agean turned and took one last look at the hilltop where he last saw the Follower.

"What is it, Agean?" Gajir asked.

"Nothing, Gajir. It is nothing," Agean replied. Agean and the others then rushed back into the forest.

chapter eighteen
The True Face of Evil

The forest brush was heavy as Agean and the others slashed and hacked their way through the thicket. Flittorin flew from tree to tree, leading their path. Gajir knew that the closer they got to Napaji, the thicker the brush would become. The Napajians preferred it that way. It had proven to be an additional layer of protection from would-be intruders. Riding the horses through such thick brush would risk the possibility of a fall or a leg break. It was a risk they could not take so they walked them carefully, holding tight to their reins.

After hours of following Flittorin's lead and cutting through thick brush, Agean looked up and saw before him the Napaji Village. A stunning sight to behold.

"Napaji," Gajir said. "We must hurry! Look there!" All eyes turned to the hacked-away brush nearby. "I fear they may already have visitors." They all quickly proceeded to the village.

Agean and the others walked their horses into the village. Not a single Napajian was in sight. Gajir's senses told him that something was terribly wrong. He visually scanned the tree village and saw nothing - no one. This was not right.

Gajir told the others, "Wait!" They all stopped. Gajir released the reins of his horse and moved forward. "Something is wrong."

Gajir took a few more steps forward when suddenly a flurry of both spears and arrows descended upon him. But instead of causing harm, they crisscrossed, forming themselves into a perfectly square prison cage around him. Gajir was taken by surprise and spun within the cage, looking for a way out. Agean, Quilin and Istya immediately took a defensive stance around Gajir's prison to protect him. Gajir struggled and soon realized he was trapped. Flittorin activated his Hamen Talons and took a position atop the cage.

Istya called out, "Master Gajir!"

Then a voice came from the trees. "What is it you want here?"

They looked up to the pathways above, and found that dozens of warriors brandishing spears and drawn bows had appeared and were now poised to attack. Nafar, a strong, muscular black man in his thirties, stood forward on one of the paths dressed for the hunt.

The Napajian hunting garb was dark in color for hiding in the thicket, and lightweight for quickness and agility among the trees and the thick brush. It was made of specially treated animal skin to protect against the barbs and thorns of the many poisonous plants, as well as the bites and stings of poisonous creatures. Nafar wore it well. He also carried with him two sharp double-bladed axes with finely carved wooden handles. Instead of at his waist, their handles slid into a sheath harness strapped to the rear of his body, their blades rising from behind at angles just above his shoulders for quick and easy access.

Gajir yelled out, "I demand to be released!"

Nafar responded, "Gajir, is that you?"

"Get me out of here, Nafar!" Gajir yelled.

Nafar asked, "How do I know it is truly you… and not a Kraylen trick?"

"Trust your Hamen senses, Man! What does your Mark tell you?" Nafar paused to give thought to Gajir's words and then began making his way cautiously down to Gajir. He moved aside some of the garb around his neck to reveal his Mark of Hamen as he approached Agean.

"May I?" Nafar asked. Seeing the Mark, Agean and the others lowered their weapons and allowed Nafar to approach. Agean noticed that Nafar's hunting garb was stained with blood. Nafar peered through the cage at Gajir. "It is good to see you, my friend."

Gajir replied, "And you, Nafar." Nafar plucked a single

arrow from its position, causing the entire cage to quickly collapse, sending Flittorin into the air. They embraced. Suddenly, Agean's Hamen senses began to tingle. He looked around, searching for signs of Kraylen in the area. Istya and Quilin sensed the same and began scanning also.

After a moment, Nafar's attention turned to the others. "Well, I see that I am among God's warriors. I am Nafar, leader of Napaji. Welcome."

Quilin replied, "I am Quilin, Nafar. And this is Istya."

"Thank you, Nafar," said Istya, bowing respectfully. Nafar returned the bow.

"Istya. What a beautiful name. It is Napajian. It means Heaven Star," said Nafar.

Istya replied, "Yes. My mother told me when I was very young." Nafar smiled then noticed Istya's Hamen weapons.

"Ah. The Priya. My people have a long history with this weapon, we being hunters from the trees. I pray it serves you well." Istya bowed her head in acceptance of Nafar's words. Nafar then crossed to Agean. "And you. You must be the Sitcian. Your Mark is exquisite."

Agean replied, bowing respectfully, "I am Agean, Master Nafar."

"Master Agean, it is good to have you here. I ask that you all please forgive the less than friendly welcome from me and my people. It is unfortunately the result of something I must share with great sadness. We were visited by the enemy." Agean reacted with great concern.

"As we feared. The Kraylen. We are too late," Agean said.

"Please do not burden yourself with blame, Agean. I was taught at a young age that there is no limit to their evil.

They chose to prove that here in Napaji."

Gajir stepped closer to Nafar and said, "We are truly sorry, Nafar… for your people… for any lives that were lost."

Nafar responded, "Oddly enough, my friend. Death has paid us no visit for some time now." Gajir gave Nafar a confused look.

Many more Napajians began to appear on the paths to see who had come to their village. Agean sensed the fear that hung in the air. Something horrible had happened here.

Nafar directed Agean and the others to an above ground landing, which led directly to the front of a tree hut. Flittorin perched on a rail next to its entrance. Nafar stopped and looked at Agean and the others.

Agean said, "Nafar. I am not certain, but my senses tell me-"

Nafar interrupted, "We are not alone. Yes, I have sensed it myself."

"I believe we all have," said Gajir.

Agean told Nafar, "We can fan out... draw them from their hiding place."

"That will not be necessary, my friend. I believe I know exactly where they are," Nafar said. Agean nodded his approval. Nafar then stepped past Agean and the others and crossed over to the railing. He peered out into the trees. He knew that when the Kraylen realized they had been discovered, they would immediately try to make their escape. He scanned. Then, he locked onto his target — two winged Kraylen spies hiding in the thick cover of a tree not too far away. Nafar stared at them for a couple of seconds.

Then suddenly, they took to the air. Nafar immediately reached and snatched the two axes from his back, flipping them in the air so that their handles landed perfectly in his hands. The axes simultaneously transformed into magnificent silver axes, each with large rounded razor sharp double blades and bearing the Arc-Pen Symbol. Axes of Hamen. Using his great strength, Nafar hurled both into the air. The glistening axes whirled towards their targets with lightning speed and with deadly accuracy. They tore through the two Kraylen, exploding them into black clouds of ash and smoke in the air. The crowd of Napajians watching reacted to both the frightening creatures, and the amazing skill of their leader in destroying them.

The axes whirled around and returned directly back to Nafar's hands.

Quilin, quite impressed, said, "Well. That should certainly make one feel a bit better."

Nafar turned to Quilin. "I did not do it for myself, Quilin. I did it for them." Nafar looked around at his people, feeling sadness for them, seeing the fear in their eyes, feeling as if he had let them down. "Nothing like this has ever come upon my people. I fear that I have failed them." Nafar looked at Agean and the others and then returned his axes to their sheaths. "Please. Prepare yourselves." Nafar walked over and moved aside a draping which covered the hut's entryway.

Agean and the others entered to a truly horrific sight. Sounds of agony and pain filled the air. The Kraylen demons had hacked away at several horribly injured villagers. Gaping wounds, limbs partially severed, some fully. Blood was everywhere. They suffered terribly as several men and women tried to tend their wounds with ancient and traditional medicines: salves made from ground leaves, seeds and roots from specific plants; mixtures of certain berries, poisonous to eat, but effective for treating wounds and infection.

Istya covered her mouth in horror, turned and exited the hut. Agean, Gajir and Quilin just stood staring, stunned and saddened. Nafar walked over to a young girl who looked to be about five years of age. She suffered from what would otherwise be a fatal neck wound. He looked at her, saddened, and held her hand.

"I promised my sister before she died that I would look after her," Nafar said with a tear running down his cheek.

Gajir responded sadly, "Nafar."

Agean's eyes met the young girl's. Her sad, glassy eyes stared at him as she shivered and swallowed, trying to bear the pain. Nafar kissed the girl's hand, stroked her hair and then turned to exit the hut, followed by Quilin and Gajir. Agean lagged behind, still staring into the girl's eyes. She strained to lift the fingers on her little hand in an attempt to reach out to Agean, but she could not. She was too weak. The pain was too great. Agean paused in sadness. Then slowly his sadness began to turn to purposefulness and determination. He reached out and lightly touched the little girl's finger, and then turned and followed the others out of the hut.

Istya was standing at the railing of the landing, staring

out at the people of the village, feeling for them. Dark clouds in the sky began to swirl as drops of rain began pelting Istya's frozen expression of shock and sadness. As the others exited the hut, Quilin walked over to her and placed his hand on her shoulder.

"Are you all right, Istya?" Quilin asked. Quilin's touch seemed to calm her sadness. She reached up and held on to his hand for a moment.

"How could this happen? What creature could do such a thing to an innocent child?" Istya asked.

Gajir stepped forward. "Istya. When you defeated these demons earlier, it was because it was your born destiny to do so. Your Hamen training, instincts, and senses took hold and everything within you told you that this enemy must be destroyed. Now, for the first time, you know why."

Istya responded in anger, "This is not just an enemy, this is Lucifer himself!"

Agean stepped in, "No Istya. They are not him. But know that they are his. Remember what you said?... About the swiftness of my blade?" Agean turned Istya around and plucked one of the Priya from her waist. "The swiftness of your Priya can save mankind." Istya looked at Agean with appreciation for his newly found wisdom as she took the Priya from him.

"They know we are running out of time," Gajir said.

"Licronus must have known we were coming here." He turned to Nafar. "I fear what would have happened if they had found you, my friend."

Nafar responded, "If only they had, Gajir. Perhaps none of this would've happened. I and a few others were out hunting. I was told they came in disguise. The blood you see upon me is not from the hunt. It is from the injured. I helped carry them to this hut."

"I am so sorry, Nafar. But... their injuries..." Istya said.

Nafar interrupts, "Yes, Istya. They should be dead. We are hearing from other lands that no one is dying, not the sick, the old, not even precious children. It is like some sort of curse has been placed upon the earth."

Agean stepped forward amid the confused looks. "It is the Kraylen. They have taken the Angel of Death."

Gajir, reacting with shock, said, "The Angel? Agean! How long have you known this?"

"The Great Court was the first to fear this could be. I was told to tell no one of their suspicions until I could confirm it... until I was absolutely sure."

"Not even us?" Quilin asked.

Agean moved closer to Quilin. "When everything about my family came to light, I lost something I thought I would never get back, Quilin — trust. But you... all of you... have given it back to me. Now I know I can trust again. I also know now that Licronus is using the Great Angel to empty the Hall of Souls, and is the cause of Master Naji's suffering."

Gajir said, "This is why you sought to delay the battle we stumbled upon days back."

"I dare not think of it, Gajir. The horror was only a possibility then. Now it is real. I did not do enough to stop them."

"The pride of Kings, Agean, is a shield not easily penetrated." Although Agean knew that what Gajir said was true, it did little to wash away his feelings of failure.

"So the Hall of Souls is emptying… because no one is dying," said Quilin.

"God's greatest gift is being used against us," said Agean. "Life is what every human wants. By capturing the Great Angel-"

"Life has being redefined," Gajir interrupts. "…to mean endless suffering — and if we are not successful, it will become that which released Lucifer from Hell. Both ingenious and sinister."

Gajir turns to Agean. "And Master Naji suffers?"

"He cannot make his transition to Heaven, Gajir. He suffers and will forever if we do not find the Angel," Agean said.

Gajir said, "I see. Then you not only wish to honor him, you wish to help him."

"I know now, Gajir, that what we must do is stop Licronus, and save the Angel. Not just for Master Naji, but for mankind," Agean said. Gajir gave Agean a confirming look.

Nafar said, "One thing is sure. Find Licronus, and you will find the Angel."

"Then we must hurry. Nafar, I know that your people need you…" Agean said.

In the midst of what had now become a downpour, Nafar drew his axes from his back, instantaneously transforming them into Axes of Hamen.

He moved in, face to face, with Agean. "Master Agean. In many ways you and I are the same. We are now unable to escape our destiny, our purpose. We are forever tied together by these Marks… by God… and now by people we love. You are the Sitcian, Leader of God's Army. Lead us into battle and I, Master Agean, will fight, and die if I must, beside you."

Nafar knelt before Agean.

Flittorin landed on Quilin's arm and screeched as Quilin drew his Hamen Whip and moved in closer.

Quilin said, "As will we. I guess you really are everything you are supposed to be after all." Quilin knelt.

Istya moved in and drew a Hamen Priya in each hand, knelt and said, "As will I, Master Agean."

Gajir with his Hamen Staff moved closer and said, "You have my life as well, Master Agean." Gajir then knelt with the rest. Agean, with a strong sense of purpose, drew the Swords of Hamen from their sheaths. He placed them both in one hand, holding them by their blades just below their crossguards, and raised them to the sky. As he aimed the pummels of the swords to the heavens, Agean knelt before the others.

"I pledge to each of you… my life to this task which God has set forth. It is an honor to serve God with you. God's Army is now complete!" Agean declared.

Suddenly, the symbols on all Hamen weapons, and the Marks upon the necks of the Hamen Warriors began to glow. The dark rain clouds swarmed in the sky amidst swirling winds and bright flashes of lightning. The people of Napaji began cheering in response to what they had witnessed.

†

PART SIX
Good Versus Evil

chapter nineteen
A War of Angels and Demons

By now the rain had ceased and the forest had become less dense as Agean and the others rode fast and strong. Flittorin led the way in the air, while Agean led the way on the ground. They rode with confidence, pride and determination. They were God's Army.

They wound their way through the trees, leaping over fallen timber as they thundered forth. When they finally reached the edge of the forest, Agean raised his hand and yelled out, "Wait!" They all brought their horses to a fast halt.

"Agean, what is it?" Istya asked.

Agean directed everyone's attention to the landscape ahead. "There! Kimirin!"

In the distance, rising from the earth, The Arc-Pen Symbol; formed from the rock at the very top of the Kimirin Mountain crest.

"The Hall of Souls. Lucifer's Lair," Gajir said.

Agean said, "The Kraylen will know this as well. Licronus knows to seek the Arc-Pen Symbol."

"Then he will surely be waiting for us," said Quilin. Gajir looked to the distant sky in the direction of Kimirin and saw a winged Kraylen soaring.

Gajir said, "They already know we are here. And remember, there will be plenty of true Kraylen among them."

"My Hamen Axes will consider them all true Kraylen," said Nafar.

"Then what say you, Master Agean?" Istya asked.

Agean took a moment and then spoke with leadership. "Prepare yourselves for battle! Today we finish this fight for God and mankind! Let us go forth and crush Licronus and his Kraylen into the dirt! God is with us!" Agean and the others charged full gallop towards Kimirin.

Kimirin was a small village of indigenous people who lived off the land, cultivating their crops and raising their herds along the hillside. The beauty and fertility of the mountainside had brought their ancestors to this land and it had remained this way for thousands of years. However, it was dusk; and while one would expect the villagers to be returning in from the fields, hundreds of them appeared to be still working. Meanwhile, Hamen Marks began glowing and tingling as Agean and the others approached. They slowed to a stop.

"The village is abandoned, yet the fields are full of workers," Quilin said.

Gajir responded, "Yes. Very strange, especially since darkness comes quickly. It is almost as if we are being invited in."

"Well then, let us not keep them waiting," Nafar said.

Agean and the others started their horses at a gradual pace in order to inspect their surroundings. Slowly they moved forward, deeper into what appeared to be a deserted village. Suddenly all Marks began glowing and tingling with even more intensity.

Agean ordered everyone, "Prepare yourselves. No one and no thing is to be trusted."

They each placed a hand on their weapons as they moved deeper into the village and then stopped. They all dismounted and tied off to a nearby railing and then walked carefully along the road. Flittorin circled above.

Suddenly, Licronus appeared on a rooftop in his human form. "Friends! Welcome to our little village."

Agean called out, "Licronus! You will find no friends here!"

"Ah. The Sitcian. So good of you to come. Some of our villagers are very anxious to meet you."

Agean and the others turned to find a few dozen or so villagers approaching from behind. But all was not as it seemed. Suddenly the villagers transformed into winged Kraylen and took to the air. Soaring above with his pendant glowing, Flittorin's talons rang out as they trans-formed to Hamen weapons. The Kraylen swooped in and attacked with an assortment of swords and other weapons. Agean and the others immediately went into battle mode, utilizing their Weapons of Hamen with precision and skill to convert the Kraylen quite efficiently to black ash and smoke. Just as the last couple was being vanquished, hun-dreds of Kraylen, armed to the teeth, began approaching from every direction, on foot and by air. It turned out that the fields filled with villagers were nothing more than a staging area for the Kraylen menace; a place to lie in wait until Agean and the others were deep within the village. Now the fields were emptying as the enemy took their Kraylen form and began to converge. Agean and the oth-ers formed a circle of defense.

"Agean, this is not looking good!" Quilin yelled.

Istya looked up and found that Licronus was no longer on the rooftop. "Agean! Licronus is gone!" Agean and the others looked to see that Licronus had indeed vanished.

While Agean and the others had their hands full, Licronus, Poragon and Bralorg made their way to the Ki-mirin mountainside. They now stood facing the moun-tain with Death's coffin and the chest containing his robe and Scytheren.

Licronus reached out to Poragon, "It is time." Poragon

removed the Credara from his waist pouch and handed it to Licronus. Licronus held it up, observed that the waters had all but completely vanished, then walked the Credara closer to the mountainside and set it on the ground. He then stepped back to his Generals. Suddenly, the Credara lit brightly. A steady beam of light shot from it to the Arc-Pen Symbol at the peak of the mountain. The symbol began to glow brightly in the night sky. Then suddenly a lighted entrance magically formed in the solid rock of the mountainside.

Licronus gave an evil look of satisfaction. "Our time has come. Bring him!" The Kraylen Generals quickly gathered up the coffin and chest while Licronus retrieved the Credara. They began making their way towards the entrance.

Agean and the others tightened their circle of defense as the Kraylen got closer. All Marks were aglow as the Hamen Warriors prepared for the first sign of an all-out attack. Flittorin screeched and circled above, waiting to pounce.

Gajir called out to the others, "We must get to the Lair and find Licronus!"

"Something tells me they have a different plan for us," Quilin said. Istya, standing next to Agean, reached into her waist pouch and removed the unexpected. A Credara.

The Arc-Pen Symbol on the Credara was glowing as she turned to Agean.

"Agean!" Istya said. The look of total shock on Agean's face replaced that of extreme focus as she handed him the heavenly urn. "A Credara? Istya, where did you-"

"My father!" Istya said. "Hurry, I'll explain later." The symbol on the Credara began to glow brighter as Agean, still in shock, held it to the sky.

Agean called out, "Credara! Summon the Sitcians!" Suddenly the Credara itself began to glow brightly. A large mass of white clouds formed in the moonlit sky as lightning struck. Then, from the heavens, a stream of smoke formed, quickly winding its way down to Agean and the others.

Seeing this, the Kraylen attacked full force, yelling as they charged into battle. Before they could fully engage Agean and the others, the stream of smoke from the heavens arrived as a torrent of Sitcian Angels led by Archangel Michael. Heaven's warriors immediately went into battle on both ground and air against their age-old enemy. Agean and the others were in total awe as the Sitcians began fighting off the Kraylen with unbridled Hamen skill. Flittorin joined the battle by tearing through and vanquishing Kraylen after Kraylen as they took to the air.

Istya had put on a masterful display of Hamen skill

by single-handedly slaughtering several Kraylen in succession, when suddenly something caught her eye. She spotted the Arc-Pen Symbol aglow atop Kimirin Mountain.

"Agean! Look!" she yelled.

Agean slayed another Kraylen and then turned towards Kimirin Mountain. He paused to gaze for a split-second, then immediately refocused.

"Licronus!" Agean yelled. Agean and the others continued battling while fighting their way towards the Kimirin mountainside.

Having finally fought their way out of the main battle, Agean and the others approached Kimirin Mountain in search of Licronus and his Generals.

Istya spotted the illuminated entrance in the side of the mountain. "Look, there it is!"

At that very moment, several more Kraylen attacked and the fight continued. The Hamen Warriors were continuing to destroy the Kraylen with great precision, when suddenly the unthinkable occurred. Several Kraylen at once overwhelmed Gajir. One of their blades found its mark in his stomach. He doubled over as the blade penetrated. Istya, seeing this, rushed over and vanquished all four Kraylen in one spectacular move.

Agean saw this and rushed over to Gajir. "Master Gajir!"

Gajir, winced in pain. "I'm okay, Agean! This old man

is tougher than they think!" Agean and Gajir's talk was cut short as they all were immediately forced back into battle. They quickly killed off the remaining Kraylen in the area.

"We must hurry!" Agean yelled. They all headed for the opening and entered Kimirin Mountain.

Having no idea what to expect, Agean and the others found themselves standing in a dimly lit cavern inside the mountain. Eternal torches mounted to the rock walls provided what little light there was. At the far end of the cavern was a tunnel. But before they could make a move, several Kraylen entered from outside. Nafar turned and drew his axes, transforming them to their Hamen form. Holding each axe at the end of its handle, he pointed both towards the ground. With a quick turn of his wrist, the end caps of each Hamen Axe disconnected, revealing a connecting length of silver braided rope, allowing his axes to drop six inches. Nafar then began whirling his Hamen Axes with such great speed that the Kraylen found themselves defenseless against a weapon they could barely see. Nafar and his Hamen Axes made quick work of them.

"We should move quickly. More of them will come… many more," Nafar said.

Agean turned to Flittorin. "Flittorin! Lead us!" Flittorin screeched and headed through the tunnel at the far end of the cavern. Everyone quickly followed. Eternal torches along its walls also lit the tunnel. After a brief passage, the tunnel ended at the entrance of a magnificent chamber never before seen by man: the Hall of Souls.

Slowly Agean and the others entered. The chamber was a place beyond description, and what they saw amazed them.

"The Hall of Souls," Gajir said. They spread out within the Hall Chamber, mesmerized by everything in sight.

The spectacular chamber was filled with ornate eternal torches casting light upon beautiful crystal and rock formations. The formations were shaped to guide and contain pearls of light flowing in like a waterfall from the highest point at the very center of the chamber.

Nafar marveled at the stream. "God's gift. Life."

Gajir added, "The souls of man."

In a giant pool, souls in the form of tiny illuminated pearls swirled in a huge, silent whirlpool. Gajir noticed that the walls of the pool were much higher than the level of the swirling pearls. "The level is dangerously low and getting lower. Time is running short!"

From the pool, the illuminated pearls flowed through channels made of precious stone into several openings in the chamber walls. Agean noticed that two of the channels led to either side of a stone work of art on one of the far walls: the channel on the left flowing out; the channel on the right flowing back into the chamber and into the giant pool.

Quilin and Agean approached the stone work of art which depicted the Arc-Pen Symbol and five faceless warriors sitting on five thrones, with three Credaras before them. The middle throne was the most ornate of the five. Just above the head of the middle faceless warrior was an indentation shaped exactly like a Credara with wings. They both delicately touched the stone as Agean pondered the flow of souls at its base. Then Agean figured it out.

Loudly, he said to the others, "This must be it, the way in! These two channels must be the flow of souls that binds Lucifer!"

Suddenly, the sound of Kraylen coming through the tunnel alerted everyone.

"Agean, we need to hurry!" Istya yelled. Agean quickly ran over to Nafar, Gajir and Istya.

"Nafar. Can you hold them off?" Agean asked. Nafar drew his axes. The blades glistened in the light of the torches and souls.

"We will hold them off, Agean," Nafar told him.

Agean looked at the blood stain on Gajir's garb and then touched his shoulder.

Gajir said to him, "I will be fine, my boy."

Agean gave Gajir a hopeful look and then quickly

made his way back to the stone painting. His eyes met Quilin's.

"Be careful, my friend," Quilin said to him.

Agean placed a hand on Quilin's shoulder and replied, "I will... my friend."

"Agean!" Gajir yelled. Agean turned to Gajir. "Find Licronus and stop him!"

"I swear to you I will!" Agean yelled back. Gajir gave him a proud look. Agean briefly touched the three Credaras on the painting.

"Three," Agean said to himself. He then removed the Credara from his waist pouch and placed it into the indentation in the stone painting. Suddenly, the stone painting slowly swung open, revealing a secret entrance. Agean removed the Credara, quickly looked back at the others and then reached for an eternal torch from a set of three torch holders on the wall next to the painting. He noticed that one torch was missing. Licronus. He looked at Quilin and then quickly grabbed one of the two remaining torches and darted into the passageway. At that moment, the Hall of Souls began filling with Kraylen, and the battle continued.

With torch in hand, Agean moved quickly through the passageway, taking great care to avoid the flow of souls coursing through the two channels running along the path - until it ended at a huge closed entrance.

The circular stone entrance had no handles. Four odd raised markings adorned the stone entrance near its outer edges. Agean had not seen these markings before and could make no sense of them. In the center, just as with the stone painting in the Hall of Souls, was an indentation in the shape of the Credara. Agean took only a brief moment to stare at the entrance and then removed the Credara from his waist pouch. He carefully placed the Credara within the indentation. Suddenly, the four odd markings moved, rotating and shifting until they reached a certain position, then stopped. Agean still could make no sense of the markings. He then removed the Credara. Suddenly, the entire stone entrance separated into four sections, each containing one of the markings, all rotating and shifting at once, until the markings came together to form a giant Arc-Pen symbol. Once complete, all four sections of the stone entrance separated and receded into the rock, revealing another huge chamber within Kimirin Mountain. A blast of hot air blew past Agean as he stared into the Lair Chamber. Lucifer's Lair Chamber.

chapter twenty
The Battle for the Lair

Agean poked his head into the Lair Chamber entrance and scanned the area for Kraylen. Then, he returned the Credara to his waist pouch and cautiously entered. The Lair Chamber was massive. Its entrance, where Agean stood, was a good distance from the entrance of the Lair itself. Eternal torches lit the chamber. The walls of the chamber were comprised of dark rock that looked as if it had been burned by the fires of Hell. The path leading out to the Lair Entrance was smooth and polished rock with an endless drop-off on both sides. At the end of the path, set into the floor, was the frighteningly intimidating Lair Entrance itself. It was huge and round.

The smooth path which led to it encircled the Lair Entrance, forming a wide border around it with an endless drop-off on all sides. Four huge stone pillars carved with symbols flanked the Lair Entrance. The two thick stone halves of the entrance were met in the center by a metal disk formed to fit the base of the Credara, and crested with the Arc-Pen Symbol.

From an opening in the wall on the left side of the Lair

Chamber entrance, a channel containing the flow of souls ran up the center of the smooth path and created a narrow moat between the path and the circular Lair Entrance, as if containing the Lair Entrance within its grasp. After fully encircling the Lair Entrance, the channel flow returned back down the center of the smooth path and out via an opening in the wall on the Lair Chamber entrance's right side. It gave the appearance of blood coursing through a vein. Also to the left and right of the Lair Chamber entrance were walking paths leading to two stone thrones on each side. A rock staircase to the left of the entrance led to a center throne which sat just above the Lair Chamber entrance. This throne bore the Sitcian Mark of Hamen.

As Agean entered, he saw Licronus standing atop the Lair Entrance near the center disk, holding the Credara. The Kraylen Generals stood guard near Death's coffin and the chest, which lay near the Lair Entrance.

Without looking up, Licronus acknowledged Agean's presence. "Very good, Priest! I see you have found us, although you are too late!" Licronus held up the Credara, admiring it in the light. "Did you like the gift I left you at the stone forest? My horses tore his body limb from limb and the wolves ate him alive and yet, he still cries out in pain. And that poor child in Napaji. I believe you failed them, Priest. Wouldn't you say?" For a moment, Agean's mind returned to the Girjan Forest, and the horrid sight of the dismembered man. Then, he snapped out of it.

"Focus, Agean," he said to himself as he refocused his attention directly on Licronus."

"I think the Angel of Death will make a marvelous gift for Lucifer, don't you agree? He will have ultimate power over you weak humans. Power to sustain life for those who beg for it, and the power to end life for those who suffer and plead for death." With his hands on his swords, Agean began moving towards Licronus. Suddenly the flow of souls around the Lair Entrance began to vanish, disappearing along its path. Agean paused to observe what was happening, helpless to stop it.

"You see, Priest," Licronus said, laughing. "His precious Hall of Souls is now empty, and I possess the key to Lucifer's freedom!"

The flow of souls now completely gone, Agean drew his swords and began running down the path. Licronus knelt and placed the Credara in the center disk of the entrance.

"Licronus, No!" Agean yelled.

Suddenly a huge tremor hit the chamber as the center disk began to rotate. Agean fell, sliding to the right edge of the path, stopping just before falling over. For a second, Agean stared down into the abyss of the endless drop-off. It was unlike anything he had ever seen. He was dizzied by it. The sight rattled him to his core. He quickly gathered his senses and slid himself safely back onto the path.

Licronus called out, "Lucifer! Rise from your eternal prison!" Agean managed to quickly get to his feet. As the disk rotated, it began to rise higher and higher as a solid metal pillar.

Tremors continued as Agean yelled out, "Licronus!"

Meanwhile, the battle waged on in the Hall of Souls as Gajir and the others continued to show their superiority against the Kraylen, until suddenly, the chamber rumbled from a tremor. All at once, the Kraylen stopped fighting and began gathering at the center of the Hall Chamber to kneel. Gajir and the others were stunned.

Istya asked, "What are they doing?"

"Something's wrong. Something's happened!" Quilin said.

Gajir replied, "Yes. I'm afraid so. Look!

Gajir turns everyone's attention to the empty channels leading from the stone artwork. They then realize that the illuminated pearls were no longer flowing into the pool. The Hall of Souls was now empty. "They kneel because Licronus has done it. The Lair is opening. They await the arrival of their master, Lucifer."

"Then let them kneel. We must go and help Agean," Nafar said.

Immediately, they rushed to the entrance behind the stone painting, grabbed the last torch from the wall and exited as the Kraylen continued gathering. Everyone made it out of the room, leaving Flittorin the last to go. Just as Flittorin was about to take flight, a Kraylen, using part of his garb, approached from behind a stone pillar and captured him by throwing the piece of thick cloth over him. As Flittorin screeched and struggled, the Kraylen gathered the cloth and tied it with a leather strap. Flittorin continued struggling as the Kraylen tossed him to the ground.

"There. Let's see you fly now, disgusting bird." The Kraylen then joined the gathering and knelt.

In the Lair Chamber, Agean ran the full distance of the path and finally made his way to Licronus. Licronus drew his sword and spun, with a sinister, sneering look. They circled each other, waiting for the first opportunity to strike.

"I told you our time would soon come, Priest," Licronus said.

Agean noticed the Hamen Sword Licronus wielded and said to him, "You dishonor God by carrying the stolen Swords of Hamen."

"Yes, I dishonor God!" Licronus said angrily. "And I will take great pleasure in slaying his Sitcian Warrior, just as I slayed your disgusting family. You, Sitcian, will feel the searing pain your mother felt, the agony your sister endured as her flesh burned from her body, and the weakness your pitiful father felt as the blood drained from him. I think about it every single day, Agean. Just like you." Licronus stared at Agean, waiting for the anger to overflow like lava from an erupting volcano. Instead, Licronus saw a new Agean, different from when they last met. This Agean was focused, calm and determined.

"Instead of taking my hand, Solis should have taken my life!" Licronus said as he lunged at Agean with his sword. A magnificent battle ensued as the center disk continued to rotate and rise. This time, however, Agean fought like a Hamen Master. He was no longer controlled by anger. Only purpose and honor guided his actions. Licronus was stunned that his cruel words no longer had an effect on the young Sitcian as he defended against Agean's skillful moves. He had always thought humans to be weak, that their love for each other and their emotions made them forever vulnerable, that they could never prove to be true warriors. In this case, Licronus was wrong.

Licronus utilized all the Hamen knowledge stolen from Master Naji to meet Agean toe to toe. After a few moments, Gajir and the others entered the chamber and rushed towards Agean. As they did, the center disk stopped rotating. Suddenly, a huge cloud of smoke and a horrid stench burst forth from the Lair Entrance as the seal was broken and the two halves of the entrance began to separate. The room rumbled and shook as the sound of scraping rock permeated the chamber.

"Agean!" Istya called.

The Kraylen Generals immediately drew their swords and rushed to meet them. Gajir and Quilin took on Poragon, while Istya and Nafar did battle with Bralorg. On more than one occasion, they came perilously close to falling over the edge of the path.

In the meantime, in the Hall of Souls, the Kraylen continued to kneel as Flittorin used his Hamen Talons to tear furiously at the sack.

Back in the Lair Chamber, the battle between true Kraylen and Hamen Warrior continued. After a few more moments of intense battle, and with a skillful move, Agean kicked Licronus off the edge of the path and into the endless drop-off. Licronus screamed as he fell over the edge. Agean quickly moved to the edge of the path and looked, watching as Licronus fell into the abyss. He then turned and focused his attention on the Lair Entrance.

The Credara was now glowing bright red. Agean ran onto the slowly opening entrance and over to the Credara. He attempted to dislodge it with no success. The others continued their battle with the Kraylen Generals, when suddenly Licronus rose from the depths in his winged form and landed next to the Lair Entrance. He tucked his wings while landing.

Laughing, Licronus said, "You see, Priest? The days of the Sitcian are over. You cannot defeat us!"

Seeing this, Istya tried to use the element of surprise and turned away from her fight with Bralorg to go after Licronus. As Istya lunged, slinging her Priya, Licronus, with great precision, used his sword to capture the Priya and send her stumbling backwards. Istya, unable to stop her momentum, slid and fell screaming into the partially opened Lair Entrance. Agean saw this and reacted immediately.

Agean called out, "Istya!" Agean then turned to Quilin. "Quilin! Your whip!"

Quilin, with little time to think, turned and tossed Agean his whip as Agean tossed him his sword.

"What do I do with this?" Quilin asked, catching the Hamen Sword.

"Behind you!" Agean yelled.

Quilin turned just in time to block Poragon's blade from slashing him in half. Agean, with Quilin's whip in hand and his Mark glowing, dove towards the Lair entrance while lashing out the Hamen weapon.

Meanwhile, Licronus knelt and began to communicate to Lucifer in Latin. "Great Lucifer, the time is now! You must rise!"

The Lair itself was like a huge deep well with jagged rock walls, burnt dark like those of the Chamber. Istya was panicking as she continued to fall deeper and deeper into the Lair. Once Agean had fully extended the Hamen Whip, the tip disconnected and continued its path down towards Istya as she fell.

Agean was hanging over the edge of the Lair Entrance as it continued to open wider. He used everything in him to focus his Hamen powers.

Agean yelled down into the Lair, "Istya! Use the Priya!"

Istya was dropping farther and faster as she tried to keep her composure. She forced her arms to stretch but realized she was falling so fast she could not reach the bladed tip with her hands. Unbeknownst to Istya, far beneath her, Lucifer had begun rising to the surface from the farthest depths of the Lair. His red eyes and the fires of Hell drew nearer with each second of Istya's fall.

Just as Istya tried to draw one of her Priya to capture the tip, ghostly evil specters began to swarm her on all sides. Smokey, white, with only the essence of human form, the tortured souls began flying through her body, one at a time, causing her to scream and writhe in pain with every pass-through.

"Mother, forgive me!" Istya said. Then, all at once, the evil specters flew into her. Istya's back arched as she wrenched in pain. Still dropping, her face began transforming to a Kraylen-like appearance. Using every bit of strength she had to resist the evil attacking her very being, Istya drew and slung her Priya, capturing the bladed tip. She continued to writhe in pain as she fought off the attack, still desperately holding on.

Agean still struggled, stretching as far as he could, focusing his Hamen powers. Then, he sensed it. Istya had captured the tip. Agean focused his Hamen power to bring the tip back to the whip.

Agean screamed as loud as he could, "Hang on, Istya!" This got Quilin's attention.

"Istya," Quilin said to himself as he left Gajir to battle with Poragon and quickly dashed over to help Agean.

Istya continued struggling against the force of evil acting upon her, knowing that it was just a matter of time before she would no longer be able to fight it off.

"Hurry, Agean!" Istya yelled. With all of her might, she hung onto the Priya as it and the tip rose to the surface, till finally, the tip rejoined the Hamen Whip. As it did, her appearance began to return to normal.

Quilin, having now made his way over to help Agean, grabbed hold of his Hamen Whip and they both pulled with all of their strength. Istya was exhausted and sweating from the sweltering heat of the Lair, but hung on as she was pulled towards the Lair Entrance. Her appearance fully back to normal, Istya reached the opening and was pulled to safety. Istya and Quilin gave each other a tight caring embrace.

"Are you alright, Istya? Are you hurt?" Quilin asked.

"No. I think I'm okay," Istya replied. "I think I'm all right."

Quilin checked her for injuries and then looked her directly in the eyes. "Try not to do that again."

Istya replied, "I promise."

Agean took a second to catch his breath, then immediately returned his attention to the situation at hand: first to Licronus, who was still kneeling and speaking to Lucifer, awaiting his imminent rise; then to the slowly opening Lair Entrance through which Lucifer would soon have his freedom if Agean didn't do something to stop it; and finally to the battle being waged against the Kraylen Generals by Nafar and Gajir. He must do something, and it must be done now. Then, he saw it. The five thrones near the entrance of the Lair Chamber captured Agean's attention. "The painting," Agean said to himself.

Agean drew his Hamen Swords and then rushed over to help Nafar fight Bralorg. Agean arrived just as Bralorg forced Nafar to do a rolling move to escape being run through by his blade. Agean quickly took over the battle with Bralorg, diverting his attention from Nafar.

"Nafar! Remember, he is a true Kraylen!" Agean yelled. Nafar, understanding what Agean meant, stood with his Hamen Axes.

Nafar called out, "Agean! Now!" With a quick, agile move, Nafar hurled one of his Hamen Axes directly at Agean and Bralorg. Hearing the whir of the incoming weapon, Agean blocked one final blow from the Kraylen just in time to drop to a kneeling position and avoid Nafar's axe as it sliced through Bralorg's neck. The Kraylen's look of terror was his last as his head violently disconnected from his body and burst into a cloud of black ash. His headless body toppled over like a fallen tree, slamming to the ground and exploding into a cloud of ash upon contact. This got Licronus's attention as he witnessed his Kraylen General being vanquished. His anger escalated even more seeing Istya and Quilin join Gajir's battle with Poragon. The three quickly overwhelmed Poragon with Hamen skill. Licronus's remaining General exploded into smoke and ash, having been impaled through the chest by the deadly tip of Gajir's Hamen Staff. Licronus's anger then reached a boiling point. He again drew a Hamen Sword from his waist and immediately went after Agean. Agean rushed to meet Licronus's advance. Much to Agean's surprise, Licronus's anger was now affecting his own fighting skills. Agean made an incredible spinning move and knocked Licronus to the floor. Licronus's sword slid across the floor, stopping near the slowly opening entrance.

Agean rushed over to the others. "Come on! I think I understand!" Everyone followed Agean down the path towards the Chamber Entrance. Licronus collected himself. He watched Agean and the others while wiping away the black blood dripping from his mouth, waiting to see what their next move would be.

"Agean, what are we doing?" Nafar asked. "We must destroy him before it is too late!" Agean continued hurrying towards the Chamber Entrance.

Istya said loudly, "Agean, we haven't time!"

Agean immediately turned to the others. "Listen! It's clear to me now. Licronus is not important!" Agean's words were met with a gathering of confused looks. "It is not as important to know how to battle, as to know when not to. Licronus is doing it again. He's trying to distract me. The answer is right in front of us!" Agean directed everyone's attention to the thrones.

"The thrones!" Gajir said. "The answer is with the thrones!"

"It must be, Gajir!" Agean said.

Meanwhile, within the Lair, bursts of fire and smoke rose from the very depths of Hell. As the Lair Entrance continued to open wider, and Lucifer drew closer and closer to his freedom, his glowing red eyes grew larger.

In the Hall of Souls, the Kraylen continued kneeling, awaiting the arrival of Lucifer. Flittorin continued to struggle to escape his bonds. Flittorin was now tearing huge rips in the sack. The sound of Flittorin's efforts got the attention of the Kraylen who snared him. He stood and turned, searching for the captured bird, his vision blocked by a large stone ledge.

In the Lair Chamber, Agean had made his way up the stairs to the center throne bearing the Mark of the Sitcian in an effort to figure out what needed to be done. Then, after a moment, it struck him.

"The stone painting!" Agean yelled. "It was more than just a secret entrance!" Agean turned to the center throne and then looked all around the chamber. He then turned back to the others. "You were right, Istya. We are pieces to a puzzle. Licronus wants us to fight so that all the pieces will not come together."

Gajir began to understand and said, "Yes! We are the warriors in the painting!"

"We each must get to a throne and quickly!" Agean yelled. "Time is running out!" They all darted up the paths to the thrones as Licronus watched from a distance.

"Your pitiful efforts will bring you no victory, Priest!" Licronus yelled. He rushed back to the Lair Entrance as it continued to slowly grind open. "Great Lucifer! We await you! Rise and take your rightful place among us!"

Bursts of smoke and flames continued to rise from the Lair Entrance. Agean and the others quickly made their way to the thrones, laying their weapons upon the stone tables in front of them. They sat, but nothing happened.

"What now? What is supposed to happen?" Nafar asked.

Gajir yelled, "We're running out of time, Agean! You've got to think! Something's missing!" Agean groaned loudly as he focused, trying to think. The stone painting. Five thrones. Five warriors. The Credara. Wings. Then it came to him.

"Wings… Flittorin… Flittorin! Quilin, where is he?" Agean called out.

Quilin, suddenly aware that Flittorin had been missing all this time, answered, "He… He must still be in the Hall of Souls!"

In the Hall of Souls, the Kraylen slowly drew his sword and began making his way towards Flittorin until he finally reached the stone ledge. Sword in hand, he slowly peeked over the ledge. Still tearing tirelessly at the shredded sack, Flittorin finally ripped completely through. The Kraylen's eyes opened wide as he raised his sword to strike him. Now free, Flittorin immediately took to the air, flying up and past the awaiting Kraylen who swung and missed him as he flew by. Flittorin then soared in a circular path, returned to the Kraylen, and quickly ripped through him with his Hamen Talons. The Kraylen exploded into a mass of black ash — vanquished. Flittorin, screeching, immediately soared through the entrance in the stone wall painting.

Meanwhile, in the Lair Chamber, smoke and flames leapt from the Lair Entrance. Licronus continued watching Agean and the others while awaiting Lucifer's arrival. Quilin, having headed off to find Flittorin, had almost made his way down the steps to the chamber floor when he heard the familiar sound of Flittorin's screech.

Quilin yelled out, "He's coming! I hear him!"

"Yes, I hear him too! He's coming!" Istya yelled. Suddenly Flittorin soared into the Lair Chamber, screeching as he flew.

Quilin yelled, "Yes!" then scrambled back to his own throne just as Flittorin landed atop Agean's. As soon as Flittorin's Hamen Talons grasped the top of the throne, Marks began glowing on all Hamen Warriors, their weapons, Flittorin's pendant, and the Credara atop the Lair Entrance. Then, Flittorin's eyes began to glow a bright white. Light outlined all thrones from top to bottom as the energy level rose. Wind began to blow within the chamber and lightning flashed as the energy level rose to maximum.

Licronus growled and sneered at the events occurring before his eyes. Suddenly, the lightning and energy-light came together at the center throne. Then a single heavy beam of energy-light fired from Flittorin's pendant, directly to the glowing symbol on the Credara. Everyone held on as tremors rocked the chamber and the wind and lightning continued. The pillars swayed as Licronus reacted to what he saw.

"Nooo!" Licronus screamed as he witnessed thousands of years of planning slipping away. Suddenly, the center disk began to rotate in reverse. The motion of the two halves of the entrance stopped and then themselves began to reverse. The Lair Entrance was closing. "Nooo!"

The tremors became more intense, as did the wind and lightning. Licronus turned, drew his remaining Hamen Sword and put it directly into the path of the light beam from Flittorin's pendant. The beam of light snapped the sword in half in a burst of sparks and knocked Licronus to the floor. The center disk spun and descended like a screw into the closing entrance. Licronus got up and rushed over to the Credara, trying to snatch it from the center disk. The Credara sparked and burned Licronus's hand, knocking him back to the floor.

As flames burst forth from the Lair, Lucifer's red eyes now became huge as he continued rising from the depths of Hell. His horrid features were now visible as he sped towards the opening, which quickly grew smaller and smaller.

The full might of God's Army continued working to close Lucifer's Lair before it was too late. They held on with everything they had as the tremors continued to rock the chamber to its foundation.

Licronus knew Lucifer was close and scrambled frantically to keep the entrance from closing, even going so far as to try and slow the closing by pulling as hard as he could on one of the halves. Licronus's efforts were futile as the entrance became too small for Lucifer to escape. Then suddenly, a huge ground shaking tremor erupted as Lucifer crashed head-on into the Lair Entrance. The entrance buckled as one of his huge horns protruded up and out of the entrance. The force knocked Licronus off his feet. Agean and the others gasped as they watched what was happening, knowing that they had to hold their positions at all costs. As the Lair Entrance continued closing, it slammed tight on Lucifer's horn and strained under the pressure. Suddenly, the pressure proved too much as the horn explosively broke from Lucifer's skull, the dislodged piece flying from the Lair Entrance and landing on the path. The roar of Lucifer's horrid scream echoed throughout the chamber as he descended back down into the depths of Hell.

Licronus screamed again, "Nooo!" A huge tremor created from the event caused the Credara to tumble from its place on the disk, breaking the beam of energy from Flittorin's pendant. It tumbled towards the closing entrance. Licronus saw this and hurled himself towards the Credara just as it fell within the opening and lodged between the two halves. Licronus's arms entered the opening in an attempt to dislodge it, but it was too late. The Credara exploded into pieces as the entrance closed completely, crushing and pinning Licronus's left arm. The holy waters from the Credara splashed in Licronus's face and burned his already dark leathery skin like acid. He screamed out in horrible pain as smoke rose from his burning face, neck and chest.

Licronus lay struggling at the center of the now closed and smoking Lair Entrance. The energy, wind and lightning died down as another tremor further loosened the pillars surrounding the Lair Entrance from their bases. Agean and the others nearly went limp from exhaustion. Breathing heavily, they each looked to see that the others were okay.

"We did it, Agean! We stopped him!" Istya yelled.

Quilin called out, "Flittorin!" Flittorin flew over to Quilin who affectionately gave him a treat from his waist pouch. "Great work, my friend."

Agean and the others, gathered their weapons and began making their way down to the chamber floor. Then together, as God's Army, they walked the path to where Licronus, who was still stuck in the Lair Entrance, moaned in pain. Agean stood before Licronus and began to draw his sword. Nafar stopped him and handed him one of his Axes of Hamen.

"Agean, do me this honor," Nafar said.

Agean's Mark and the symbol on the Hamen Axe glowed when he took it. Sure of Licronus's fate, Gajir and Istya walked over and picked up the chest while Nafar and Quilin walked over and picked up Death's coffin, leaving Agean to the task at hand. Agean stared down at Licronus. Another tremor shook the chamber as the pillars continued to sway.

"Do as you will, Priest," said Licronus. "But you will find that this fight is not yet finished."

"I am Sitcian, Licronus. For me, the battle against your kind is never finished. But for you, the fight is over," Agean said.

As Agean raised the Hamen Axe, another tremor rocked the chamber, causing one of the loosened pillars to crash to the ground, breaking into sections.

Istya yelled, "Agean! Look out!"

Agean did an incredible back flipping Hamen maneuver and narrowly avoided a huge section of the fallen pillar as it slid across the Lair Entrance directly at Licronus.

Seeing the pillar barreling towards him, Licronus screamed. His voice echoed throughout the Lair Chamber as the pillar plowed Licronus from the entrance, shearing off his left arm and pushing him over the edge and into the endless drop-off. Agean and the others stood watching, shocked. A stronger tremor then hit the chamber, causing the remaining three pillars to sway.

"We must leave now!" Gajir yelled.

Agean quickly picked up Licronus's unbroken Sword of Hamen as yet another huge tremor hit. Agean ran and grabbed one end of Death's coffin and began moving towards the Chamber Entrance.

The Hall of Souls was also being shaken to its core as tremors continued. Large chunks of crystal and rock formations broke off and tumbled to the ground. Eternal torches fell from the walls as Kraylen attempted to escape the Hall Chamber. The falling rock and crystal crushed and vanquished any Kraylen caught in their path. Agean and the others entered from the stone painting carrying Death's coffin and chest. They skillfully vanquished every Kraylen they confronted, one after the other. As the tremors continued, they found themselves fighting Kraylen and dodging falling rocks as they made their way to the entrance of the Hall Chamber and exited.

chapter twenty-one
Setting Things Right

Kimirin Mountain had now become the backdrop of an epic battle of Sitcian versus Kraylen. The Kraylen menace made a valiant effort to win purely by the numbers as they continued to pour into the fray against the Sitcian Angels. Thousands of Kraylen swarmed as they did battle with Archangel Michael and his Sitcian legion. Despite their numbers, Kraylen after Kraylen disappeared in bursts of smoke and dust as they were vanquished by the Sitcian Angels. How long could they keep this up, with what seemed like an endless stream of Kraylen Warriors pouring in from all directions?

A few Kraylen exited the entrance from Kimirin Mountain ahead of Agean and the others, all barely making it out alive. God's Warriors quickly discovered that Licronus had, for once, been telling the truth. The fight was not yet finished.

They immediately found themselves fully engaged in battle once again. They set the coffin and chest down near the rock face of the mountainside and then turned to fight against the Kraylen onslaught.

"Agean, their numbers are too many!" Nafar called out as he sliced through a Kraylen.

Agean responded, "Every Kraylen on earth must be here!"

"Not even close, my boy!" said Gajir. Agean and the others killed a dozen more Kraylen.

Istya yelled, "Agean, we must do something!"

"She's right, Agean!" Quilin said as he vanquished several more Kraylen.

Agean yelled, "I know! First, we must protect the Angel!" Agean and the others formed a tighter defense around the coffin and chest and continued vanquishing Kraylen.

Istya yelled out, "Agean! The Credara! We cannot let the Kraylen get their hands on it!"

"I know, Istya! Just keep fighting!" Agean responded. Still battling, Agean quickly removed the Credara from its pouch on his waist and held it high. "Flittorin!"

After ripping through two flying Kraylen, Flittorin screeched and deactivated his Hamen Talons. He then soared down and grabbed the Credara from Agean's hand.

Quilin yelled, "What's he doing? Where is he going?"

"He's the Protector! He'll know what to do!" Agean replied.

Istya yelled to Agean, "What about us? How are we going to make it out of here alive?"

Agean replied, "The Angel comes first, then we worry about us!"

Quilin said to himself, "Of course. Why not?" They all fought with extra passion, skill and determination. Meanwhile, Flittorin soared upward, high into the sky with the Credara in his grasp. Beneath him was Kraylen movement from all directions numbering in the tens of thousands, moving towards the battle at Kimirin Mountain, converging on Agean and the others like a swarm of locusts.

Flittorin continued flying to a high position. Then, he began circling directly above the center of the battle. Suddenly, his Hamen Pendant began to glow, as did the Arc-Pen Symbol on the Credara. Then, the Credara itself began to glow bright like a star in the sky. Suddenly, a flash of lightning struck it. Then loudly, clearly, Archangel Gabriel's horn sounded from the heavens. All at once, a massive, blinding burst of energy was emitted from the Credara and began flowing straight down towards Agean and the others. Hearing the horn, Michael and his Sitcian Angels knew what was about to happen. They began kneeling, mid-battle, and folding themselves beneath their protective wings. Several of the Sitcian Angels, including Michael, grabbed Agean, Gajir, Istya, Nafar and Quilin and folded their wings around them to protect them. Blows from Kraylen swords bounced off their wings as if striking stone. The energy from the Credara struck the earth like a meteor. It then spread out like a tidal wave in all directions. As the wave of energy extended out from its center, it vanquished instantly every Kraylen in its path. Thousands of them burned to dark ash and smoke as the energy cut a swath through the converging mass. Then, as quickly as the energy came, it was reversed and sucked back up into the Credara.

The battle was over. All Kraylen in the area were now gone. Michael and his Sitcian Angels unfolded and released Agean and the others from their protective wings. Agean and the others were stunned as they watched the last of the energy disappear into the sky. The other Sitcian Angels unfolded themselves and looked to the sky as well. After a moment, the brightly lit Credara, like a glowing meteor, fell from the sky in slow motion, landing in the dirt at Agean's feet. Its light slowly dimmed, then extinguished. As they all looked down at the Credara, it was slowly joined by Flittorin's sacred pendant, landing on the ground next to the heavenly urn. Agean and the others looked at each other, saddened. Quilin, visibly hurt, stepped forward, knelt in the dirt and picked up the pendant. He then looked to the sky. Istya, with tears in her eyes, knelt next to him and tried to comfort him with an embrace. Agean picked up the Credara and stared at it.

Gajir gave a solemn look to the others as Archangel Gabriel glided in, with Michael approaching on foot. After sharing the sadness of the moment, Gabriel approached Quilin and extended his hand. Quilin looked at him with a tear on his cheek, then reluctantly placed Flittorin's pendant gently into Gabriel's hand.

Michael then approached Agean. "Agean. You have done well and have proven yourself a true Sitcian. We are proud to have you as one of us." The Sitcian Angels bowed in honor as Agean showed a look of pride.

"But Sitcian, remember Master Naji's words to you," Gabriel said. Gabriel directed Agean's attention to the Angel of Death's coffin. Agean suddenly realized what Gabriel meant.

"The miracle. The miracle is broken," Agean said.

Gabriel nodded, affirming Agean's words. "Without him, all is lost." After a moment, Gabriel stepped back, blew his horn and all Sitcian Angels took flight with their injured and streamed back to the heavens.

Agean placed the Credara into his waist pouch, then turned and walked over to Death's coffin and the chest.

Agean gestured for Nafar and Quilin to join him and together they stood Death's coffin up and leaned it against the mountainside. Agean then drew his sword and struck the lock, breaking it open. He opened the coffin lid to find Death, arms crossed, staring forward with a despondent look. Against the dark interior of the coffin, the Angel looked so pale that he appeared to glow.

Agean acknowledged him, "Angel." then struck the lock on the chest and opened it. He reached in, removed Death's robe, unfolded and presented it to him. Death's head tilted as his eyes slowly turned to meet Agean's. He slowly uncrossed his arms and struggled to take a step. Death then stepped forward as Agean allowed the robe to flow down over his head and down his entire body. Immediately, thunder clapped and lightning flashed in the sky as Death began to reclaim his skeletal form.

Everyone was stunned at the miracle being witnessed. Death then emitted a loud visible breath that streamed out of his hood and seemed to travel in every direction. Gajir reached into the chest, took out the Hamen Scytheren and stood face to face with Death.

Gajir said to him, "Great Angel. I believe you and I have unfinished business." Everyone was taken aback by Gajir's statement.

"No! Wait, Master!" Quilin said, saddened.

"There is no need to interrupt, Quilin," Gajir said as he opened his garment to fully expose the terrible bloody gash inflicted by the Kraylen. "It is my time, my son. I have had a very full life in service to God, and can think of no better ending than the victory we share here today."

Agean asked, "Master Gajir. Is there nothing we can do?" Agean then turned to Death. "Great Angel-"

"No, Agean," Gajir said. "This is to be, my boy. God's mission for us is to set things right. Not change them. And this is right." Gajir handed his Hamen Staff to Agean. "You see, Agean, I miss my beloved wife. If it is His will, I will see her again. I only ask that you please give my staff to my son. He will know what to do with it." Agean took the staff from Gajir. Gajir then placed a hand on Agean's shoulder. "Agean. Try to find it in your heart to forgive Solis. It is because of him that you were able to know your heart before it was filled with hatred for Licronus. He allowed you another path to choose. One of purpose and destiny, which you chose like the true Sitcian you are." Agean stared into Gajir's eyes, thankful for his undying wisdom, but knowing that it was the last he would share.

Gajir turned and bowed his head while handing the Scytheren to Death. Death took the Scytheren and transformed it into the Hamen Scythe. He pointed his finger into the air. Then gently, he touched Gajir on the head. A strong wind stirred as Gajir's eyes closed slowly. He then collapsed. Agean caught him before he fell and laid him gently on the ground. Quilin knelt by him, saddened. He crossed Gajir's arms gently over his chest. Death then took the Hamen Scythe in both hands and raised it to the sky. The wind began to blow stronger.

The sounds of ailing and pain still filled the air in the Napaji hut as the maimed villagers continued to suffer. Nafar's young niece lay almost motionless, staring at the ceiling. Her breathing was terribly labored as her watery eyes no longer even blinked. The beads of sweat that formed on her forehead ran down her hairline and disappeared behind her ears.

Then, a sudden and strangely cool feeling came over the room. The several men and women tending to the injured stood straight up and looked around as Death's wind blew in. They saw its effect on the hair and clothing of the injured, but on nothing else in the room. Nor could they feel it themselves. From nowhere it came. There were no uncovered windows or doors to allow such a wind to enter. Yet it was there.

Nafar's precious little niece, not yet old enough to understand life's injustices, but old enough to want what any child would want under her circumstances — for the agony to end, opened her eyes wide as the cool breeze slipped across her ailing skin. She almost smiled as her existence cracked open like the most delicate of eggshells, and her very essence poured out of her tragic circumstances as she welcomed the better of the two. She welcomed death. Then... her suffering ended. The suffering of the others ended as well. They all died peacefully as those tending them sobbed in relieved sadness.

∽

Solis and several monks were holding a prayer vigil at Master Naji's bedside. There were many candles lighting the room as Master Naji lay in silence, still breathing. Suddenly the flames all began to flicker as if a wind was in the air.

While leading the prayers, Solis noticed something strange. Tears had begun streaming from Master Naji's eyes. Solis halted the prayer and leaned in closer to see. Then slowly, Master Naji's arm raised and his hand grabbed Solis's arm. Solis was both happy and stunned that this was happening and he held Master Naji up. Master Naji's eyes sparkled in the candlelight as his eyelids struggled to part.

He looked into Solis's eyes and spoke in a scratchy voice. "He did it. Solis, he did it."

Solis, realizing what Master Naji had said, began to smile.

"That's wonderful Master. We knew he could. We knew he could," Solis said happily.

Then, staring directly into Solis's eyes, Master Naji said, "Hamorem."

Solis teared up and said to him, "Yes Master. Hamorem." Master Naji slowly drifted off into death, finally moved on to Heaven by the blade of a Sitcian's sword.

As Solis lowered Master Naji back onto his bed and covered him, extreme sadness replaced his fading smile. He then stood as he and the monks crossed themselves. Then, all at once, a gust of wind filled the room and all candles were blown out. Complete darkness.

ଓ

In the same relic filled room where Licronus and his Kraylen Generals captured The Angel of Death, an old woman soaked a few bloody rags in a bowl of water. Across the room on a pallet lay Gabris, tortured and suffering. She wrung out the rags, then walked over to the old man and began wiping his forehead. She saw the terror in his eyes. She stared woefully at him, wondering what he must have done to cause such a horrible circumstance. Gabris's pain came not only from his gaping stomach wound, but from what he had allowed to transpire. The horror he had helped bring to mankind. He feared he would never receive forgiveness.

Then suddenly, through an open window of his room, Death's wind blew in, bringing with it his ghostly image.

As Death floated closer, Gabris began to smile, happy to see the end of his suffering. As Death reached him, Gabris reached out to touch him. Death's ghostly image extended its finger and then suddenly withdrew it just before they touched. Death then slowly backed away, his smoky image fading from sight. Gabris was left to his horrible suffering.

Gabris, still reaching out, yelled, "No! Please take me! Pleeeeease!"

❧

The battlefield where the two kings had ignored Agean's plea was covered with bloodied bodies with every imaginable injury. Sounds of agony arose from the bloody landscape like the morning steam of a swamp. Days had passed and the slashing and maiming had now ceased — not because of victory, but because finally it was realized that continuing would only bring more unimaginable horror, none of which would result in death.

King Soranem, injured himself, stood over one of his knights who suffered from a horrible gaping chest wound. His internal organs visible, he struggled with every breath. The Sovereign held no power to relieve the terrible suffering that surrounded him. He looked around, still trying to understand why such a horrible thing had happened.

Death, he could understand. Death was an honor for a warrior in battle. But this, he could not comprehend. He had never before seen so many men who deserved to die — not because of misdeeds, but because death was a better result than that which they were suffering.

As Soranem looked around, his eyes met those of King Gassan in the distance. Soranem was unaware if Gassan had suffered any injury. The two had not spoken since that fateful day, the day the Priest came and asked, in the name of God, that they delay their war. The two kings gazed at each other over the distance with tragic regret. Then, suddenly, a wind started blowing in from all directions. It was a strange, whipping wind that brought with it a thin smoky white fog that raced about, swirling in and around and through everything, covering absolutely every inch of the battlefield, touching everyone.

Suddenly, Soranem felt a hand grasping his ankle. It was his knight. He was trying to tell him something. Grimacing from the pain of injury, Soranem knelt so that he could hear his words.

"Thank God," the knight said to him. Then, suddenly, the life drained from the knight's body. Soranem's eyes widened when he realized that finally, he was dead. Still kneeling, he looked around and saw others taking their final breath right before his eyes. In the distance, he heard great sighs of relief for the death of fallen warriors as both comrade and foe expressed happiness that the suffering had finally ended.

Soranem looked to the Heavens and smiled. "Yes! Yes, thank you!" Soranem stood with a relieved smile on his face and looked to Gassan. Just as he again spotted him in the distance, Gassan collapsed dead on the ground. Soranem's expression returned to that of sadness and regret as he stared solemnly off into the distance.

◈

Agean and the others watched as Death stood, arms outstretched, his Hamen Scythe aimed to the sky. The powerful winds continued to blow as everyone watched Death make right the horrible wrong Licronus had caused. Agean removed the Credara from his waist pouch. The Credara lit brightly as the waters swirled and began rising to the top.

◈

The tremors had ceased as the Hall of Souls lay practically in ruins. Then, a wind stirred and grew within the mighty Hall. Immediately, the damage to the Hall began to reverse, with chunks of rock and precious stones magically flying back into place. Once all was restored, the flow of souls began again – illuminated pearls poured forth from the top of the chamber, filling the pool. Once again, souls flowed through the channels to the entrances and exits as before. The Hall of Souls magically returned to a place of exquisite beauty, and Lucifer's Lair was once again... Locked.

Agean and the others continued to marvel at Death as he lowered his Hamen Scythe. The winds receded.

Death turned to Agean, silently bowed his head in gratitude and then faded away. After a moment had passed, several human figures appeared at the edge of the forest. Quilin spotted them.

"Agean!" Quilin said, directing everyone's attention to them.

Quilin, Istya and Nafar prepared to draw their weapons.

"No! It's all right!" Agean said. He then turned to the human figures.

"You are safe now!" Agean called out. "God Almighty has won this battle!"

Embraces and sounds of joy came from the Kimi-rin villagers as more began to appear out of the forest. Agean and the others shared the bittersweet moment.

They all looked at Gajir's peaceful face.

"It would have made him happy to have seen this," Nafar said. Istya put a comforting arm around Quilin.

The sound of rushing waterfalls filled the air for miles as Agean, Quilin and Istya approached Gannus with Gajir's wrapped body aboard a wagon. As they reached the kingdom's entrance, Tordin, Kisara and their newborn child greeted them. Once they saw that Gajir was not riding among them, Kisara dropped to her knees and began crying. Agean dismounted and approached Tordin, who stood strong, but bore a sad look for the loss of his father. Agean and Tordin embraced. Agean then retrieved Gajir's staff from his horse and presented it to Tordin. Tordin looked at his father's staff with pride for a moment, then walked over and stood before Kisara and their newborn child. He extended the top of the staff to them. Kisara looked up at Tordin, realizing what he wanted. She then partially unwrapped the child to free its hand. Tordin moved the staff to the child's hand and it grabbed hold. Suddenly, the Arc-Pen Symbol on the staff glowed and the staff immediately transformed from its wooden form to a Hamen Staff. Agean and the others were shocked as Kisara opened the child's wrap further to reveal the Sitcian Mark of Hamen upon its neck. They all just stared in amazement. Agean's look then turned to one of pride and honor. He, Quilin and Istya bowed in honor of the next Sitcian.

❧

Many large candelabras were in place in the Great Foyer for a special occasion. A new monument had been put into place. Solis, Nafar, Gradore, Brand, and the Court of Seven looked on proudly at the newly erected statue of Patharus. Solis now wore the honorary garb of the Great Court as its newest member.

Solis walked over to Nafar and received Patharus's Sword of Hamen, taken back from Licronus. He then crossed to Patharus's statue and placed the sword in the palm of its hand. The statue's hand immediately grasped the sword as Solis and everyone looked on with pride.

chapter twenty-two
Something Far More Sinister

On a beautiful and sunny afternoon, Agean, Quilin, and Istya made their way down the Bridge of Eternity to Quintana. By now, Agean had returned the white and gold sleeve to his hair.

The sound of rock scraping against rock rang out from the closing entrance as Turon, Agean, Quilin and Istya entered Quintana. Janirin, along with two others, awaited them with a look of gratitude for their return. Istya ran up and lovingly hugged her father.

"Father!" Istya said.

"Istya! Thank God! Thank God," Janirin said as he embraced his daughter, practically in tears over her return.

Quilin and Agean smiled at the happy reunion between Istya and Janirin. Then, something wonderful caught Agean's eye. A group of children were playing just beyond where Istya and Janirin stood. Suddenly, one of the happy little girls turned around and looked directly at Agean. It was the injured little girl from Napaji,

Nafar's niece. A rush of happiness surged through Agean like nothing he had ever felt before. He smiled at her as she waved at him and then resumed playing. Agean and Quilin then approached Janirin. Just as Quilin was about to say something, Istya took him by the hand and snatched him away.

"Wonderful to see you again, Sir!" Quilin said as he strolled off, hand in hand with Istya. Caught totally off guard, Janirin stared in complete shock. He immediately turned his shocked look to Agean.

Agean said, "You asked that I do all I could to return her to you. I made no promises as to what condition." Agean shrugged his shoulders as Janirin turned to look at Istya and Quilin in amazement. "Janirin. It is with much regret that I bring sad news."

"Yes... Yes, I know, Agean. Gajir was a friend," Janirin told him with a somber look.

Agean asked, "How did you know?"

"Here, we always know, my boy. Remember where you are, Agean. As with Nafar's niece, do not be surprised should you see him again someday," Janirin replied.

Agean smiled as the realization of Janirin's words filled his heart with a feeling of peace. Janirin then turned towards the horse drawn carriage where Istya and Quilin sat giggling between themselves.

"Now, whatever shall we do about this situation?" Janirin asked as he and Agean strolled over to join them.

⁂

A cool wind swirled in from every direction through the majestic range of mountain peaks. The stagnant dry weather had allowed no snow to form for months on the jagged crowns that reached for the sky. A solitary figure, clothing fluttering in the breeze, stood atop one of the peaks, staring out into the distance. A tattered Kraylen, dark, winged and missing its left arm — Licronus. The level of hatred and evil which burned from his eyes could scorch the mountain peaks in the distance.

Defeated? Evil has a way of always surviving defeat. As long as there is goodness, there is a path for evil. It is this unending balance which pits one endlessly against the other. For without one, the other cannot exist. Licronus knew this, but he was unsatisfied with the thought of this constant cycle in which evil fed off of goodness, and goodness off of evil. This would not do. It would never be good enough. One had to rule over the other. Licronus craved victory and nothing less. So ponder he did. His next move would be enviable. Lucifer himself would be impressed. He already had a plan – and an unwitting pawn with which to execute it.

Suddenly, Licronus's senses keyed in on a distinct change in the wind patterns which swirled about. Wings in the air. He knew that only one of his kind, or one of theirs, could cause such. If it was one of his, it had better be important. If one of theirs, perhaps God had sent one of His Sitcian executioners to finish him. The latter seemed too easy. Then, the sound of crunching gravel as footsteps approached. It was Barejis – burned and scarred from his recent encounter at Shao-Tan. He stopped just a couple of feet from Licronus.

"Barejis," Licronus said. "What did you bring me?"

"I could not get what the monk carried, Licronus," Barejis replied, lowering his head in disappointment.

Licronus spun around in anger and knocked Barejis to the ground in a heap. "You dare fail me?!" Barejis scuffled along the dirt as Licronus moved towards him, huffing in anger. Barejis wiped the black blood from his mouth then spat.

"Yes, great Licronus. I failed you. But who are you for me to fail?" Licronus blazed an angry look at Barejis. "Who made you our leader?" Barejis slowly gathered himself as Licronus glared at him. Barejis finally made it to his feet and dusted himself off. "Many of us, the half breeds, are sick of following your orders and listening to your arrogance. We follow Lucifer just as you!" Barejis's words infuriated Licronus. He clenched his fist and stepped towards Barejis. Just as he took his first step, Barejis drew one of his blades and sent it hurling towards Licronus. The blade hit its mark, landing squarely in the center of Licronus's abdomen. Licronus stopped in his tracks and lurched forward in pain. At first, Barejis was taken aback by what he had just done, but quickly welcomed his newfound courage. Licronus rose up to face Barejis, with the blade still buried deep into his abdomen.

Barejis, drawing two more blades, said, "Look at you with only one arm. Tens of thousands of us have died because of you. I say it's time for a new leader." Barejis proceeded to hurl two of his blades into Licronus's chest. Licronus buckled in pain as he stumbled backwards. Barejis wasted no time drawing and sending two more blades into Licronus's torso. Licronus growled in pain and spun around, dropping to his knees. His back to Barejis, he breathed heavily, holding on to the blades protruding from his chest and stomach.

Barejis approached Licronus from behind, drawing his last blade. "You can't destroy us. Only the weapons of God's pitiful warriors can destroy us. And you no longer have them. You, a pitiful excuse for a warrior, lost them in defeat." Barejis spat on the ground next to Licronus and then rammed his final blade through his back. Licronus screamed out in pain as the blade made its way through his dark, thick flesh. After a couple of breaths, and much to Barejis's surprise, Licronus raised his head and stood. He then began to laugh – low and evil.

"You are correct, Barejis. It is good to know you've been paying attention." Licronus then turned to face Barejis. With the blades still buried deep within him, Licronus's hand drew from his waist the broken Sword of Hamen which he had retrieved from The Lair. Barejis's eyes bulged, knowing what it was – and knowing it was the last thing he would ever see.

Licronus, with a powerful forward motion, drove the broken blade directly into Barejis's chest. Barejis's mouth opened wide, yelling in pain as individual parts of his face began to quickly break down. His teeth and tongue all turned to dust and blew from his open mouth as if a wind had swept them away. His eyes turned to grey sand and poured from his eye sockets. His head began to implode as his bones became brittle, causing his jaw to fall from his skull just before the remainder of his body disintegrated into a mass of ash and smoke. Licronus stood with the broken Hamen Sword still in its position as Barejis's body crumbled and fell away from him onto the ground.

Licronus, for a moment, reveled in what he had done. He then stood straight up and began flexing all of his muscles. Suddenly, Barejis's blades slowly began sliding out of his body. Licronus pressed with all of his might, growling and mustering all of the strength he had until the blades, one by one, exited his body and fell to the ground. Once the final blade fell free, he exhaled and began panting, catching his breath. He paused a moment to inspect the pile of ash which was all that was left of Barejis. Licronus then turned back to look out at the mountainous land-scape.

Just as Licronus thought he would be left to his thoughts, his planning, another Kraylen landed nearby and approached. It was Jirsa. She stopped for a moment to stare at the pile of vanquished Kraylen before making her way to Licronus. She stopped several feet away from Licronus.

"Barejis, I assume?" Jirsa asked, referring to the pile. "I told you. You should have left the Shao-Tan monk to me," Jirsa said. "Now their numbers increase."

"Their wise Warrior has fallen. The young monk, like the others, will fall as well."

Jirsa moved in closer. "This God's Army - these chosen humans - have proven a formidable foe, Licronus. As their Sitcian grows stronger, so do they."

"Do they impress you, Jirsa?"

"They do not, Licronus. They are filth that needs to be swatted like flies. But I say to you as our leader, this enemy deserves respect. It will take our greatest effort to destroy them."

Licronus pondered Jirsa's words. "There was once a time when I felt I owed them the sharpest edge of my sword and nothing more." Licronus reached deep into an outer pocket of his garment and pulled out the unbelievable. The Horn of Satan which broke off during Licronus's attempt to free Lucifer at the Lair. Licronus held the item out into the sun so that God himself could see it. "Now I see things differently."

"What is that?" Jirsa asked, trying to seem unmoved, but feeling a powerful energy and a sudden inescapable connection to the item.

"Feel its power surge through you, Jirsa. It is because of this that we, the true angels of Heaven, grow ever more powerful," Licronus replied as he gazed upon the horn. The sunlight revealed small worms crawling through its cracks and strange dark beetles running along its broken edges. "Come, Jirsa. I want you to hold it – to feel for yourself the immense power Lucifer himself has bestowed upon us." Jirsa walked closer to Licronus.

"Lucifer. What shall become of him?" She could feel the energy of the horn intensifying as she approached. Jirsa stared at the horn for a moment, then raised her hand to take it. The surge of energy was almost too much for her to bear as she took hold of the horn. "What plan do you have now to release him?"

"Speak to me no more of Lucifer!," Licronus lashed out angrily. "He shall serve his purpose when the time comes." Licronus took the horn from Jirsa and gazed upon it again. "This is just the beginning, Jirsa," Licronus said with an evil sneer. "It is the beginning… of the end."

Istya and Quilin were already in the main room of Janirin's home when he and Agean entered. Janirin, still quite taken by his daughter's newfound fondness for Quilin, stared at them for a brief moment.

"Yes, well, you must be hungry after your long journey," Janirin said. "I trust that on this visit you will be able to dine with us?"

"I could definitely eat," Quilin said. Istya playfully smacked him on the head as Janirin watched, confused. Quilin and Istya laughed.

Janirin continued, "While we wait for dinner to be prepared, Agean, I would like you to take a ride with me."

"A ride? Where are we going?" Agean asked.

Janirin replied, "Not to worry, my boy. It isn't far." Janirin and Agean moved towards the doorway. "Oh, and Quilin. I believe someone would like to say hello to you."

At that very moment, Flittorin landed on the sill of the window and screeched.

"Flittorin!" Quilin yelled, overwhelmed with happiness. Quilin and Istya rushed over to see him. Agean and Janirin smiled at their excitement.

Janirin said to Agean, "Come with me, Agean." He then turned to Istya and Quilin. "We will return shortly."

Quilin and Istya were so excited for Flittorin's return, they didn't even look up as Janirin and Agean exited.

Sweating and breathing heavily, Jirsa took in the surge of power being emitted from the Horn of Satan. Every second she held onto it, her hands felt as if they were becoming part of it. When she could hold onto it no longer, she quickly returned it to Licronus.

"What will you do with it?" Jirsa asked.

"It is a tool, Jirsa. I will use it to unleash the greatest power of evil there is upon His kingdom, and rain death upon the filthy creatures of this earth." Licronus returned the horn back to an outer pocket of his garb and then reached into its interior and pulled out a cloth covered item bound by chord. As Jirsa watched, he untied the chord binding with his teeth and allowed the cloth covering to fall aside.

"This, Jirsa, will show us the way." It was the Bisalis.

Jirsa's expression lit up as she cast her eyes upon the holy book. How did he get the precious text? Licronus gazed at Jirsa with an evil smile as he observed her reaction.

"Our Sitcian enemies believe they have won. But as you can see, this battle is far from over."

Jirsa stared in awe at the Bisalis.

"May I?" Jirsa asked.

Licronus paused for a moment to admire Jirsa's enthusiasm, then handed her the text. Jirsa carefully took the thin leather book into her hands. Then, she opened it ever so delicately.

"I was to have one of my own," Jirsa said as she slowly turned the thick pages of the text.

"When the time comes you shall have everything." Licronus said. "Everything He took from you will be yours again. This book of lies will enable us to return to our rightful place — to a kingdom which is rightfully ours." Suddenly, Jirsa's expression changed as she closely inspected one of the pages.

"There might be a slight problem with your plan, Licronus." As Licronus turned his gaze to Jirsa, she turned the open Bisalis towards him to show that a page had been torn out of it.

"It seems that they are always one step ahead of you," Jirsa said.

Suddenly, Licronus's expression changed as he ran his thick dark fingers along the remnants of the missing page. Then, his eyes turned jet black as his anger rose to an explosive level. His jet black wings sprouted from his back and spread slowly towards the sky. His fist clinched so tightly that Jirsa feared he might break his own fingers. Then, he let out a horrid angry scream that echoed throughout the range of still mountain peaks.

"Aaaaaaaahh!"

Even Jirsa could not believe the frightening level of anger Licronus displayed. She took a few steps away from the edge of the cliff, in case Licronus decided to direct his fury at her. Then, wings fully spread, Licronus grabbed the Bisalis from Jirsa's hands and raised it to the sky with the intent of hurling the book from the cliff. Jirsa quickly stepped in and grabbed his arm before Licronus could finish the deed.

"No! Licronus! It may still be the way back!" Jirsa pleaded. Then, something occurred to Jirsa. "In fact, I think I may know why this page is missing… and where it might be.

Licronus, still growling with anger, allowed Jirsa's words to curb his fury. He slowly lowered his arm and turned his evil look back to the mountains in the distance.

"Before we are finished, rivers of Hamen blood will

spill upon this putrid land," Licronus said. Licronus again reached into his garb, only this time pulling out the other of the only two Credara now left on earth. The one stolen from the Shao-Tan many years back. He then stared out into the distance.

"Istya. We have much to discuss." Jirsa displayed a demonic grin as the wheels of her mind continued to turn.

Istya and Quilin had decided to make the most of their time before dinner with a romantic walk through Janirin's garden. This day, the flowers and trees would not serve as a target for Istya's practice. Instead, they both enjoyed time with each other among the beautiful foliage as Flittorin perched on a nearby tree branch.

Suddenly, Istya began feeling strange and faint as Quilin held her. This feeling, powerful and overwhelming, rose from the very core of her being and coursed through her veins. Istya was not unfamiliar with this feeling. She had felt it once before. Inside the Lair.

"Istya! Are you all right? What's wrong? Is it the Mark?" Quilin asked.

Istya, breathing heavily, shook her head, "No." Istya then looked up to the Quintana sky and stared in horror. Tears streamed down her cheeks. Then, all at once, ghostly white specters shot out of Istya's body, causing her to writhe in pain. Quilin stumbled back at the sight of the swarm of evil souls. As quickly as they appeared, they shot back into her again. Then, for a split second, Quilin saw an instantaneous flash of Kraylen in Istya's face. Quilin was stunned and overwhelmed with shock at what he was witnessing. Istya cried out as she doubled over in pain. As she was about to fall to the ground, Quilin came to his senses and ran back in to catch her. What had just happened? Did he really see what he thought he saw? It happened so fast and then just like that… it was over. Istya had begun to recover as Quilin held her tight. Then, still breathing heavily, she looked at him with tears in her eyes; no evil specters, just a look of helplessness on her face.

Agean and Janirin rode alone in a small horse drawn carriage along a lush and beautiful path. After a few more moments, they stopped alongside a splendid grassy hill.

Janirin said, "Here we are."

"What is this place?" Agean asked.

Janirin smiled at Agean and said, "Come along! You'll see."

Janirin and Agean exited the carriage. Agean followed as Janirin began walking up the hill.

After a few moments' hike, Agean and Janirin reached the top, overlooking a beautiful lush green valley. In the distance was a modest farm with a small farmhouse. Agean took in the beautiful view but could not yet understand its meaning.

He turned to Janirin. "Janirin, I don't understand."

"Open your heart, Agean. Look!" Janirin said. Agean looked again at the small farm. Suddenly, a man exited the horse stable. Immediately, memories flashed in Agean's head. Visions began tossing about, bringing him something which previous visions had never provided — clarity. After only a few seconds, Agean realized the man was his father. A rush of emotions welled up in Agean.

Agean said softly, "Father." Then, a teenage girl with her mother exited the front door of the house to join the man. They were all very happy. A tear ran down Agean's cheek. "My family."

Janirin said to him, "Yes, Agean. You see, Master Gajir was correct. Quintana is… Heaven on Earth."

Agean stared, teary-eyed, for a few moments. "Why did you not mention this before?"

"Because, my boy, the Sitcian's journey was yours and yours alone. I could do nothing to make your path easier or more difficult. That war… you had to fight on your own. You did it, Agean. You saved us all." Agean paused a moment to take in Janirin's words, and enjoy the miracle of seeing his family.

"How long have they been here?" Agean asked, still gazing out at the farm.

Janirin replied, "Ever since that horrible day. You need no longer fear their memory, Agean."

Agean asked, "How long will they stay?"

"Well, that is for Him to decide," Janirin said. With a nod, Janirin directed Agean's attention to the far right of the valley and there, before his eyes, was the Follower on horseback. Agean and Janirin peered out at him. "You're very fortunate, Agean. We do not see Him often. But somehow He always lets us know He's there."

Agean said, "Yes. I too have felt His presence." Agean squeezed a smile through his tears and emotions as the Follower turned his horse and slowly faded from sight. Janirin placed his hand on Agean's shoulder.

"Take your time, Agean. I'll be waiting for you," Janirin said as he turned to walk away.

Agean stopped him. "Janirin! I almost forgot." Agean reached into his waist pouch and handed Janirin the Credara. "It saved our lives. The other was destroyed. "Thank you, Agean. I am grateful to have it back in Quintana."

"There are only two now. Do you know what has become of the other?" Agean asked.

The third was kept by the Shao-Tan Order. It was taken deep into the secret caverns of a volcanic mountain. Sadly, through deceit and corruption, that holy urn fell into the hands of the Kraylen many years ago."

Suddenly, thoughts began rushing in like a huge wave crashing down on Agean's mind. Agean now stood before Janirin with a shocked and confused look. "The Kraylen? Then why would Licronus-" Agean's thought was immediately interrupted. His eyes opened wide as he realized that Licronus had yet another motive. He quickly searched his waist area and pouch and realized... it was gone. The Bisalis was gone.

The memories began rushing in again as Agean recalled his battle with the Kraylen at the river. He recalled the Kraylen Generals and their attempt to take his life. The slash cut into his clothing, just at the waist. The one he deemed of no consequence had turned out to be more than he'd previously thought. He then envisioned the thin, lightweight holy text tumbling from the opening in his clothing. He imagined that it must have happened this way. In his mind, Agean saw Licronus picking it up from the shore where it must have landed during their battle. So distracted by the Kraylen's brutal attack, the urgency of the situation so dire, Agean had not noticed. Until now.

Agean's mind rushed back to the reality of the moment. All this time it was never just the Credara. Licronus wanted something more.

"Agean. What is it?" said a concerned Janirin.

"The Credara. It wasn't just the Credara he was after," Agean replied.

Janirin said to him, "I don't understand."

"The key to Lucifer's Lair. Janirin, you just said Licronus already had it. But what he didn't have was The Bisalis. The Bisalis given to me by the Council is gone, Janirin!"

Janirin gazes at Agean with even greater concern.

"But why would he want to release Lucifer, and steal the Bisalis?" Agean asked. Janirin paused a moment, but then it came to him.

"The blank pages, Agean," Janirin said with a concerned look. "The blank pages of the Bisalis reveal the way to heaven for the Sitcian. Only a Sitcian can actually read these pages."

"And Lucifer... was Sitcian," Agean said.

Agean and Janirin stand frozen, staring at each other with looks of terror on their faces.

&

With the sun high in the sky, accompanied by a smattering of smoky cloud cover, Tan rode with newfound purpose. He was now chosen. He was now a Hamen Warrior. Somehow, he knew exactly what to do. For years without realizing it, Solis had been preparing him for this moment in time. The Arc-Pen Symbol crested on the scroll case now had greater meaning. Tan also knew that the scroll within meant so much more now. When he placed his hand upon the case, it drew his entire being closer. He could not understand why Solis sent the precious item away with him, but now was not the time to question Solis's wisdom. Had it not been for Solis, he would be dead.

Tan's Hamen senses burned with acute accuracy. With little effort he felt aware of everything that went on around him. A new type of energy surged through his veins: one of pure truth, goodness and honor. As he thundered along, Tan retrieved one of his Bouma from his waist. As he held it forward, he embraced the fact that he was no longer simply an expert at the use of the Bouma, but a Master of the Hamen Bouma. The newly endowed Mark of Hamen on Tan's neck tingled, connecting every cell of his being to it. With simply his will, Tan transformed what was once a precision balanced weapon carved from the finest ebony on the planet, into a glistening, razor sharp, metallic weapon crested with Arc-Pen Symbols on each side. Its perfect form fitting almost magically into the protective leather hand covering given to him by Solis during his years of training. With a quick move, Tan launched the Hamen Bouma into the air. Sparks spewed out as the weapon whirled at an incredible speed, cutting the air like a blade through flesh. Then suddenly, the Bouma split in half, sending two deadly bladed weapons whirling in two directions. Tan was humbled by the enhanced capabilities of the weapon he'd spent years mastering. His mind and the Hamen Bouma were connected in a way he had never before imagined. With the purity of his will, Tan brought the two razor sharp halves back together in the air. The weapon then circled back to Tan's awaiting grip. He transformed the Bouma back to its normal form and returned it to his waist.

As he continued to race along atop his steed, the only thing on which he could now focus — the only thing that now mattered — was the precious scroll case he carried, and what the Old Man on the horse had said to him: "Protect the scroll. Beware the Kraylen. Find the Sitcian. There will be a place for you with God's Army." This was Tan's new mission. His Hamen Mark continued to tingle with each stride of his stallion, confirming something which would now remain a part of his life forever: The enemy was everywhere.

Before now, a dutiful daughter was her only responsibility. Before now, her love for her parents had superseded all of her own dreams for love and family. Before now, she was strikingly beautiful… and tragically ordinary. But Jie never complained. As Tan's sister, she knew her duty was to her family while Tan was away at the Holy Order. This had been God's purpose for her. Now, in what seemed like a split second, everything in her life changed. With her hair whipping in the wind, her stallion carried her forth on the first deviation from ordinary life she had ever known. As she galloped top speed along the path laid out by her loving older brother, she knew that life from this day forth would be different. The scroll case she carried, whether authentic or fake, was an exact duplicate of that carried by Tan. And despite which was in her possession, she was now a moving target to the greatest force of evil in existence. Jie knew she was risking her life, but she understood the grave nature of everything Tan had explained to her. "Find the Sitcian." She did this not only for Tan — she did this for mankind — she did this for God.

THE BEGINNING OF THE END

www.ingramcontent.com/pod-product-compliance
Lightning Source LLC
Chambersburg PA
CBHW030339120726
47901CB00007B/1837